Fall Into You

SEASONS OF LOVE:
BOOK 1

CAROLINE FRANK

PRAISE FOR
Fall Into You

If When Harry Met Sally is the quintessential fall movie, Fall Into You is the quintessential fall book. So many quirky, funny episodes, romantic scenes and steamy, heart-racing moments.

AMAZON REVIEWER

I loved, loved, loved this book! It has spice, it has the brother's best friend trope, and it has the instalove, but done in a way that doesn't make me cringe. Liza and Matt's chemistry is over the top awesome, and I'm insanely excited to see that it is book one in a series!

@ROMANCEBOOKSFAN

If you're looking for a rom-com with a Fall feeling, look no further 🍂 I'm looking forward to the next install-ment in the series.

@LISSTHEBOOKLOVER

PRAISE FOR
Shall We Dance?

This book easily moved to my favorite rom com spot. Barbara and Theo are such a fun couple. I'm a sucker for enemies to lovers and Caroline Frank did a wonderful job nailing this with the perfect amount of banter, spice, and tension. I found myself thinking about this story constantly, and couldn't wait to finish it, but also wanted to savor every word.

@VICWITHTHEGOODBOOKS

This book is everything a romance novel should be. It had all the pieces for a perfect love story. Enemies to lovers, grump and sunshine, and a detrimental miss communication. What more could a romance lover want?? I loved the characters and how real and relatable they were. Shall We Dance is a 10/10.

AMAZON REVIEWER

I'm swooning over this book!

JENG

Per mia madre, che diceva sempre che
sarei diventata una scrittrice.
Love you, Mah.

Life Starts All Over Again When It Gets Crisp In The Fall

F. SCOTT FITZGERALD

Chapter One

LIZA

"...In conclusion, I think we would be better suited with other people."

I stare, open-mouthed, at my now ex-boyfriend sitting across from me, looking incredibly smug.

"You're kidding me, right? Or did you seriously just *read* me your break-up?" I ask, dumbfounded.

"Liza." Jeremy removes his glasses and sets them on the table next to the piece of paper with his break-up speech. He brings his hands together in front of him, pursing his lips before saying, "I just thought it would be less messy if I organized my thoughts and laid them all out in a structured fashion, rather than let you lead me off on a tangent and not let me explain myself properly—as you tend to do."

I blink at him. "What does that mean?" I ask.

He sighs, as if holding back. "I never seem to be able to properly express myself around you without it turning into a scene."

A scene?

To Jeremy, a scene means expressing any type of emotion, good or bad, apparently.

"Ah," I say in understanding. "So, you bring me to my favorite restaurant for lunch, knowing full well that I would not want to risk embarrassing myself by causing a scene so that I could keep coming back after?"

"Yes, that is correct," he says in agreement, sitting up straight in his seat.

I can't blame him for that unnecessary line of thinking. Though, it just emphasizes how much of a spineless tool he is.

You know what? This break-up might not be the worst thing ever. I mean, look at him. He is so...so...*meticulous*. Which is to say, he is such a perfectionist asshole with his perfect Ken-doll hair and perfect teeth. Everything in his life needs to be planned, detailed, calculated. I mean, seriously? Who brings a script to a break-up? A man with no passion or heat—cold-hearted, too in his head.

"Jeremy, I'm disappointed in you." I *tsk* and take a sip of my wine. I feel like getting under his skin a little.

"Oh?" He lifts an eyebrow, intrigued. Jeremy is a type-A personality and overachiever. He is severely allergic to disappointment.

"I thought you were an intelligent man—you know, what with you being a tenured Physics professor at Columbia and all."

He scoffs. "Are you implying that I am not?" He sits back in his chair as if I've just pushed him.

"I'm *saying* that you're not. You've overestimated just how emotionally invested I was in this relationship." I take another sip of wine, trying to act cool. "You don't want to be with me anymore." I shrug. "No biggie."

"No biggie?" he asks, frowning. "We've been together for three years. We were engaged, Liza."

Ah, yes. I guess you can't really 'no biggie' an engagement break-up, can you? But oh, how I love how peeved he is at the thought of me not caring about the fact that he's breaking up with me. It gives me an incredible—admittedly, petty—sense of satisfaction.

"Oops," I say with a fake laugh. "Right. Here you go—before I forget." I slide the ring he gave me a year ago off my finger. A gold band with a heart-shaped diamond.

To be fair, that should have been the final red flag in a sea of red flags. No offense to women who love heart-shaped jewelry, but I am not a heart-shaped-diamond-engagement-ring type of gal.

Jeremy takes the ring and looks down at it, confounded. "I truly did not expect you to take it so well," he says, frowning. He inspects it as if I had it switched with a fake stone, expecting this exact moment to happen or something.

"Oh, really?" I chug the rest of the contents of my wine glass and reach for his. Jeremy is smart enough not to complain. He just broke up with me, after all. He'd be an even bigger dick if he were to not let me have any of his wine.

"You know, that is a three-hundred-dollar bottle of wine. It is meant to be savored and enjoyed, not chugged like a box of Franzia that's being passed around between people at a college party." He laughs once, and I roll my eyes at him, chugging more of his wine to make a point.

I always hate it when he makes incredibly snobby comments like that—like anyone who can't afford his lifestyle is below him, and he is absolute perfection. Ain't nothing wrong with the occasional box of wine. Not everyone can afford to live the lifestyle that he lives.

Who even has the kind of money to buy a three-hundred-dollar bottle of wine??

I'm so happy I don't have to deal with this crap anymore.

"Seeing as you are taking this so well, I feel as though I can be honest with you now. I have actually been seeing someone else," he says cheerfully. His grin widens, and he sits up taller in his seat.

I stop breathing. "Excuse me? Why would you tell me that, Jeremy?"

"Well, you seem to be taking this break-up pretty easily." He shrugs, surprised. "I mean... Y-you seemed okay with it." He runs his fingers through his hair, smoothing it down, making sure that it's neat. "I thought you would be happy for me."

"*Why* in the world would you think that I would *ever* need to hear the fact that you *cheated* on me, Jeremy? Do you know the damage you could have just caused to my psyche? Now I'll probably never trust anyone ever again."

"Pfft, come on, Liza. Let's not be dramatic," he says as he adjusts the cuffs on his tweed blazer. It's painful how I never realized how big of a cliché he is—his jacket even has elbow patches! "I know you are a psychologist, but you cannot expect me to believe that this simple fact can affect your '*psyche*.'" He air-quotes with a look of disgust in his eyes. "You and your social sciences." He shakes his head at me with a patronizing smile on his lips. "I told you that your psychology master's program was a mistake the day I met you. You should have at least gone for psychiatry. I mean, it is still a joke, in my opinion, but at least it contains *some* actual scientific study."

"Oh, *gawd*," I say, standing up. "You know what? I don't even care. I am just *astounded* by the fact that you could find another woman to even put up with you and how *boring* you are." I toss back the rest of his glass of wine and pick up my purse, digging for my coat check number and five bucks to give to the attendant.

"Let's not exaggerate now, Liza." He laughs a little. "I don't think that a Columbia University Physics professor could *ever* be deemed as *boring*."

I burst out into hysterical laughter, scaring the waiter trying to get by me. "Oh my god," I laugh. "Just listen to yourself." I grab a couple of mini-baguettes from the bread basket to take to-go, devastated that I can't take the French butter with me, too. "You are *incredibly* boring, Jeremy—in *and* out of bed. You know there are more positions out there than missionary, right? I promise you that. You could probably afford to allocate some of your research time into studying them." At this, I realize we have started to garner some attention, but I don't care. I will definitely give him a scene now. "I want to personally thank you for this break-up, given that I admit I did not have the lady-balls to do it myself. But I want to let you know that *you fucking suck* for cheating on me."

"No need to use foul language," he whisper-yells at me, looking around nervously at the other tables.

"Goodbye, Jeremy. Thanks for the boring memories. I'm pretty sure I'll soon forget them."

"So, he just *read* you your break-up? Just like that?" my brother, Vinny, asks as he sips his wine in our mother's kitchen. The smells coming from her stove bring back warm and comforting childhood memories. Ones of sitting at this very table with my parents and brother, eating my mother's home-cooked meals, essentially ruining all Italian restaurants for me because *no one* cooks Italian like my mother.

"He freaking pulled out a sheet of paper as soon as they served us a drink *and proceeded to read it out loud to me.*" I am still shocked. Vinny just snorts and shakes his head. "I mean, Barbara always said he was nuts, since day one, but I just thought the guy was just a little eccentric. Plus, it's not like she has such a phenomenal grasp on what normalcy is, if you know what I mean." I raise my eyebrows at Vinny, and he nods thoughtfully.

Barbara is my best friend and the wildest person I know. She was also the first person in my life to meet Jeremy. Two minutes into meeting him at dinner, she texted *Get out! Get out now!* under the table. But she's always had a unique personality, so I didn't take her too seriously.

"The worst part—besides the fact that he couldn't wait until we were done with our entrees so that I could at least enjoy my Cajun chicken—was that I didn't understand what was happening at first, so I just let him go on and on while I sipped my wine, listing off all the things I had to do the next day in my head, until I heard him say my name."

"What do you mean?" He raises an eyebrow at me, taking another sip of his wine.

"I mean, I thought he was reading me another one of his boring articles or letters to the editor. You know how he liked to send in stupid stuff whenever he thought journalists were wrong or their research was lacking?" Vinny nods with a smirk. "Well, he started off saying something about how romance is overrated, and that certain people want romance more than they want the actual person that they're with. So, naturally, I thought he was going off on one of his rants about the social sciences and some study he read up on or something. But then I heard him say my name, and he got my attention. He said that I didn't seem to be really into this relationship because of him, but more the idea of him, and that we should just break up."

Vinny takes a sip from his drink and looks the other way, avoiding my gaze. He shifts uncomfortably in his seat.

"What?" I ask. "Why are you being weird?"

"I mean..." He clears his throat. "Let me just preface this by saying that I never liked the guy. No one did."

"Except Dad," I remind him sadly, and he winces. Dad only met Jeremy once before he passed away, but before he died, he had told me how much he loved Jeremy for me, and that meant everything. To tell the truth, I'm not sure that I was all that into Jeremy until Dad told me how great he thought he was.

"Right." He scratches the back of his head. "Whatever. The point is that I didn't like him, *but*...the thing is, Liza...I don't think that he was necessarily wrong, you know?"

I lift an eyebrow at him. "Excuse me?"

Besides the sound of meatballs simmering in the pan and the low bubbling of my mother's tomato sauce, there are no sounds in the kitchen. Mom's in the dining room, setting the table for us, and Vinny and I are hiding here, like children. I'm hiding to avoid any type of housework while I'm back home for fall break, while my brother is hiding from his wife and kids. I'm guessing by how uncomfortable my brother looks now, though, that he's praying for Danielle to walk in here with some sort of childcare crisis—not bad enough that it's scary, but just enough that he would need to walk away from this conversation.

I kick one of the legs of his chair and throw him a menacing look. "*Vinny*. What do you mean?"

He exhales deeply and runs his fingers through his dark-brown hair. "I'm just saying that maybe he has a point. I think all those romance novels and rom-coms you watch are messing with your perception of what love really is, you know?"

There might be a *little* truth to what he's saying. I might have been going through a 'Hot for Teacher' trope phase in my reading when I met Jeremy at a prospective students' school event. But still. There were tons of reasons why I dated Jeremy.

I just can't think of one right now, that's all.

"What are you talking about? I really cared about him. And he was plenty romantic." I frown. "I mean, he brought me

7

flowers every Friday and then took me to nice restaurants, told me I was pretty, blah blah."

Vinny scoffs, raising a bushy eyebrow at me, and takes a giant sip of wine. "*Now* I know what your problem is. You don't know what love is."

He says it so matter-of-factly my jaw drops. This coming from the bro-est of bros, the epitome of frat boy himself, the man who won the fucking lottery by meeting a woman as amazing as Danielle and getting her to love him, marry him, and start a family with him. I never thought he would ever settle down, and now he's talking to me as if he were the ultimate authority on love.

I'm about to say something not so nice when the kitchen door swings open, and my sister-in-law walks in holding one toddler in her arms while another trails closely behind her, gripping her pant leg.

"This is for you." She hands my nephew, Leo, to my brother like a football. Vinny takes him and recoils at the scent of what I can tell is a very poopy diaper.

"See?" he says, holding up his son as evidence. "*This* is love. *This* is romance. Love is not reminding your wife that it's her turn to change the diaper, that you've changed the last ten poop diapers because you love her so much and know that, after two kids, she still has a hard time not gagging when she changes them."

"Please." She rolls her eyes at him. "I was up all night with Clara while she vomited, and where were you? Sleeping like a baby," she says with her hands on her hips. Danielle looks back and forth between the two of us. "What are we talking about?" She pulls her naturally blonde hair up into a messy high bun at the top of her head and still manages to look perfectly polished. How do other women *do* that? If I tried that with my thick curly hair, it would look like a giant cinnamon roll stuck on the top of my head.

Vinny gets up from his seat and settles Leo on his hip. "Just telling Liza here that she's never really been in love," he says casually with a shrug.

"Oh, yeah, totally. I thought this was common knowledge," she says, and Vinny throws his head back in laughter as he walks out of the kitchen, presumably to change Leo's diaper.

"What are you even talking about?" I screech. "I was *engaged* to the guy. I was with him for three freaking years, you guys!"

Danielle looks bored and ignores me as she picks up Clara and sets her on my lap. "I need to pee. Please take her before I lose my mind." I sigh deeply and wrap my arms around my niece, holding her to me.

I look down and catch Clara staring up at me with the same big brown eyes and huge smile on her face that Dad had. She looks so much like him it's almost eerie. Of everyone in the family, she's the one who looks the most like her grandfather. Despite being twins, Leo looks more like Danielle's side of the family than ours. Where her brother is blond and blue-eyed, Clara has curly brown hair that is often pulled up to the side with a crooked clip. Poor Danielle grew up with Pantene-commercial hair and doesn't know how to handle so much of it, so her daughter often looks like a mess.

I fix Clara's hair and hold her close, giving her a kiss on the forehead.

"You definitely have the Castelli hair, kid." I smile fondly at her. "You and your daddy look so much like your *nonno*."

"No-no," she says with a smile.

I sigh. The door swings open, and my mother walks into the kitchen in a huff as I say, "No, you have to say it right. *Nonno*," I repeat, emphasizing the double-N.

"They're never going to learn Italian, are they?" she asks me in her native tongue, and I shake my head with a smirk.

"I don't think so. Vinny only ever speaks to them in English," I reply back in Italian.

"Then *you* should be the one to teach them. It's your job to keep traditions alive when I'm gone." I roll my eyes at her. My mother grunts in frustration as she stirs the sauce.

"I need you to add one more place setting, by the way. Your brother just invited someone over for lunch."

I bounce Clara on my knee while she plays with the gold necklace my dad gave me a few weeks before he passed—a gold medallion with my initials engraved in it on the back.

"What do you mean he invited someone over? I was just talking to him, and he didn't mention anything." I switch back to English.

Mom looks over her shoulder at me, exasperated, and shakes her head. "It was last minute, apparently," she sighs. "More like last second," she adds, muttering under her breath.

I feel bad for my mom. She's always giving, giving, giving, and we never notice how much we're taking, taking, taking. I make a mental note to start showing my mother how much I appreciate all that she does for us.

But not right now because I have a baby on my lap, and she is so damn cute.

"Who did he invite?" I ask, smiling down at Clara. "I didn't realize he was still in touch with people from high school." I definitely am not. I hated high school. It was just four years of torture and mean girls and football players and bullies. You could easily say that I wasn't very popular growing up, due in large part to my huge, frizzy hair and nerdy tendencies. I preferred to stay in and watch *Buffy the Vampire Slayer* reruns than go out partying, thank you very much (*Team Spike* all the way).

Vinny, on the other hand, was the high school golden boy. A jock, a genius, class president—you name it! Thankfully, the fact that my brother is six years older than me meant that he never had to see how big of a loser I was. Though, I sometimes wonder whether he would have given me some sort of street cred, like being his sister would have somehow made things better for me.

We both grew up here in Long Island, but Vinny and I live in New York City now. My brother got a scholarship to Columbia for pre-med *and* med school and is now a doctor at Cornell-Weill.

I went to NYU for undergrad and am currently in my last year of my psych graduate program at Columbia. We visit often to see my mom, but we haven't really hung out with any of our high school friends since graduation, which is why I'm confused. Who could he have invited that lives in town?

"It's not a high school friend. It's one of his old college roommates who was apparently in the area," she tells me.

Holy shit.

"Which one?" My heart starts beating out of my chest suddenly, and my stomach churns. Vinny had a lot of roommates throughout his eight years of college, but there were definitely some stand-out candidates—one in particular.

"Auntie Liza?" Clara slaps my face lightly so I pay attention to her. "My tummy hurts."

"Hold on, kid," I say on the verge of a panic attack. "Mom, who is it??"

TELL ME, WOMAN. I MUST KNOW NOW.

"I don't know," she sighs, stirring her sauce and lowering the heat. "I think it's Mark? Max? I can't remember."

"*MATT WILSON??*" I yelp, suddenly finding it hard to breathe.

"Yes?" I turn to the voice standing in the doorway and see my brother's college best friend and former roommate standing

11

there, looking down at me with the sexiest smirk I've ever seen, with Vinny in tow.

I'm momentarily paralyzed with shock. Clara grabs me by the shirt, shaking me as much as she can, but I'm still trying to recover here.

Words. I need to remember how to say them.

Play it cool.

"H—" I start to say but am interrupted by Clara vomiting all over my shirt.

What—and I cannot stress this enough—the actual fuck??

Chapter Two

LIZA

"Did he see? How bad was it?" I ask Danielle desperately while we attempt to clean some of the mess on me.

"Uh, considering he was pretty much right in front of you when it happened, I'd say pretty fucking bad," she laughs, blotting at my hair. "*It. Is. Everywhere.* Wow," she says with wide eyes.

"You know, your sarcasm isn't really helping. And this is all your fault. You gave me the sick baby who threw up all over me in front of Majestic Matt!"

Danielle snorts at me as she gives up trying to wipe the vomit from my hair. "You call him Majestic Matt? What?" She laughs at me.

I sigh deeply. "That was the nickname I had for him when he was living with Vinny during med school. I rarely saw him, but whenever I did, he always looked majestic. So, he became Majestic Matt." I shrug. "*Obviously* neither my brother nor Matt himself know about this nickname, so please let's keep it that way."

"Oh my god, this is so cute. You had a crush on him?" She smiles, clapping her hands together. I sigh in frustration.

"Yeah, when I was, like, a *teenager*. I'm a mature adult woman now. I'm over it. I'm totally, absolutely unaffected by his presence, so don't go planning anything weird or whatever." I wiggle my finger at her.

She laughs and pats me on the head—the part that's not matted in vomit, that is—and says, "It's just as well. I think your brother would have his balls if he comes anywhere near you, to be honest. I've heard some wild stories about Vinny and your Manly Matt's nights out."

I glare at her and hiss. "It's *Majestic* Matt, not *Manly*. And he's not *mine*," I say. I mean, I absolutely, positively would not mind him being mine—or me being his, for that matter. Even if it's just for one night, if you know what I mean. But Danielle is right. Even if I *did* ever get Matt to give me the time of day, Vinny would lose his shit.

Stupid bro code.

I sigh and push Danielle's hand away. I give up. "Yeah, I'm gonna need you to leave so I can shower."

She waves at me dismissively and leaves my childhood bathroom with a laugh. "Lunch is in twenty minutes, by the way!" she calls over her shoulder.

I look in the mirror and assess myself. I am an absolute and total mess. My favorite sweater is completely destroyed (I hope Vinny is aware that he will be getting a bill for its replacement), and my hair is incredibly gross. I start feeling annoyed that I need to shower, redo my hair, makeup, and get dressed when I realize...I get to redo my hair, makeup, and pick a cuter outfit.

All of a sudden, I want to run downstairs and kiss Clara's head (she's doing great now, by the way) because I wasn't prepared to see Matt before, but now I can be by using my niece's vomit as an excuse!

I dive quickly into the shower, scrubbing the vomit out of my hair, rinsing and repeating at least three times, being extra careful. I condition with the super-expensive orange hair mask I stole from Dani while I lather my body in coconut body wash and rinse everything out. I only have about ten minutes left to blow-dry, do my makeup, and get dressed, but it's doable. I can absolutely make it to the table, like, five minutes late.

ONCE I'M DONE, I BREATHE A SIGH OF RELIEF. I LOOK SO much better than the last time he saw me. Pre-vomit and post-vomit. By some miracle, I was able to fix my hair in a reasonable amount of time to the point that it looks good! Shiny! And most importantly, clean! I wear a cream ribbed turtleneck bodysuit and high-waisted olive jeans. I'm trying to pull off *cozy fall* meets *trendy fall* with the little I had packed for this trip, and I think I've managed it. I know I'm being ridiculous, but hasn't everyone acted a little crazy in front of a childhood crush?

"She lives!" Vinny says when I approach the table.

"Ha-ha," I say sarcastically and stop dead in my tracks when I realize the only free seat at the table is next to Majestic Matt, and holy crap, does he still live up to his nickname! Between the initial shock of seeing him for the first time after at least six years and the projectile vomit, I completely forgot to check him out properly. Now that I'm up close, I can truly appreciate him for the god that he is.

He's changed some since the last time I saw him. Like fine wine, Matt seems to have improved with age. Even through his burgundy cable-knit sweater, I can tell by how his muscles flex when he turns to look at me that any trace of baby fat or a beer belly he might have had in med school is gone and has now been replaced with broad shoulders, a muscular back, and what I suspect is a very defined six-pack under all that knit material. The smooth olive skin on his face is now covered by a trimmed, dark-brown beard that he wears like a hot, sexy lumberjack.

Mmmm. I've never kissed a guy with a beard before.

Whoa, okay. Calm down.

Though this Matt is definitely more man than boy, his dark-green eyes still shine with mischief. He faces me with a smile and a simple, "Hi," and I'm done. If I could barely handle Matt when he was an annoying frat bro, how the hell am I going to be able to control myself and act like a normal human with this Majestic Matt 2.0 situation? I mean, I can tell you right now that I will not be at my most verbose throughout this entire lunch.

"Hi," I say back as he stands to pull the chair out for me. I look up at him, surprised, while Vinny's fork stops midway to his mouth. Mom doesn't notice anything weird, but I catch Danielle covering her mouth to hide a smile.

"Uh, thanks," I say. I can't say that I remember the last time a guy pulled out a chair for me. Jeremy refused to do things like open doors and pull out chairs, because he said women couldn't have it both ways.

"You either want to be respected and treated like an equal, or I can treat you like the weaker sex," he told me one night after an argument.

I obviously wanted to be respected and treated like an equal, but does that necessarily exclude any type of chivalrous behavior? Is it a crime for me to want a guy who will help me put on my coat after dinner?

For the millionth time since breaking up with Jeremy last night, I thank my lucky stars that we're over.

I take a seat beside Matt and look down at my plate, in a trance.

He's just being polite, Liza. Don't get ahead of yourself. It's not a marriage proposal.

Although, a girl can dream. I wouldn't mind waking up next to him every morning for the rest of my life. I mean, *look* at him.

"I'm Matt," he says, sticking his hand out.

Disappointment hits hard in my stomach.

He doesn't remember me.

"Yeah, I know," I say with a small smile, feeling my cheeks blush. "We've actually met before."

I see Matt's skin redden under his beard, all the way to the tips of his ears. "Oh, sorry. I—I don't remember you. You know... college," he says by way of explanation—as in, he was probably not sober the times I met him?

"It's okay." I shrug. "We only saw each other a couple of times, and you might have been hungover for most of them." I laugh awkwardly, trying to appease him—he doesn't look too happy with himself right now.

"Right." He furrows his brow at me. "I was kind of a mess back then."

Vinny snorts, and it's only then that I register, since Matt first pulled out my chair, that we are not alone and are actually surrounded by my family. "*Kind of* a mess?" He smirks at Matt. "Matt here has the record for most *almost* arrests in our frat."

Vinny likes to use any opportunity to bring up the glory days. Normally, I ignore him, but this time, I take the bait.

"What do you mean? What constitutes an *almost* arrest?" I ask, trying not to sound too eager for more information.

Matt scratches the back of his neck and shifts in his seat. "It's stupid," he says.

"He's being humble. It just means that he almost got arrested several times but was able to bullshit himself out of them. I don't even know how many times you managed to get away with it, but it was impressive. Matt is the shit." He shakes his head in laughter.

"Shit!" Leo parrots with a huge smile.

"Oh my God, Vinny! What did I say about cursing in front of the kids?" Danielle yells. "I swear to God, this is why the other parents in daycare hate us." She throws her napkin in frustration on the table. "You *know* they're at that age where they repeat everything."

"Yeah, but it's like they know to repeat *just* the curse words. It's so annoying." Vinny sighs.

I bite my lip, trying not to giggle, but I can't keep it inside anymore once I hear Matt's deep, throaty laugh. I look up at him, awestruck. He looks down at me and stops laughing immediately.

Oh, man.

My skin feels hot, like you could melt butter on it.

"Leo, buddy," I hear my brother say. "You can't say that word. We talked about this."

"Shit! *Shit!* SHIT!" Leo yells, but Matt and I don't laugh this time, too focused on each other. I look down at my plate, doing my best to avoid eye contact. I'm scared if we keep at it, my skin will burst into flames. From the corner of my eye, though, I see him stare at me. I see his gaze travel from my face, down my neck, over my chest. It's like laser beams. I can feel the heat of it, and *God* it feels great.

"Leo! If you keep this up, then we won't go to Tom's Pumpkin Patch after lunch!" Vinny says, sighing heavily.

"Maybe the pumpkin patch isn't the best idea, huh?" Danielle says over her glass of water. Vinny looks up at her with wide, disappointed eyes. "Don't give me that face. Clara literally threw up less than an hour ago, Vinny."

"She's *fine*! Look at her!" He points at his daughter, who—to his credit—is looking a little less green than she did only half an hour ago. "Babe, I am a *doctor*, okay? I think I know more about this than you do."

The table goes quiet, and Danielle glares at him, gearing herself up for a fight. She opens her mouth to say something when Matt interrupts in the nick of time: "Pass the meatballs, please?"

I look up at him and smile coyly. He just successfully stopped World War III from starting here, in my mother's dining room, by reminding them that we have company. We all hate it when my brother pulls the doctor card—*especially* Danielle, and especially when it concerns him going against her maternal instincts.

"Will you join us?" I ask Matt as casually as possible, changing the topic to a much more important one. "At the pumpkin patch, I mean?"

He smiles crookedly at me and places the plate with the meatballs back on the table. "Yeah, if you'll have me. I was planning on going back to the city after lunch, but I can stay a while. Never been to a pumpkin patch before." He shrugs.

"I think you'll love it," I whisper so no one can hear, impressed with my forwardness. I'm not usually like this.

I bite my lip and look away from him. His smile is like the sun; I can't look at it for too long because it starts to hurt.

Is this flirting? Are we actually flirting right now? Just the thought of having something with Matt blows my mind. I mean, is that even possible? When I was a senior in high school, it seemed so farfetched that my brother's best friend would even pay attention to me for one second. And I was right—he didn't even remember meeting me. But I am a grown woman now, and Matt is all man.

I definitely felt a spark there. Did he feel it too?

I've *never* felt this before.

"I'm sure I will if you're there," he leans into me and whispers. His breath on my ear sends shivers down my spine, causes my skin to blush, and I panic. There is no way no one at the table just noticed that. I raise my head and look around to the others, but they're too wrapped up in their own world to notice what just happened. Mom is spooning more meatballs onto Vinny's plate while he feeds Leo, and Danielle is trying to get a fussy Clara to eat her applesauce.

Well, then.

I smile up at Matt, wondering how the hell I got so lucky that Jeremy broke up with me right before my fall break. I *never* felt this type of spark or energy with him.

What even is this?

Chapter Three

MATT

I THINK I'M IN TROUBLE.

No. I *know* I'm in trouble.

Vinny's sister is...amazing. Pretty fucking amazing, actually. She's smart, well-read, and quick-witted. I think a normal girl would have been mortified, but she handled the whole covered-in-vomit thing amazingly well, cracking jokes instead of freaking out. Normally, I find self-deprecating humor to be annoying, but on her, it's...adorable? Plus, she's beautiful, which really does nothing to help my case.

It's funny. I usually go for the tall, stick-thin girls—a habit from college, I think—but Liza is different. She's petite, curvy in all the right places, and has big, dark, unruly hair that makes me want to lean in and stick my face in it and smell the back of her neck.

I'm freaking myself out here. This is not stuff I should be thinking about.

If Vinny found out I was thinking about his little sister in this way, he'd kill me. The guy *lives* by the bro code, and I bet you *Thou shalt not date another bro's sister* is up there in the top ten most important rules of the whole book.

I could tell from the minute she sat down next to me at lunch that we had something, though. Not to sound like a girl, but we clicked the second I turned to look at her at the lunch table—maybe even before that, when we made eye contact before she ended up covered in vomit.

I was dying to get to know her better but was scared it would be too obvious if I focused only on her, so I did everything I could to get information on her as casually as possible.

First thing I had to find out was whether or not she's single, which, luckily, she is. Unfortunately, it seems like she literally just broke up with someone, and while Vinny said she was still getting over it, Danielle made it clear that Liza never loved him.

I can definitely work with that.

Second thing I had to make sure was whether she'd be interested in me, which had me worried. I know I'm a nice-looking guy, but looks aren't everything—personality is more important —which is why I panicked a little at first when she said that we had met before. It was the second time today that Old Me had screwed things up for Present Me, and it was getting annoying.

I wanted to kick myself for not remembering her, but more so for her having met me when I was a complete ass more than anything else.

You could say that I wasn't the sweetest guy in med school. The stress from school really got to me, which meant that whenever I wasn't studying, I was drinking and sleeping around. It was the only way I knew how to deal with the pressure. I knew once she said that we had already met that it was going to be tough to convince her that I wasn't that guy anymore. Nowadays, I try to balance the stress and anxiety in a healthier way through a mix of yoga, meditation, and cycling.

Hopefully, she'll understand that we all make mistakes and go through phases we regret. I mean, we all have to grow up eventually, right? Not to sound like Vinny here, but I'm a doctor now. I'm responsible. People's lives literally depend on me. It's a lot of pressure, but it should work in my favor, right?

I know it's not cool since it goes against the rules, but the second they mentioned the trip to the pumpkin patch, I immediately canceled all of my plans for the rest of the day to make sure I got to spend more time with her. For a minute there, though, she almost didn't make it, claiming she wanted to stay and help Catterina, her mother, to clean up after lunch.

Luckily, her sister-in-law all but pushed her into their SUV and said she would stay and help with the clean-up. I honestly could have kissed Danielle then, but I'm pretty sure *Thou shalt not kiss another bro's wife* is also up there next to the sister rule and would not have turned out so great for me.

I'm a little embarrassed about how nervous I feel at the thought of spending the rest of the afternoon with her. I mean, I've done this a million times, right? She's just another girl. I'm just super disappointed that I didn't get to sit next to her on the car ride over.

Because there are two car seats for the twins, there's only one seat available in the back, which she takes. This, I find out soon into the car ride, is not the worst thing in the world, given that it gives me access to look at her through the reflection in the rearview mirror. After a few minutes of lurking, she looks up and meets my gaze. Both our eyes widen, and we look away at the same time.

Shit. That was embarrassing.

Not cool, Matt. Totally not cool. Now she's going to think you're a creep.

I lift my gaze back up to the mirror again to check whether she looks angry or freaked out, but I catch her looking at me at the same time. She flushes and looks away, looking so adorably embarrassed that I laugh once, doing my best to cover it up with a cough.

I try to control myself, but after a minute or so of doing my best to look absolutely anywhere but in the rearview mirror, I cave. And there she is. Again.

This time, neither one of us looks away, though. I smile broadly at her, and she blushes, biting down on her lip to keep from smiling back. I take a chance and wink at her, and she shakes her head with a low laugh, turning away from my gaze just as we pull into the farm with the pumpkin patch.

She's definitely into me.

AS SOON AS WE PARK, VINNY JUMPS OUT OF THE CAR TO frantically start unbuckling Clara from her car seat while Liza works on Leo's.

"Hurry, Liza! Can't you see how long the line for the hayride is? We need to *move*," he says desperately.

"Oh my God, chill, you psycho! You're thirty-one years old! Your kids aren't even as excited as you are," she points out to him, rolling her eyes. "Can you help me get Leo out?" she turns to ask me.

Anything. I'll do anything.

"Sure," I smile and lift him out of his seat while Liza tries to exit over Clara's now-empty car seat. Liza crawls over it carefully, slowly, on all fours, and I catch myself staring at her ass (which looks incredible in those tight green jeans, by the way, in case you were wondering). Leo starts to squirm, so I settle him on my hip while I casually ogle at his aunt. I'm like a deer caught in the headlights. I barely take in the seas of different oranges from the pumpkins all around me.

Liza finally manages to jump out of the car when I hear a throat clear beside me and jump.

"Hey." Vinny narrows his eyes at me. *Shit.* I guess I really wasn't being subtle at all.

If looks could kill... But honestly, he can't really blame me for it, can he? His sister is a total babe, and her ass was right *there*!

Sigh.

I'm an asshole. A total fucking asshole. Maybe I haven't changed.

"Hey, man." I clear my throat, mortified. I set Leo down on the ground, and he reaches for his dad's hand. Vinny takes his Leo's hand and narrows his eyes at me.

You'd think a man holding two toddlers by the hands would not look intimidating at all, but you'd be wrong. Vinny is still about six-four and works out a lot. He was a jock all throughout high school and undergrad, good enough that I think he went to school on a scholarship, so you could say he's a little physically intimidating.

We don't say anything for a while, a silent exchange occurring between the two of us.

Don't look at my sister like that again.

I'll do my very best not to.

"Hey, so where do you guys want to start? Food? Ride? Pick a pumpkin?" I hear Liza ask beside us. I want to look at her but realize I should probably tread lightly right now.

Vinny keeps his eyes on me, not replying for a beat. Finally, he drags his eyes off my face and turns to his sister. "Hayride," he says with significantly less enthusiasm than when we first arrived. Liza seems to notice, too, furrowing her brows and looking between the two of us.

"O...kay," she says, choosing not to ask what his problem is. "Should we go, then?"

"I DON'T *WANT* TO GO ON THE RIDE!" LEO SCREAMS AT HIS dad, stomping his foot, refusing to get on the back of the truck.

Vinny looks around to the people giving us death stares, embarrassed by his son's behavior. "Leo," Vinny begs. "Hayrides are so fun! *Please* get in the back. Look at your sister. She's so excited!" I look over to Clara and notice she's looking a little lethargic.

Oh boy. Kid still looks a little sick.

"NO!" Leo says. This kid has a phenomenal set of lungs, I tell you.

"Vinny," Liza says with a calming, soothing voice. "He doesn't want to. You guys go ahead, and Leo and I will go pick out pumpkins. Does that sound good, buddy?" She pulls him to her, and he wraps his arms around her waist, smooshing his face in her stomach.

She looks so beautiful in her turtleneck and leather jacket, surrounded by a kaleidoscope of warm browns, light oranges, and bright yellows coming from the gourds all around us. The occasional chilly wind gust pulls at her hair, making her look like a movie star.

My breath literally hitches in my throat.

"Fine," Vinny grumbles, jumping onto the back of the truck. "Let's go," he tells me.

This is my shot to have some time with her without her brother, maybe ask for her number. "Uh, I'm gonna stay too. I don't want to get motion sickness or anything, you know?" I lie.

Good job, Matt. You sound super convincing.

I expect Vinny to say something, but he's too preoccupied with wanting to hop on the ride.

"Let's get some doughnuts first, yeah?" I ask Leo as the hayride pulls away with a suspecting Vinny and a green Clara. "And..." I turn nervously to Liza. "Can I, uh, buy you a glass of cider, too?"

Liza looks up at me, eyes wide, lips parted, while Leo pulls on her hand. "Yeah." She smiles. "I'd like that."

Yes!

We make our way to the stand by a huge pile of pumpkins in every size and color and order enough doughnuts to feed an army and a cider for each of us. Suddenly, we hear a very loud and distinct, "WOOOOO!!" coming from the hayride. We turn to see Vinny from afar with one hand around Clara and another in the air.

We burst out laughing, and I shake my head, running my fingers through my hair.

"I swear, I think his favorite part of being a parent is that he gets to play like a kid again," she says, laughing.

"I've never heard a more accurate statement in my life," I say, paying for our ciders and baked goods. I hand her a glass of cider and a doughnut before crouching in front of Leo. I hold out the doughnut in front of him. "This has a lot of sugar in it. Are you allowed to have this?"

He nods excitedly, salivating over the doughnut like a dog with its treat. "Yes!"

"Not really," Liza whispers to me and smirks.

I shrug and laugh. "A little sugar rush won't hurt him. Go crazy, kid." I hand him the doughnut, and he stuffs it in his mouth as far as it can go. He manages to stuff it halfway through, and I gotta say, I admire the effort.

"Thanks for this." She smiles, eyes shining through her long lashes.

"Anytime you need doughnuts or cider, I'm your guy." I throw a thumb in my direction.

WHAT. WAS. THAT?

She laughs once. "What?"

I groan and run a hand down my face. "I have no idea why I just said that." I used to be so smooth. What the hell has happened to me?

I open my eyes to look at her and assess the damage that I've caused, expecting her to look at me in confusion or disgust. Instead, I'm met with a sort of bemused expression. She smiles and is about to say something when we hear Vinny's voice from far away.

"Red alert. We got another regurgitation situation! Coming through! Coming through!"

People start to stare in the direction of her brother as he jogs toward us with Clara in his arms—who now happens to have her lunch all over her coat.

Poor kid.

"Oh no," Liza says with a grimace.

"We gotta *go*, guys!" Vinny stops in front of us, almost slipping on a puddle of mud. "Clara just threw up again. They made us get off the hayride! Danielle is gonna kill me."

I truly feel bad for Clara, but I'm really disappointed that we have to go back now. I was looking forward to getting to know Liza better without her brother hovering around. I need to think of a plan B.

"But Daddy, pumpkin!" Leo says.

He makes an absolutely fantastic point—this kid is a genius. I don't think I've ever loved a kid as much as I love Vinny's son.

"Vinny, why don't you take Clara home and come pick us up after? Leo wants to stay and play. Plus, Mom really wanted us to pick pumpkins to decorate the house. I'm not going home until we pick them."

Yes, Vinny. GO. HOME. Leave us here alone to "pick pumpkins."

"Fine," he sighs, exasperated. "I just need to get her home. I'll pick you guys up as soon as I leave her with Danielle." He stalks toward his car in a hurry.

We watch as Vinny runs to the parking lot, straps his daughter into the car seat at lightning speed, and drives away.

I've never spent much time with kids before, but I'm excited to spend the rest of the afternoon with Vinny's son, too. He looks like a trip—especially with the whole cussing thing.

I turn to Leo and ask him if he's ready for pumpkin-picking fun, whether he's pumped for us to go crazy and find the wildest and best pumpkins around.

"YES!" he screams, and I laugh at him his enthusiasm as he shoves the rest of his doughnut into his mouth. He takes my hand and pulls me toward the entrance of the actual pumpkin patch.

Chapter Four

LIZA

I MIGHT BE DELUSIONAL, BUT I'M REALLY STARTING TO think that the attraction I feel for Matt is not completely one-sided. Between the stolen glances in the rearview mirror on the drive over and the cider, I think I can safely say that we're both on the same page here.

I'm also pretty sure I caught him staring appreciatively at me when I reached down to pick up a mini pumpkin from a huge pile of them on our way into the actual patch. It was quick, but I definitely saw his eyes on my butt right before he tripped and almost knocked Leo over.

There's a huge contrast between the Matt of six years ago and this 2.0 version, and I don't just mean physically. Matt from med school was a total bro. He was attractive and nice, but I rarely saw him without a beer in one hand and a girl in the other. The guy tripping over his own two feet from ogling my butt is not the same one as the Matt from med school who would not hesitate to ask whomever he pleased out. This version of Matt is more mature, confident, yet oddly more self-conscious at the same time. It's like he's more calculated with his decisions rather than motivated by impulses—a fact that I really, really like for some reason.

When we reach the entrance to the patch, he lets go of Leo's hand to grab a wheelbarrow and tells him to get in it, to which Leo almost loses his mind.

"We're going on a ride!" Matt says enthusiastically, and Leo practically screams with glee.

Wait? What's that? Oh, it's just my uterus calling me to let me know that I need to marry this man. Super chill. No problem. I'll get right on that.

"WOO!" Leo cheers as Matt pushes him in a serpentine fashion, garnering the attention of strangers smiling all around us. They both look so adorable playing together that I can't help it. I pull my phone out and take pictures of this beautiful moment while I run after them, hoping one day I get lucky enough to find a man who will be as good a dad as Matt seems to be able to be.

After a few minutes of running, though, Matt tires and stops to take a breath.

"More! More!" Leo looks up at him with a pouty face.

Matt leans over and puts his hands on his thighs, panting. "Gimme a second, kid. I gotta recover," he practically wheezes.

"You okay there, champ?" I snort and pat him on the back—big mistake, as the feel of his muscles, even hidden under his coat, send me into a sudden frenzy. They have me wondering what it would be like to slip my hands underneath all those layers and feel his warm skin on my palm.

And that would be crazy, right?

Matt coughs out a laugh and stands up straight. "I promise I'm in much better shape than this. I just had an exhausting day today." He starts pushing the wheelbarrow forward again, stopping every so often so that Leo can meticulously evaluate each pumpkin before dumping it in his lap.

"What'd you do today?" I ask casually as I tread through the vines and mud next to him. But of course, none of this feels casual, for some reason. I'm trying to play it cool, but I'm dying to know every bit of information I can get from him, his life, anything that will give me insight into the man that he's become. I want to peel him like an onion, find out what he's like under every single one of his layers.

"Uh..." He winces. "I woke up really early today and drove all the way to Sag Harbor from New York to stay at a friend's house for the weekend, only to be promptly kicked out as soon as I got there." He looks extremely uncomfortable, but there's absolutely no way that I'm not gonna ask.

"Kicked out? Why?"

He stops and takes a deep breath, and I can tell he *really* doesn't want to go into specifics, but I don't care. I want to know. "I was kinda invited to my friend's house under the pretense that it would be a long weekend trip with a *group*, when in fact it was just the two of us and...I just wasn't into it." He shrugs.

"Ah," I say in understanding, and start walking ahead of him. He starts to follow behind, ignoring Leo as he stretches a little, swiping at a pumpkin and missing. "A friend of the *female* variety. An ex?"

And immediately I want to die because who asks that? He's gonna think I'm crazy, because the only type of person who asks something like that is a CRAZY woman. I've officially shown my card here, making it flat-out obvious that I like him—or am at least *interested* in him.

Although, is that really such a bad thing? I feel like he's into me too.

Matt winces. "Yes? I mean, she and I had a...uh...fling one time?" To his credit, he looks extremely uncomfortable about it. "But that's all it was, and it was a long, long time ago—about a year ago, when I was in the city for a long weekend, just visiting," he adds quickly. "And we were supposed to remain friends, just a one-time thing, you know? But I don't know..." He shrugs. "I guess she thought that doing it once meant it was a green light to do it whenever, and she never expected me to ever want to say no."

"So, what, you wouldn't sleep with her again, so she kicked you out?" I ask, shocked.

"I guess?" He shrugs, looking embarrassed. "I think she's not used to rejection."

I try to ignore the uncomfortable feeling in the pit of my stomach caused by the thought of Matt with another woman. It's completely irrational, I know. He's not anything to me, but I just can't help it. I don't like thinking about him with someone.

"I was about to leave and go back to the city when I remembered your brother was from around here, and I hadn't seen him in a while. I gave him a call from my car, and low and behold, you were all spending Columbus Day weekend in Sag Harbor!" He smiles sheepishly at me, and I flash a grin at him.

I want to switch off the topic of this other woman, and I'm guessing Matt does too, so I ask him what he's been doing since graduating from med school. I think he sees right through me, because he grins at me before answering.

"I was doing my residency in cardiology at a hospital in Boston. Just finished my fellowship and got a job at NYU - Langone a couple of months ago. I'm actually really excited to be back in New York. I've missed the city."

We reach a small playground in the middle of the patch, and Leo squirms in the wheelbarrow, trying unsuccessfully to get out. Matt notices and stops to help him. Leo runs toward the slide, and I yell out for him to be careful. I don't take my eyes off him when I ask Matt why he chose cardiology.

"My dad," he replies quietly.

I turn to look at him questioningly but try not to make it so that I'm pressing him for information.

"He, uh, died from a heart attack when I was about fourteen." He shrugs. "I was always into medicine, and I guess I thought I would honor my dad by trying to save other people from having a heart attack too. It's stupid," he says, shaking his head and running his fingers through his hair.

"It's not," I say. "I get it." I shrug. "My dad died a few years ago, too," I say, my hand flying automatically to the necklace around my neck like it always does when I talk about him. "But he died from lung cancer." Dad's fight with cancer was long and drawn out. Painful for him but also exhausting for my mother. It was years of treatments and doctor's visits, of spending every weekend out in Long Island for fear of it being the last time that I saw him, watching him deteriorate from one week to the next.

I try to rid myself of those thoughts by taking a deep breath, letting the crisp air fill my lungs and expand my chest. I close my eyes and briefly focus on the cold wind on my face, on the sweet scent of hay, and on the sound of leaves shaking with each gust.

After a few steadying breaths, I look over to Leo. I don't think I've ever been jealous of a two-and-a-half-year-old kid, but I am. I envy his innocence and the fact that he doesn't know that type of pain yet.

There is nothing like the pain of losing a parent.

Matt and I are quiet for a few minutes, both watching and not watching my nephew at the same time.

"What do you think is worse?" I ask out of nowhere. "To die suddenly like your dad did, where none of you were prepared for it? Or to die like *my* dad, long and drawn out but with enough time to say goodbye to everyone?"

Matt doesn't answer, choosing to take his time and think on what to say.

"I guess it depends on who you're asking—the family or the patient."

I sniff, and he reaches out to take my hand. I wipe my eyes, embarrassed. "God, I'm so sorry. It's just that being here is hard. It was tradition to come here when we were kids, and this year is the twins' first time, and Dad never even got to meet them. Danielle was just a few months pregnant when he passed away."

"It's okay." He pauses. "I mean, it's *not* okay, but it's okay that you're sad." He squeezes my hand and breaks the tension by asking, "Do you want another doughnut? I hear emotional eating is amazing."

I look up at him and laugh, wiping a final tear from my cheek. "No, thanks. I'm good."

He pulls a doughnut out from the paper bag and shoves half of it in his mouth, much like Leo. He chews on it for a couple of seconds and stuffs in the other half, causing the sugar to fall all over his face. Matt's beard is now covered in cinnamon-cider powder, and I've never wanted to lick someone so much in my life.

"What?" he asks self-consciously, his eyes gleaming with that signature mischief.

"Your beard." I point to his face with a smirk.

"What's wrong with my beard?" He starts patting his right side with sugar-covered fingers, making the whole thing worse.

"You're covered in sugar." We both laugh, and I shake my head at him. "Here," I say, reaching up on my tiptoes to brush it off, but when my hand meets his beard, grazing it softly, we both stop laughing. He gazes straight down into my eyes, and I'm hit with an intense array of dark greens, golds, and yellows that hypnotize me, making me forget where I am for a split second. His hand goes to the one resting on his cheek, and he holds it there.

A sudden gust of wind shakes the branches of the trees above, and the leaves come twirling down all around us, encasing us in a flurry of warm oranges and browns, leaving me hypnotized, eyes stuck on the face of this perfect and adorable man.

What is happening?

"Auntie Liza!" I hear Leo yell, and just like that, the moment is gone. I turn to my nephew to check that he's alright. "There is a big turkey over there!" He points behind me. "Can we go take a picture with him? *Please?*" he begs.

"Sure, buddy," I say cheerily as I help him jump off the playhouse. But really, I want to ask him why he couldn't have waited two minutes for me and his dad's friend to see where that moment would have led had he not interrupted it. Matt wipes his hands on a napkin as he clears his throat, scratching the back of his head before helping Leo back into the wheelbarrow. He tries to make a game out of it again, but it's so full of pumpkins that there's no way he can push a wheelbarrow with a toddler and about a million pounds of gourds through the mud.

WE TALK ABOUT EVERYTHING AND NOTHING AS WE SLOWLY make our way to the ten-foot wooden turkey. I think he's trying to prolong our time together, which makes my heart squeeze in my chest. Eventually, we reach our destination, and Leo runs to find a bale of hay to sit on for the picture. I don't get what all the excitement is about, but hey, I'm not a child anymore.

Matt laughs as he watches Leo jump from one hay bale to another, practically bouncing from excitement.

"I blame you, you know," I say to him in mock horror.

"*Moi?*" He points to himself. "What did I do?"

"You gave him the doughnuts, and now he's on a full-blown sugar high. You're gonna have to answer to Danielle when we get home, and he crashes."

He smiles back and raises his hands as if I were about to shoot. "I have no issues with that. Danielle seems to really like me, for some reason."

I noticed this too. She practically pushed me out the door, claiming to want to spend "alone time" with my mom and that I needed to bond with my niece and nephew. But I know that woman. She was trying to push me and Matt together.

Something I have no issue with, by the way.

"Picture!" Leo demands, stomping his foot.

"Alright, alright," I sigh and pull out my phone to take a picture of him with his arms and legs spread wide in front of the turkey. "*Perfect,*" I say, about to pull him off the bale.

"Hold on," Matt says, smirking. "What about you? You need to be in a picture with him, too." He pushes me and Leo back toward the bale of hay and asks us to sit, taking out his phone.

"Okay," he says to us both. "I want to see your best duck-faces, people."

"What's a duck-face?" Leo asks.

I've never felt so old in my life.

"What's a—? I can't believe you don't know this. It's the expression you absolutely *have* to do in every picture," he says. I snort at how serious he sounds. Their mom is going to *love* this. "You gotta put your lips like this." Matt purses his lips into the most beautiful duck-face imaginable. I never thought it would be possible for anyone to look good like that, but here I stand corrected.

I burst out laughing as he starts taking pictures of us.

"Stay still!" he tells me with a laugh.

"Do you need me to take a picture of you three?" an older woman with white hair pulled up into a perfect bun asks.

"Excuse me?" Matt replies, phone still in hand and pointed at us.

"Do you want me to take the picture so that you can be in it?" she asks.

Matt hands her the phone with a, "Sure," and a dazzling smile, leaving the woman momentarily awestruck.

Totally feel you, lady. It's been happening to me all freaking afternoon.

He sits down closely beside me and wraps an arm around my waist. My skin ignites, and my heart starts beating wildly. I know he's looking down at me right now, but I can't stand to make eye contact with him. Between his touch, woodsy scent, and just overall general proximity, my mind has momentarily turned to mush, and I just can't process anything that's happening right now. I'm barely able to keep a hand wrapped tight around Leo to make sure he doesn't run away. I cannot lose my focus by looking at Matt now. I'm so dizzy. My brain is so foggy... This man should probably come with a warning to avoid operating heavy machinery while in his proximity.

"Hey." He shakes me a little. "You need to smile. Pretend like you're not having the worst time ever sitting next to me and your nephew."

I have to look up at him now and smile because he sounds nervous, like he actually thinks there might be even a small chance that I'm currently not having the time of my life. He doesn't know that if I were someone who journaled, I'd spend the next two months *Dear Diary-ing* about this exact moment in time over and over and over again.

When my eyes meet his, he holds my gaze until the stranger taking the pictures interrupts us. "Well, I think that does it," she says proudly, handing Matt back his phone. "You three make such a cute family."

"Oh, actually—" I start to say, but she quickly walks away, leaving the sentence in the air. I run my fingers through my loose hair over my shoulder and help Leo stand.

Do not look at Matt. Do not look at Matt.

"Hey," he says as he picks up the wheelbarrow handles. I can hear his breathing speed up a little, voice shaking like he's nervous. He wipes one hand on his jeans before continuing. "I was wondering... Maybe when we're both back in the city, we might be able to, I don't know—"

"Hey," I hear my brother's voice behind us.

I've never wanted to commit murder in my life, but I can say with absolute certainty that today is the closest I've ever come to doing it.

I want to kill Vinny.

For a minute there, it felt like Matt was about to ask me out, and now we'll never know, will we? Thanks for nothing, Vinny. Between the vomit, Leo and his stupid turkey, and my brother, I have not been able to catch a break with this guy, I swear. Timing has definitely not been on our side today.

"What are you guys doing?" Vinny glares at Matt and looks back and forth between the two of us.

"Taking a picture with a giant turkey. Duh," I say, rolling my eyes at him, pretending like not everyone here—with the exception of clueless Leo—knows that Matt and I were definitely having a moment. And that Vinny just screwed it up.

"Right." Vinny looks down at the bales of hay, nodding slowly, lips thin. "Clara is really sick. Let's just pay for these fucking pumpkins and go home."

"Fucking!" Leo yells, and Vinny groans, running a hand down his face in frustration.

"Danielle is gonna kill me," he mutters under his breath.

39

Chapter Five

MATT

I NEVER THOUGHT A FIFTEEN-MINUTE DRIVE COULD FEEL SO awkward and tense, like trying to cut an ice cube with a butter knife.

I can feel the guilt of being caught mid-asking Liza out painted all over my face—and hers, for that matter. The anger and disappointment oozing from Vinny's entire being is obvious as he drives the car back home while I sit up in the front seat next to him.

I see Vinny chew on the inside of his cheek from the corner of my eye, watch him as his hands grip the steering wheel a little harder when I ask how his daughter is feeling, and I flinch from the coldness in his voice when he grunts out, "Not great, but she'll be fine."

Liza notices Vinny's change in mood as well. We keep subtly meeting each other's gaze in the rearview mirror, but instead of exchanging exciting and flirty glances like the ones on the way to the pumpkin patch, these looks are full of anxiety and concern. Her brother caught us right as I was about to break the bro code, and he knows it.

But I'm a grown man, for Christ's sake, not a teenager! And his sister is a grown woman. I shouldn't feel like a fifteen-year-old who was just caught by his parents, making out with his girlfriend in his car. Can't we all be adults here?

I resolve to talk to him tonight after dinner, see if he would be cool with me asking her out and get ahead of this thing. Maybe if I'm up front about everything, he won't mind so much. We're not college students anymore, and I think Vinny's a smart enough guy to understand that things like the bro code belong in the same category as keg parties. It's in the past. We've matured, evolved. We drink wine now, have serious relationships. That type of stuff.

I'm sure once I talk to him, he'll understand. He *has* to because I just spent one of the best afternoons of my life with this girl, and it wasn't even a date. We clicked, and talked, and played, and had an amazing time. I was dying to kiss her the whole afternoon and hope to do so sometime soon today. Maybe after I get her number?

When we reach the house, none of us say a word as Liza helps Vinny unbuckle Leo from his car seat and lift him out. Danielle greets us at the door and takes the baby from him while Liza follows closely behind.

I make my way toward the door, but Vinny stops me by placing a hand on my chest, lightly pushing back.

"What are you doing, man?" I ask, pretending to be confused but knowing full well what's about to go down.

"I should be asking you the same question, Matt." He glares at me.

I sigh and push his hand off me. "I don't know what you're talking about."

"Don't do that, man." He shakes his head at me. "Don't pretend like you don't know what this is about." He takes a deep breath. "Listen, you know I like you and that I'm happy you're back in the city so we can see more of each other, but..."

"But?" I ask after a relatively long pause.

"But I can't have you sniffing around my sister, man." He glares at me, hands on his hips, and I want to smack the look of self-righteousness off his face.

Really?

I scoff. "*Sniffing* around your sister? What am I, a dog?" I ask, offended.

"Hey, if the dog collar fits..." He shrugs.

"I resent that," I say, blood boiling now. One thing is to tell me that it would be weird for me to date his sister—which I totally get. Another is to tell me he doesn't want me dating her because he thinks I'm a fucking *dog*.

He exhales deeply and looks over my shoulder for a beat before looking me in the eye again. "Matt. Come on. I lived for four years with you in the same apartment, took the same classes, went to the same parties, saw a different girl leave your bedroom every morning. And it was fun, you know—when we were college students. But not anymore. And not with my sister."

"Why do you just assume I'm still like that. I mean, are *you?*" I know I've made a horrible mistake by turning it around on him, but I can't help it. I'm pissed now, rage coursing through my body, my hands fisting at my sides.

"Obviously not, man. I have a wife now, a *family*. But you're not there yet. You were just kicked out of your booty call's house, for fuck's sake!" He throws his hands in the air.

"*Ex*-booty call," I remind him through gritted teeth. "And she wasn't even a booty call!" I throw my hands in the air. "I slept with her *one time*, and it was a mistake."

"Whatever," Vinny sighs and runs his fingers through his hair. "I don't want Liza to be another one of your 'mistakes.' I don't want you with my sister, Matt. She acts all tough, but she's not, okay? She might not be hurting over her break-up, but she's still not in the best place. I've seen her slowly recover, but I can't have you ruining her progress. Not now, after everything that she's been through, and certainly not after a break-up—no matter how annoying her ex was."

I'm momentarily sidetracked. My newfound concern for Liza's well-being makes it so that I can't stop myself from asking what he means by that.

"She's still, you know, not in the best shape over my dad." He shrugs and shoves his hands in his coat pocket. "They were really close, and it really affected her when he passed away." He sighs and looks down at his feet. "I don't think she's really...been able to kind of...rebuild herself."

I just stare at him for a second while we both process this information, and I realize that, by the looks of it, Liza isn't the only Castelli sibling still struggling with their father's death almost three years later, because I don't think for one second that Vinny is only talking about his sister.

"Okay," I say reluctantly. "I'll stay away."

He looks up and nods quietly before replying with, "Thanks, man."

Vinny slaps me on the shoulder once and tells me to come inside and have dinner because his mother is making her famous butternut squash risotto, and I'm gonna love it.

I smile back, faking enthusiasm, absolutely gutted by my conversation with Vinny. He wasn't just asking me to stay away and respect the bro code. He was asking me to stay away because he's concerned about her, which is fair. But what he doesn't know is that he's just made it even more difficult now for me to stay away from Liza. I want to tell him that I know exactly what she's going through because I went through it too. I want to tell him that I *want* to help her through this, I *want* to be there for her, I *want* to be her person, and that I know this just after spending one afternoon with her.

I should've fought harder. I should've told him that I'm not that guy anymore, that I haven't been in a really long time. I want to tell him that, just like *he's* changed, so have I.

But he doesn't really give me the chance, because Vinny turns and quickly makes his way back into the house through the front door, leaving me standing outside in the cold like an idiot.

I'm rattled by our conversation, but I take a deep breath, trying to calm my anger and frustration, and head back inside where my eyes immediately go to Liza who is playing on the couch with her nephew. She turns to look at me and smiles broadly. I can't help myself; I smile back. I'm just automatically drawn to her, like a fucking magnet.

I make my way toward the couch, planning to sit next to her, fully aware that it might earn me an ass-kicking from Vinny, when Catterina walks through the door.

"*Elisabetta*," she says with authority.

"*Si?*" Liza asks her mom, and they proceed to have a conversation in Italian.

Oh, God. She speaks Italian.

Now I'm even more attracted to her. She is so fucking sexy.

I suppress a groan.

"Can you watch him?" she interrupts the fantasies currently playing in my head of her naked with me on a terrace in Capri overlooking the Tyrrhenian Sea. Hearing Liza speak Italian makes me want to drink wine and eat prosciutto and pizza and make love all day every day.

"Huh?" I ask. She must think I'm slow.

"Can you watch him? Leo? I have to go help my mom with dinner." She stares down at me with concern. "Hey, are you okay?"

"Yeah, sure." I pull the kid toward me, but he hops off the couch and crawls toward the twins' toy bin. "I'll watch Leo. No problem." I try to manage a smile, but I think I've been turned into goo.

"You okay?" she asks again in a low voice this time.

"Who is *Elisabetta*?" I ask in a near-trancelike state.

Liza smirks. "That's my name," she laughs. "*Elisabetta* is the Italian *Elizabeth*. Which is why people call me Liza."

I try to unsuccessfully swallow the knot in my throat and force a smile. "Cool," I say.

Cool?? COOL??

Something is seriously wrong with me.

"Uh, yeah, cool," she chuckles and walks away, looking over her shoulder once before disappearing through the swinging door.

Elisabetta.

I fall back on the couch and groan, rubbing both hands down my face.

"I am royally fucked," I mutter under my breath.

"Fucked! Fucked!" Leo parrots as he plays with his blocks on the floor in front of me.

Shit, Danielle is gonna kill me.

Chapter Six

LIZA

Mom invited Matt to stay over so he wouldn't have to drive back to the city alone at night (he had a packed weekender in the trunk of his car, so it was no big deal), and I was really excited to use that time to get to know him better. But after spending an incredible afternoon with Matt at the farm, he proceeded to ignore me most of the night, speaking to me only when necessary. *"Pass the risotto, please." "You dropped your napkin." "Can I use the shower now?"*

The frustration and confusion from last night made it really difficult for me to sleep soundly, leading me to wake up when it was still dark out.

Despite the freezing temperatures, I decide to go for a run early this morning, seeing as though it doesn't look like I'll be getting any more sleep today. I bundle up and run all the way down to the wharf, take a break, and make it back all before six am. Considering how long it's been since I've been out for a run, I think I did pretty well.

The exercise gave me some time to mull over everything that happened last night, which has left me incredibly confused.

I don't know what happened yesterday after the pumpkin patch. I mean, I thought he would ask me out later or at least keep flirting with me a little, but to completely ignore me?

It left me reeling, wondering whether every single dating instinct I had was faulty. I mean, they did lead me to Jeremy, after all.

Maybe it's just time for me to come to terms with the fact that I am just not good at dating. Period.

I should give up, just never go on a date again.

I daydream about what that would mean for my life, the amount of free time I would have. I wouldn't have to worry about texting the right thing to a guy, doing my make-up, dressing cute, or God, *shaving my legs*. It could be winter all year round as far as my legs are concerned, if you know what I mean.

Determined to give up on dating for the rest of my life, I walk into the dark kitchen after my run to get a bottle of water. Panting from exhaustion, I jump about twenty feet in the air at the sight of Matt seated at the kitchen table on his phone.

"Jesus!" I gasp, terrified. "You scared me!" My hand is on my chest, grasping a boob as if whoever I thought was there was gonna steal it. I drop my hand *immediately* after realizing my indiscretion but not before he notices with a smirk.

"Shhh!" He puts his finger to his lips. "You're gonna wake everyone up," he whispers and chuckles at my expression.

"I think you just took about five years off my life," I say quietly, taking a seat opposite him, trying to catch my breath.

Matt smiles at me and wordlessly gets up to go to the fridge, pulling out a bottle of water. He hands it to me and sits back down, crossing his arms in front of him.

He got me water, and I didn't even ask.

"Thanks," I say, trying to control my goofy smile by biting my lip and failing.

I suddenly feel extremely self-conscious. *Jesus.* I'm a sweaty, makeup-less, frizzy-haired, morning breath mess. Not exactly my most seductive look.

I chug the water, hoping it helps dispel some of the rank currently living and breathing in my mouth.

He chuckles and groans, running his fingers through his super-sexy bed hair.

"What's wrong?" I ask.

He stares at me for a moment with a soft smile on his lips. "Nothing." He shakes his head. "It's fine. Just a little frustrated, is all." He quirks half his mouth up and half down, like he can't decide whether to grin or frown.

I don't know why, but that little admission sends shivers down my spine.

I shrug, take another sip of my water, and ask what he's doing up so early.

"I had an emergency call from a patient." He waves his phone in his hand.

"Oh, I'm sorry," I say. Honestly, I don't know how doctors and other healthcare workers do it. Even when they're not on-call, they have to be on-call. You truly have to have a calling in order to be able to survive. In my opinion, it needs to be your passion.

"No, it's cool," Matt says. "My patient will be fine, thankfully. What about you? Why are you up so early?"

"Couldn't sleep. Thought I'd take advantage of my insomnia and work out for the first time in months," I say with a shrug.

He laughs, his dark eyes shining despite the early morning darkness.

We're quiet as we stare at each other over the table, never breaking eye contact. I want to swim in the dark-green waters of his eyes, dive into them and never come up. His eyes are low-lidded as he twirls his phone in his hand, and I dream about those fingers on me, about rubbing my face over his beard, dream about running my hands all over his body, ripping his t-shirt off, straddling him right here, right now.

Okay, calm down.

I'm practically panting again, heart racing. If I were a cartoon, my tongue would be hanging out of my mouth now. He looks so good in his white t-shirt that I'm afraid I'm going to spontaneously combust. Every time his muscles flex, I want to groan, pull him to me, and bite him. I don't know, but he makes me feel primal.

"So..." I say, needing to break the silence, needing to get my mind out of the gutter—and quick! Because look at those forearms sprinkled with dark hair.

"So?" he parrots in a gravelly voice. The air between us crackles.

"Are you gonna..." *Ask me out,* I want to say. "Are you gonna send me the pictures you took yesterday?"

Of me and Leo. Of you and me and Leo. Of us.

He grimaces and exhales deeply. "I don't think that's a good idea, Liza."

I sit back in my chair, confused. "Why's that?" Why on earth would sending me pictures not be a good idea?

He sighs and stares back at me intensely. "Because if I have your number, I'll be too tempted to call you later and ask you out."

My heart is definitely racing now, and I feel really light-headed. I marvel at how he can string a few words together and cause such a reaction in me. "Oh," is all I manage to say.

I'm the queen of wit, here, folks. Pull out pen and paper—take notes!

"Yeah," he sighs and looks down at the kitchen table, tracing patterns on the wooden surface with his fingers.

"And why is that a problem exactly?" I ask in a small voice. I'm totally down for you to ask me out, Matt. Been waiting my entire life, it feels like.

He looks up at me and furrows his brows, willing me to understand. All of a sudden, I get it. "Ah." I nod and take another sip of my water. "The bro code."

Vinny must have said something after seeing how cozy we had gotten at the farm.

He grimaces and half-smiles at me. "Yeah, I was reminded of its existence last night."

I knew it.

"I understand," I lie. "You can't ask me out. No biggie." I shrug, but it really is a biggie. It feels like a bigger biggie than breaking off my engagement did.

He sighs deeply, his frustration visible in the way his brows come together.

"There are ways around this, you know," I say, channeling all those years of watching *Suits*. I'm gonna lawyer my way into finding a loophole in this damn bro code if it's the last thing I do. I cannot just let the fact that Matt likes me roll over me like it's nothing.

He chuckles and scratches his neck. "Oh, yeah? Do tell, because I've been coming up short since yesterday afternoon."

I think for a minute and go for the most obvious option. "Um, I can ask *you* out?"

He shakes his head. "Nope, sorry. Can't go out on a date with you at all, even if you ask." He takes a deep breath and expels a groan. "That is definitely not allowed either."

"Hmmm," I say, absolutely thrilled to see that he seems to want this as much as I do—and that's saying something. It gives me hope but also reminds me how annoying my brother is.

I hate Vinny. I hate Vinny. I hate Vinny.

Just as I'm about to lose it and offer up a crazy idea like

running away to another country—because of course there's probably some regional stipulation, right?—an idea forms in my head. "What if we were to casually run into each other on accident? And then just happened to hang out?" I ask. "Does that count as breaking the bro code?"

Matt smiles broadly and sits up straight in his chair. "No, there's nothing in there about running into a bro's sister in public and saying hi, maybe talking to her for a few minutes. If you think about it, it would be incredibly rude of me *not* to say hi to you."

"Great!" I say. "So, now that that's clear...I just want to casually mention that I have brunch every Saturday at Angelina Cafe on Sixth Avenue at around eleven am. Just in case you were wondering. About what people do. On Saturdays. Since you haven't lived in New York for quite some time."

He laughs quietly at me and shakes his head.

"Nice to know that's where you'll be for sure next Saturday at eleven. I always wonder what people do around that time on the weekends."

We're both laughing when the kitchen door opens, and my sister-in-law walks in. In true Danielle fashion, she looks incredible even at six in the morning with no makeup, just her pajamas and a robe.

She glances back and forth between the two of us with a Cheshire Cat smile on her face before saying, "Don't let me interrupt. I just came down to get a glass of water." She snickers.

Snickers!

Matt and I are both quiet as she fills up a glass of water, never removing her eyes from us. She takes a sip and looks at Matt first, then me, and says, "You know..." She waves her finger back and forth between us. *Don't say it, Danielle. Don't freaking say it, PLEASE.* "You two make *such* a cute couple."

I roll my eyes at her, and she chuckles as she drops the bomb and walks away from us without looking back.

"She's such a pain," I mutter under my breath. "But I freaking love her."

He smiles fondly at me, and my heart squeezes in my chest. Matt reaches out to hold my hand, and the electricity is back.

I would love nothing more than to spend the rest of the morning sitting here talking to him, but I don't want to risk getting caught by anyone else. Mom is an early riser, and the twins get up around seven, which means Vinny does, too. Plus, I'm still sweaty and gross, a fact that Matt might not have noticed yet due to the early-morning sun but certainly will soon as more and more light fills the kitchen.

I sigh and say, "I'm gonna go take a shower now."

And do my very best to not think of you in it with me.

"See ya later," he calls out to me as I leave the kitchen.

Chapter Seven

MATT

I check the watch on my phone for the time and see that it's only 10:58 am.

She hasn't stood me up—yet.

Honestly, I don't even know if she's coming. When we talked about it that morning in her mother's kitchen, it *seemed* like she was being serious, but we didn't talk about meeting up again during the rest of my stay. I should have confirmed that we would be going through with this "chance" encounter plan that she devised, but I could never catch her by herself. Vinny had eased up a lot after our talk, no longer glaring at me every time I spoke to her, but he definitely did everything to keep us from being in the same room alone. And it's not like I had her number to confirm that she'd be showing up or anything. Nope. That would be against the rules.

Is this what people did before cell phones? Because it is a *nightmare*. Now I just have to stand here and wait, not knowing whether she was being serious or not.

What if she doesn't show? I had to switch shifts with another cardiologist at the hospital in order to get this Saturday free, and it would suck if I had to pull a double next week for no good reason.

I stand in front of the cafe's display of chocolates and candy, pretending to shop, while I take another sip from my coffee.

This really is amazing coffee. No wonder she comes here every weekend. Plus, the restaurant is beautiful and vibrant, full of people. The smell of butter and baked goods makes my mouth water.

I take comfort in knowing that I can just drown my sorrows in pounds of flaky croissants if she stands me up. I can just order a bunch of the ones in the window of the cafe, bring them home, and eat them all day.

I check my phone again and groan. 10:59 am.

Get it together, Matt!

I crack my neck on both sides and shake my arms a little, being careful not to spill a drop of this delicious coffee. Maybe I should have gone for some tea or something. This much caffeine was a bad idea. I'm all wired up.

Yup, must be the coffee. Definitely not because I'm nervous or anything. Definitely not because I know that, even though I'm *technically* not doing something wrong, I'm *definitely* doing something wrong.

I check my surroundings again, sorting through all the faces around me. I'm six-three, but I still stand on my tiptoes to look around the crowd for her face. I crane my neck left and right, completely losing hope and cursing myself for being dumb enough to show up. And then...

I see her.

She sees me.

She smiles.

I smile.

She looks *incredible*.

Her hair is in a braid this time, and she's dressed in loose denim overalls and a baggy long-sleeved tee underneath with cream high-top Chucks. I like that she chose a casual outfit for our non-date. I love that she's comfortable in her own skin. I love her style.

I do hate the fact that her current outfit is hiding all of her curves, though, but it's okay.

She bites that beautiful lip of hers and waves for me to come over.

No need to ask me twice.

I keep my eyes on her as I weave through the people waiting for a table. I can't believe she's actually here. I can't believe we're actually going to have our non-date. The anticipation is building in me, and suddenly, I'm nervous, my stomach turning, my heart racing.

After what seems like ages, I finally reach Liza, stopping right in front of her.

Do I hug her hello? Do I lean down and kiss her on the cheek? Handshake?

God, what is wrong with me?

"Hey," she says all breathily.

Hey it is, then.

"Hey," I hear Vinny's voice practically grunt beside me.

I do a double-take.

Fuck.

I try my very best to control my expression when I look at him, try my hardest not to show exactly how disappointed I am to see him standing here, crashing my "chance" encounter non-date.

Did she ask him to come? Did I misunderstand what this whole thing was?

"What are you guys doing here?! This is such a coincidence!" My voice is too high-pitched, shaky. I feel like it's betraying me savagely.

"Uh, having brunch?" Vinny says as if I were dense.

"Cool, cool, cool," I say, bobbing my head, completely *not* being cool. I start playing with the keys in my coat pocket with my free hand.

"What about you?" Liza asks cheerily.

"Was just getting coffee. Maybe brunch, I don't know." I shrug nonchalantly. *Just casually in the same place at the same time after spending the entire week pining away at you. Is it stalking if she told you where to stalk her?*

"Do you want to join us?" Vinny asks.

I'm momentarily taken aback by his invitation. It's not like we haven't spoken since last weekend, because we have. I even stopped by his house for dinner on Wednesday. But it's the fact that we're with his sister, who he deemed as completely off-limits, that shocks me. Is he just being polite? Or are we really back to being cool about his sister? Does he really think that, after that one conversation, I would never go near her in that way again?

Dude, you are so wrong.

But I take whatever I can get.

"Sure! If you think there's room," I say. I catch Liza smiling hopefully up at me.

"Lemme check with the host. We actually have a reservation," he says before disappearing in the crowd toward the host stand.

"What the hell, Liza?" I whisper-yell. "You didn't say your brother was coming!"

"Um, I didn't know he was coming until yesterday. I was supposed to meet him later today, but he wanted to eat before. And I don't have your number, remember? So there was no way I could warn you." She giggles. "But I'm glad I didn't tell you—you wouldn't have come otherwise."

I shrug. "To be honest, I've thought about you so much since

I last saw you that I don't think there is a single thing in the world that would have kept me away from you today. Not even your overprotective brother."

Her breath hitches, and she stares at me, eyes wide, lips slightly parted.

"Look at me, trying and failing to act cool." I laugh nervously, scratching my beard. This really isn't going as planned. I'm being too intense.

"No," she says quietly. "I—I feel the same way, I guess. I'm not gonna deny that I thought about you a lot as well. I was wondering whether you'd actually show." She smiles softly. "I'm glad you came."

"Yeah?" I ask with a grin, stepping closer, breathing her in as best I can with so much space between us.

"Yeah." She nods. My chest tightens in the best possible way, and I'm fucking aching to touch her, hold her, *anything*.

I slowly reach out my hand toward hers but drop it as soon as I see Vinny come back to us.

"Okay, I've got good news and bad news," he says. "The good news is that they can make space for Matt at our table." My heart speeds. I get to have a kind of date with Liza! Chaperoned by her brother, of course, but I get to see her and talk to her just the same.

God, I'm pathetic. But I'll take whatever I can get.

"What's the bad news?" she asks.

"The bad news is that the head of neuro at the hospital just called, and they need me to fill in for someone, so I can't join you for brunch. I have to go." Vinny kisses the top of his sister's head and shakes my hand.

Not to sound like an asshole, but how is this bad news? It's the most amazing news I've heard all day. All year, even. This is the best news ever.

"I'm really sorry, Liza. I'm not gonna be able to help you

move today," he tells her nervously. "Maybe we can find some last-minute movers to help? Or do you have any friends you can call that can manage heavy lifting? I'll offer them some cash."

"You're moving?" I ask her, ignoring her brother.

"Yes," she says sheepishly. "I, uh, used to live with my ex. Had to find my own place."

Jealousy courses through my entire body, heating it, boiling the blood in my veins. I'm surprised by how much that little statement—the little "*I used to live with my ex*"—turns me into an irrational, green monster. It also hits me just how recent her break-up is.

Shit, am I a rebound??

No, I can't be. There's no way that I am. If she feels even a fraction of the connection I feel with her, there's no way I could be *just* a rebound to her.

"I can help!" I offer a little too enthusiastically, wanting to push away any more negative thoughts from my mind. "I mean, if you need help, I can help you. I have the afternoon off today."

Vinny looks at me and nods. "Okay...well...I guess you'll have Matt here to help you out. Thanks, man."

"Great!" Liza says. I silently beg her to tone down the enthusiasm. I realize that we both want to spend time alone together, but she's got to control it! He's going to notice! "I'm sure I'll be in good hands."

"Right. Matt knows exactly what to do with his hands. And where *not* to put them," he mutters, eyes like daggers, sending me warning signs.

Don't you fucking dare touch her, Matt. Remember what we talked about.

I ignore him completely.

He kisses the top of his sister's head again with a final warning glare in my direction, and we watch him walk out.

"Did he just subtly-but-not-so-subtly threaten you in front of me?" she asks, giggling. I'm glad one of us finds this funny.

"Kind of," I laugh nervously. I really do care about Vinny. He's a great friend and a smart guy, but I think he's being unreasonable. And I don't want to be sneaking around forever, just long enough for Liza and me to build a solid base so that we can go to her brother and show him...proof of concept? Like a start-up.

Yup, that's what I need.

Sigh.

I don't even know what I'm saying anymore.

"Let's get our table."

I put my hand on the small of her back and guide her over to the host so that he can seat us.

The fact that I can touch her is almost as exhilarating as the action itself. I feel an electric current run up and down my arm. I'm in complete disbelief that we're here, and my hand is there, and we're so close I can smell the coconut scent of her shampoo in her hair. I lean over subtly and inhale, closing my eyes, and thank God she's so short she can't see me do it. I momentarily feel like a creep, but then I remember that I'm here with her because she wants me too, and I stop caring.

When we reach the table, I pull out her chair, and she takes a seat, smiling up at me as she scoots in.

"Hey," she says as I take the seat in front of her. "We're kinda on a date."

I smile broadly and laugh. "Nope, not possible, remember? This is a chance-encounter, non-date situation."

"Ah." She nods, placing her napkin on her lap. "My mistake." She grins.

I reach out for her hand—*finally!*—and kiss it. Considering we've never even kissed on the lips before, it's a bold move, I know. It feels so intimate but like the right thing to do, so I do it again—and I know she likes it.

Liza blushes and shakes her head at me with a smile. "You're trouble."

"Am I?" I ask, smirking. I love that she thinks I'm trouble. It means she feels something there, quite possibly as deep a connection as I do.

"Yes." She bites her lip, and it gives me a strange thrill.

"I'm okay being trouble so long as I get to spend time with you," I say, meaning every word.

She laughs. "You know that means you actually have to help me move, then, don't you?"

I decide to go for it and lay all my cards out on the table for her. I don't care about her brother forbidding me from seeing her anymore, and I don't want to play any more games. I like her, and I want her to know it. I want to own up to it.

"Liza." I bring her hand to my lips with both of mine this time. "I really could not give a shit what we're doing so long as we're together. You need me to spend the entire day building IKEA furniture with you? No fucking problem. I'll build the shit out of your MALM wardrobe or your BILLY bookcase. I don't care. I want to get to know you better and spend time with you, and if that's what I have to do to be able to get it, then I will do it."

She blushes, and a slow smile spreads across her face.

"Okay, then," she says simply. "But just as an FYI, I didn't get a MALM wardrobe. I wasn't into that line."

Chapter Eight

LIZA

I DON'T THINK I'VE EVER HAD SO MUCH FUN BUILDING furniture in my life, and I freaking *love* building IKEA furniture. I'm the crazy person who volunteers to help her friends when they move or buy new stuff. The simplicity of the process and the sense of accomplishment you get as you stand in front of the bookcase or dresser you built is almost incomparable. It's the same reason why I love doing my paint-by-numbers sets. I have tons of them (don't judge—I already got teased by Matt).

I mean, it's *genius*. They make the instructions so simple for something that ends up looking so great *and you made*. How can you not love it? Add the guy you're crushing hard on to the mix, and you've got yourself the best day ever. *Especially* when said man is building most of the furniture for you while you unpack. I mean, is there really *anything* sexier than a man building something for you? Is it the power tools? Is that it? It must be that because, *my God*, look at him holding that orange Black & Decker drill.

Plus, he basically unloaded everything in my U-Haul by himself. He would only let me carry the light stuff.

Sigh.

He's such a good provider.

It's also been an amazing day because we've been able to get to know each other more. I've been able to ask him the million questions I wanted to ask and learn more about him—something I've been dying to do since the first moment I laid eyes on him over six years ago.

He asked me what it was like to grow up with Vinny (we didn't spend too much time together because of the age difference, but as we've gotten older, we've gotten closer), what my dad was like (the best guy in the world), why I picked Psych (I'm fascinated by human behavior), what the hell all those paint-by-numbers were (I explained how working with your hands is supposed to help with anxiety and depression, and I hardcore went through a painting phase after Dad died), and what my relationship with Jeremy was like, that I only recently figured out there was always something missing. I was pretty open about everything and threw back as much as I took—except I chose not to ask him about *his* exes. I knew his reputation and really didn't feel like having it confirmed. I wanted to go off of the Matt I was getting to know now and not the Majestic Matt who partied with my brother all those years ago.

I did ask about a million other things about his life, though. I learned that he's from Florida, which I joked I wouldn't hold against him. I learned that his mother, who owns a fairly successful jewelry line, remarried a couple of years after his dad passed and that it was difficult for him to accept, that it's still sometimes hard to see her with someone, but that he's happy that she's happy. I learned he prefers The Rolling Stones over The Beatles but respects the commercial value of the latter. I learned how meditation and yoga saved him from a mental breakdown his first year of residency. How, when he was in college, he used drinking and partying as a way to blow off some steam, but as a resident, he couldn't act the same way, and he had to find healthier ways to deal with the pressure.

This topic turned him glum, to which I had to ask why. He was quiet at first, like it pained him to admit what he was going to say, but he told me anyway.

"I was an immature ass up until I started my residency. I really couldn't deal with anything in my life at the time. I don't even know how I made it through school with good grades. I was acting out in so many self-destructive ways... I'm not proud of who I was then." He shakes his head. "I was just...lonely, I guess. Mom was traveling all the time with her new husband, and I don't have any siblings... I don't know. I...I kinda felt like an orphan."

My heart breaks for Matt, and I walk over to where he's kneeling over the bed frame he's been putting together for me. Losing my dad was horrible, but I was lucky enough to have my family to get through it together. I can't imagine what it must have been like for him to go through that all alone.

I place my hand on his back in an effort to comfort him, to let him know that he's not alone—not now, at least—feeling every muscle under my fingertips, wanting to touch him under his t-shirt.

"I don't really remember you being that bad of a guy, but I don't think it matters anymore. I think the guy you are now is pretty amazing—and that's all that matters to me," I say.

I feel his deep sigh rumble through his back before he turns to look up at me with a pained smile.

"I hate that I don't remember you from before," he says sadly.

"It's just as well." I shrug, trying to lighten the mood, aching to run my fingers through his hair, touch his beard again, lean my head on his shoulder. "I looked hella awkward senior year of high school."

My plan works. He chuckles a little and runs his fingers through his hair, kneeling up straight. I lean down and kiss him on the cheek, his beard tickling my lips, as if it were nothing, as if we do it every day, and walk back over to my box of books while leaving him stunned on the floor. I feel his eyes on me as I quietly stack my Psych textbooks into a neat pile, waiting to be shelved, but he doesn't say much.

Eventually, he breaks the silence. "Can I turn on some music?"

"Sure," I say, disappointed. Music means he doesn't want to talk anymore, means he wants to fill the silence with someone else's melodies and voice, and all I want to do is hear his.

I walk over to my laptop currently resting on the nightstand we built a few hours ago, and he walks over to join me.

"Here. Go nuts," I deadpan as I open Spotify and slide my laptop to face him.

"You're gonna let me peruse your Spotify without supervision? Let me look at your playlists?" he asks in wonder. I raise a questioning eyebrow at him. What's the big deal?

"Going through someone's music without supervision is akin to looking through the window of someone's soul without permission, did you know that?" he tells me, completely serious.

I laugh once and suddenly feel a little nervous. "Well, you have my permission to look into my soul."

I guess he's a little right. What will he say? I mean, I have a really weird combination of music in my library. If he were to make an assessment on my soul based on my playlists, he'd think I have a split personality disorder. I have everything in my collection from Britney Spears (because she's eternal) to Luis Fonsi, to Frank Sinatra, to Credence Clearwater Revival, you know? I even have a ton of Red Hot Chili Peppers and Green Day (a byproduct of having an older brother from that generation). I love them all.

I have a playlist for every mood, every theme, every situation. I have a playlist for when it rains, for when I'm sad, for when I'm studying. I have decades playlists. I have a #GirlBoss playlist. *Everything.*

Luckily, I number them, so I don't make it easy for him to know why I picked different songs to go into a specific grouping, and that alleviates some of my nerves.

"Ooh, cool. This is one of my favorite songs," he says and hits play.

The Rolling Stones's "Wild Horses" starts filling my new apartment with a melancholic guitar intro and Mick Jagger's distinctive voice. My stomach plummets to the ground.

"Hey, this is a really good playlist," he says, scrolling through it, brows furrowed in concentration.

It's my wedding playlist.

He turns to look at me with a smile. "You want to dance?" he asks, and I can feel the blood drain from my face.

It takes a while for me to process his question, but I eventually take his outstretched hand, and he pulls me to him. I lean my head against his chest and inhale a deep, unsteady breath. He smells like cedar, like nights by the fire drinking wine. He puts a hand around my waist and one in my hair, holding me so close I can barely breathe—but it's not from how tight he's holding me. No. It's because this is the song I've always wanted to dance to as my first dance with my husband.

Jeremy hated it. He wanted something more conventional, like Sinatra. I tried to explain to him that, though unconventional for a first song, The Stones are my favorite band, that I listened to them all the time with Dad, that this is my favorite song ever. But he never got it, and the one time I convinced him to try it out, to dance with me, it was all wrong. We didn't even make it past the first verse before he pushed me away.

But Matt.

Matt picked it out for us without having a clue what the song means to me.

"To be honest, I just wanted an excuse to hold you, and I think this is the perfect song," he whispers, his voice low and gravelly, tickling my ear.

He wanted to dance with me, and he picked *this song*. He couldn't have possibly known what this song means to me, could he? Is this seriously just coincidence? I feel a knot in my throat and try to stifle a sob.

Why couldn't we have had this earlier? Why couldn't my dad have met *him* instead of Jeremy before he passed away? Would he have been opposed to me dating him like Vinny so clearly is? Or would he have understood that he's not the same guy he was in med school?

I'm so overcome with emotion, both loving and hating that I'm in his arms, swaying to the song I always saw myself dancing to with the right man at our wedding, that a sob breaks through me—I can't help it. He gently pushes me back to look me in the eye. When I meet his gaze, his eyes widen with concern at the tears in my eyes. His hands graze up my arms to cup my face.

"Hey, what's wrong? What did I do?" he asks as his eyes bounce between mine.

"Nothing, nothing," I say, sniffling. "You didn't do anything wrong. I just need a moment." I feel like I'm on the verge of having a full breakdown and want to kick him out so he doesn't have to see me like this, but I don't want to hurt his feelings.

"I came on too strong. I'm so sorry," he says, his voice anguished. "I fucked it up."

"No, you really didn't," I say, shaking my head. I squeeze my eyes shut, trying to keep from crying. "It's not you; it's me," I say.

I just realized that if we keep going like this, I'm gonna end up falling for you, and it pains me that my dad will never get to meet you.

This is so ridiculous.

I walk toward one of my suitcases and rifle quickly through my clothes, pulling out the first things I see.

"What are you doing?" he asks softly.

I take a deep breath, steeling myself. I'm afraid I'm going to start crying the second I open my mouth, so I do my very best to control it when I say, "I'm gonna take a quick shower, okay?"

"What?" he asks, eyes wide and confused, looking at me like I've lost my mind.

"Yeah, just a quick one. I'm so sweaty and gross, you know?" I start backing into the bathroom with my clothes, leaving him in the middle of my bedroom by the unfinished bed.

I turn on the shower, willing it to heat quickly so I can cry, get it out of my system without having him hear me. I strip quickly and run my fingers under the stream. Once the water is warm enough, I practically throw myself into the shower. Under the hot water, I press my forehead to the cold tile and let the tears stream down.

WHEN I LEAVE THE BATHROOM IN A PAIR OF CLEAN DARK jeans and a dark-green sweater, I find Matt sitting on the edge of my new bed. In the time I spent in the shower, trying to recover from a mild breakdown, he not only managed to finish building it, but added the mattress and a fresh set of sheets for me.

He's incredible. Majestic Matt is nothing in comparison to this Matt 2.0.

His eyes are stuck on the floor, holding his head in his right hand and a hammer in the other. When he hears me approach him, he looks up to meet my eyes.

"Hey," he says softly, brows furrowed. "You okay?"

I walk slowly over to him and put my hands on his shoulders, standing between his legs. Matt drops the hammer on the floor and puts his hands on my waist. I press my forehead to his. I close my eyes and inhale, letting the combination of his natural cedar scent combined with the one of particle board reach every corner of my body, soothing my heart and soul.

"Yeah," I whisper. "I'm fine now."

He takes a deep breath but thankfully doesn't ask me to elaborate.

"You made my bed," I say.

"I didn't know if you wanted me to leave, but I didn't want you to have to finish it on your own or leave you to sleep on the mattress," he says softly.

My heart glows in my chest, doing backflips and chanting, *"I want him!"*

We stay like this, unmoving and quiet, until his stomach breaks the silence with a grumble, and we both separate with laughter. Matt's entire face flushes in embarrassment.

"Sorry," he says. "We just haven't really had anything to eat since brunch." He lifts a shoulder.

Man's gotta eat.

"Let me take you out for a beer and a Wiener schnitzel." I smile.

"A Wiener schnitzel?" he asks, amused. "That's...oddly specific." He smirks at me.

I laugh. "I want to take you to one of my favorite places in New York as a thank you for all of your help today. It's a German bar on the Upper East Side with the best beer. They have some amazing food, but they're best known for their Weiner schnitzel."

"All right." He grins, kissing me on the neck, making my knees buckle.

This man...

It's weird. We haven't even kissed on the lips yet, but already I know how he feels against my skin. I can't even imagine what it would be like to actually have his mouth on mine. I'd probably spontaneously combust. I stifle a moan when he kisses right under my ear and do my best to control my breathing as heat courses through my belly.

"I would've guessed you would take me somewhere Italian," he whispers against my skin, punctuating his sentence with another kiss and a light lick of his tongue.

I push him away by the shoulders and look seriously into his surprised eyes. "I need you to understand something right here and now if we're to have any type of relationship, friendship or otherwise."

He looks up at me seriously, expectantly.

"My mother makes *the best* Italian food in the world, and no one else's cooking comes close. So, we will never go to an Italian restaurant together. Got it? It's just a waste of money."

"Okay, understood." He laughs and stands. "I agree that your mother's cooking is unreal, having had the pleasure of recently experiencing it." He nods. "I have never been so well fed as I was last weekend." And I believe that he's being serious. She's just that good.

He kisses me on the forehead and pulls me toward the front door.

Chapter Nine

LIZA

Matt wraps an arm around my waist, pulling me in as we wait for our table. I go willingly, snuggling into him. I want to savor this moment, take a picture—*something*. I'm on a non-date with Matt! How did this even happen?

He's so tall.

"Your table is ready," the hostess announces, glancing at me knowingly, apologetically—I think she can tell I was kind of having a moment. I flush at the thought of the goofy grin I must have had on my face. But can you really blame me? Matt is incredible and handsome. There's no way I could have resisted him, no way I wouldn't be on cloud nine now.

When we reach our table, he pulls the chair out for me again and sits across.

His phone starts ringing in his coat pocket, and he says, "Sorry, I need to check this. Might be the hospital." He pulls it from his pocket and checks the screen. His brows furrow, and he chooses to ignore the call.

"Not the hospital," he mutters, tension clear in his voice.

O...kay?

"Okay. So, you said I need to order the Wiener schnitzel?" he asks in a forced cheerful voice. Matt pulls up the menu and reads with seemingly great concentration.

"What's wrong?" I ask.

"What? Nothing. Why?" But it doesn't look like nothing's wrong.

I narrow my eyes at him. "Why are you being weird all of a sudden?"

Matt hesitates for a minute. "I'm not being weird."

I raise an eyebrow at him. "Matt. Come on. Tell me."

He sighs and shrugs. "Your brother's been calling me all afternoon, is all. Probably checking in on us."

"He has? That's weird. I don't have any missed calls from him." I pull out my phone to double-check. Nope. Nothing. Not even a text.

"No, Liza. You don't get it." He shakes his head with a small smile on his lips. "He's not calling to see how we're doing with the move and whether we managed to finish. He's probably calling to make sure I didn't try anything," he says, guilt clear across his face.

"I mean, you didn't. We didn't," I say curtly.

He tilts his head at me. "Come on, you know that's not true."

I think back to him holding me close as he whispered his confession in my ear, how it felt to be in his arms, his lips on my skin. We didn't *do* anything, but we also didn't *not* do anything. Matt and I definitely made it clear that we have feelings for each other, even if we didn't flat-out *say* it. Which is definitely not going to be okay with Vinny, considering he flat-out asked Matt not to pursue me.

"Just answer the phone next time he calls. It's no big deal. Or better yet, call him. Tell him the truth—without the details. You helped me move and build furniture, just like you said you would, and now I'm taking you out for a beer as a thank you." I shrug. "All of this is true. You're not lying."

He frowns, looking down at his phone uncertainly. "You mean I should call him now?"

"If you call him while we're together, it will make it seem like we're not hiding anything—which we aren't."

"Except the fact that I felt you up to the voice of Mick Jagger, made you cry, and then made out with your neck," he deadpans, and I burst out laughing. Matt chuckles awkwardly, like he still can't trust that my breakdown wasn't his fault.

"Seriously," I say. "Call him back right now."

He takes a deep breath and dials Vinny, putting the phone to his ear and keeping eye-contact with me while the phone rings.

"Hey, man, sorry. I didn't see your calls. We've been busy all day." Matt closes his eyes as he listens to Vinny on the other end. "No, yeah. We pretty much got everything done. It went by really quickly because we were so focused, you know?"

I stifle a laugh.

"Yeah, I'm, uh, actually with her right now." He winces in anticipation of Vinny's reply. "Yeah, I know it's pretty late, but we hadn't eaten, and she just wanted to buy me some food and a beer as a thank you." I check my phone. It's only 8:30! My brother is being completely ridiculous.

Matt looks anxiously at me. I shoot him two thumbs up and add an encouraging smile.

You got this, Matt!

"Yeah, I'm gonna go home after this." I roll my eyes at his line of questioning. "Okay, I'll talk to you tomorrow, man." He hangs up and looks down at his phone.

"I don't like lying to him, Liza." He looks at me seriously. "Do you want whatever this is?" He waves a hand back and forth between the two of us. "Because I do. And I don't want to lie to your brother. If you want to do this, if you want to pursue this...I'm going to have to ask him if it's cool."

"Matt, you don't need *permission* from my brother to date me," I say, annoyed. This is such a ridiculous, antiquated thing. I know that my family is very Italian and traditional, but Jesus. Just because he's *technically* the oldest male of the Castelli family doesn't mean we need to act like we're in a movie or a different century. He's not Vito Corleone, for fuck's sake. And I am a feminist—I'm not about to let my brother control my life.

"I like your brother, Liza. And he's always been a good friend to me. We stayed in touch after school, and I was actually really excited to get this new job because one of the perks was that it meant I got to hang out with him again. I don't want to be a bad friend to him by going behind his back. I also don't want to give him any ammo, anything that he can use against me.

"Vinny is an adult. I'm sure that once we explain that this isn't some random fling, he'll be okay with it." He says it with such determination, with such rational thought supporting his theory, that for a split second I almost believe it. But that's not how things are in real life.

I shake my head at him. "He's not going to see it that way, believe me. I know my brother. Ever since my dad died, he's had this protectiveness come out with me and my mom. It's like he feels it's his job to shield us from all the things he considers could hurt us in the world. I'm telling you, it would be best if we just see where this goes first before rocking the boat." I take a deep breath and look down at my hands. "I really, *really* like you, Matt. But I'd rather chase this for a little bit, see where it goes, before stirring the pot and upsetting him or ruining your friendship. Like you said, Vinny means a lot to you, and you don't want to mess things up. If you go to him with this and we don't work out in two weeks because you don't like my quirks or we have zero sexual chemistry..." He snorts, because there is obviously a ton of chemistry here. "...then you will definitely fuck up your friendship.

"Properly rekindle your relationship with him now that you're both in the city again. We can hang out and date a little and reevaluate on December first," I say.

Matt smirks. "You're setting a deadline for us?"

"More like a checkpoint. It's the academic in me." I smile with a shrug. "It's also the day before I start finals, and I don't want to have to worry about this while I enter hell week."

He laughs. "Fair. We can reevaluate on December first, then."

"So...can we call this a date, then?" I ask, biting my lip and looking up at him with pleading eyes.

"Mmmm, I don't know. I don't even have your number yet," he teases.

"Take out your phone right now, then. You owe me some pictures anyway." I slap his arm playfully.

He laughs and takes a minute to scroll through his phone.

"Alright, I'm ready. Give me your number."

I list off my digits and immediately get a ping. I expect to receive a picture of me and Leo or at least one with the three of us together, but what I get instead is a picture of Matt mid-laugh, staring down at me as I look up and beam at him. My heart starts doing backflips in my chest.

We look so *happy*.

I feel a goofy smile spread across my face. "What is this?" I ask, completely smitten.

He looks down at me with soft eyes and shrugs. "I don't know. I guess the woman who was taking our photo really did think we were a couple and decided to take one of just us, too." I catch him glance at my lips before his eyes meet mine again. "I spent all week looking at that picture, Liza. All week thinking about you and our connection and wanting to see you again."

Whoa.

"I was so happy when Vinny relaxed toward the end of the weekend, and I was able to spend time with you—even if it was practically chaperoned. And then, after I got back to the city, I kept counting down the days to see you, hoping to God you weren't joking about brunch or that you would change your mind." He puffs out a breath and scratches his beard. "Sorry, I'm being incredibly intense. I'm embarrassed." He squeezes his eyes shut and pinches his nose between his thumb and forefinger.

I'm speechless. I think about maybe saying something dumb to relieve the tension but decide I don't want to ruin the moment. Instead, I snuggle closer into his side and stare at the picture of the two of us on my phone, marveling at how two people can meet again at a different point in time and hit it off, how different things can be.

It makes me wonder whether everything in life really is about timing and how happy I am that we got a second chance to meet in order to get to this.

"Jesus Christ, you were right. This place is amazing," Matt says around a mouthful of Wiener schnitzel. He swallows it down with a chug of Hofbräu beer.

"Wow," I laugh. "You're really going for it, aren't you?"

He laughs a throaty laugh and wipes some beer foam off his beard with the back of his hand. "Sorry, I know I must look like a wild hyena right now. I was just *really* starving."

"You should have told me!"

"It's okay. It was worth the wait. This food is incredible, and the beer is so good." He cuts another piece and shoves it in his mouth. "Plus, the whole Bavarian decor and overall over-the-top theme of the place is hilarious. I really dig this vibe." He laughs, and we look around at the decorated walls of the restaurant and the waitresses dressed in lederhosen with their braided pigtails.

"I'm glad you like it. They also have a two-liter boot-shaped beer glass if you're down to try it one day!"

"Oh my God, you mean like from that movie *Beerfest*? The Das Boot? I don't think I can handle something like that anymore. I swear, I might only be a couple of years past my twenties, but as soon as you hit thirty, *it. Is. Brutal.* It is so hard to recover from a hangover."

I laugh at him. "Well, I'm smack in the middle of my twenties, so I think I'm still good."

"Enjoy your final years of youth!" he says with a smirk.

I'm about to say something funny about how he's obviously not old yet, what with being thirty-one and all, when I spy Jeremy, of all people, getting up from a table with another woman in my direct line of sight.

"*No way,*" I mutter under my breath.

Matt looks over his shoulder in the same direction I'm looking. "What? What is it?"

"Jeremy is here. What the hell is he doing here? He had a list of places he wasn't allowed to go back to, ever, and this was in the top five."

"Huh?"

"My ex. Jeremy," I whisper. "He hated this place. Why is he even here?" He squints in our direction and smiles wickedly when he spots me, changing course. "Oh my god, he's coming over. I apologize in advance for what's about to happen, because it's bound to be bad."

Matt stares at me, wide-eyed. "What is—"

"*Elisabetta,*" Jeremy says, and I wince. He only calls me by my full name when he's trying to impress someone, to make them believe that he knows how to speak Italian, when the most he can say is, "*Potrei vedere la lista dei vini?*" ("May I see your wine list?") because, according to him, all you need to know in Italy is how to order wine.

Just thinking about it makes me want to roll my eyes.

Sometimes, when I think about our relationship, I wonder why I ever thought I could be happy with him. I mean, *look* at him. He's dressed in his Indiana Jones attire again, minus the bullwhip and the Harrison Ford good looks. Like, we get it, you're a professor. Get over it.

"I believe this was on my list of restaurants, Jeremy," I say curtly.

He scoffs and says, "I thought we could be adults about this. You know I always loved this place." I snort. He always fought me tooth and nail whenever I wanted to come here. "Plus, Heidi here was homesick." He points to the redhead clinging to his side.

I'm assuming Heidi is from Germany?

"And who is this?" he asks with a raised eyebrow. "A date? How lovely. I was so very concerned you would end up alone, to be honest."

I scoff in disbelief. Is he kidding right now? Is he seriously so petty that he has to try and undermine me in front of a guy?

"Actually," I hear Matt say. "I'm not her date. I'm her boyfriend."

What now?

"Boyfriend? But we have only been broken up two weeks." Jeremy frowns.

"Sorry, and the redhead is?" Matt asks pointedly. He's allowed to have a girlfriend after two weeks, but I'm not?

"Well, but that's different. Heidi and I, uh..."

77

...started seeing each other while Liza and I were still together?

He doesn't finish the sentence, though. Instead, Jeremy clears his throat and says, "Well, I hope you like a challenge, because she is a piece of work, my friend." He puts his hand on Matt's shoulder.

Matt stares down at Jeremy's hand and pushes it off, rising from his seat.

Oh no.

"I think *you're* the one who's a piece of work here, *friend.*"

Jeremy snorts and looks at me. "Wow, Liza. *Brava.* You have actually found someone as dramatic as you," he snarls. "Let's go, Heidi." He takes the redhead's hand and drags her out of the restaurant, looking over his shoulder once at us before disappearing into the cold October night.

"Thanks for standing up for me," I say as Matt takes his seat. "He's such a loser." I shake my head.

"He really fucking is." Matt's eyes are still on the front door, on alert in case Jeremy comes back. "I don't get what you ever saw in that tool."

I flush, embarrassed. "Honestly, I don't really know *why* I was with him. I think I first started dating him because I was sad Dad was sick and looking for a distraction or companionship. Also, the idea of dating a professor was kinda hot at the time." He chuckles at my confession. "Then, when Dad passed away, Jeremy was actually really supportive. Once I started getting better, though, I started seeing his annoying side, and I guess I started wondering what we were even doing together. But then he proposed, and I remembered my dad saying how much he liked him for me, and I guess that's how I wasted three years of my life."

I shrug casually, like it's no big deal that I spent the last three years in a boring relationship with a horribly conceited man. I wash away the bitterness with a giant gulp of beer and smile half-heartedly at him.

"It's okay," I say. "Thanks for standing up for me and for pretending to be my boyfriend," I say again. "It wasn't really necessary, but thanks anyway."

He laughs a little, embarrassed. "I just *hated* how he just assumed you would basically die alone. He's such a tool."

"Definitely." I smile coyly at him.

"What?" he asks.

"It's nothing. It's just...this wasn't the first time you helped me with a breakup."

He looks at me, confused. "I don't understand. What do you mean?"

"It makes sense for you not to remember this, since you don't remember me at all, but the reason I visited New York to see Vinny the first time I met you was because I had just broken up with my ex. I was really sad and embarrassed and took a train into the city without telling my parents. I showed up at your apartment, crying, looking for my brother, but he wasn't there. You answered the door and invited me in, asked me if you could do anything for me. I told you I just wanted my brother, that my boyfriend had broken up with me. You said Vinny wouldn't be home for a couple of hours, told me to sit in the living room, and left.

"I thought you had left to go to class or something, but you came back fifteen minutes later with a Big Mac, fries, a Coke, and an apple pie for me." The memory makes me smile, makes me feel all warm inside. I fell massively *in-crush* with Matt then, never having forgotten the kindness he showed me, even over six years later.

"I—I'm so sorry. I don't remember any of this," he says sadly.

"It's okay." I shrug. "I was just a kid then. I don't know whether you did that with many girls, but regardless, it cheered me up and made me feel cared for when I felt alone and sad. My point is, you've always been a nice guy, Matt—even during your d-bag days." I reach across the table to grab his hand.

He squeezes my hand with a soft smile, and we say nothing more about Jeremy or Matt's drinking days as we finish our meals.

Chapter Ten

LIZA

After dinner, he walks me home, hands in his coat pockets, keeping his eyes on the ground, only holding my hand whenever we need to cross the street—after which, though, he drops my hand and shoves his hand back into his coat.

It's like the night turned south for some reason, and I'm at a loss as to why. I thought we were having a good time.

When we reach my apartment door, the silence has grown uncomfortable, and I'm a little pissed. He waits patiently while I unlock my front door and push it open. We both stand in the doorway, and I look up at him expectantly.

Can I at least get a goodnight kiss? Jeez.

He looks down into my eyes, his gaze occasionally slipping to my lips. I stand on my tiptoes, lifting my chin. I'm definitely going over the 90/10 rule, where the man leans 90% of the way into the kiss and the woman goes the last 10% (thanks, Will Smith, for the lesson). I feel like I'm embarrassing myself—I must be at 40% now. He *has to* know what I'm doing, right?

Jesus.

When it becomes excruciatingly obvious that, despite the

81

incredible sexual tension that can be cut with a knife, he will not be kissing me tonight, I huff in frustration and say, "Thanks for your help today." It's childish, I know, but I don't understand where this is coming from. I feel like we were having such an amazing time and then...nothing.

"You're welcome," he says softly. "I guess I'm gonna..." He throws a thumb over his shoulder and twists in the opposite direction.

I frown. "Right. Have a nice night." I slam the door in his face, completely embarrassed.

"Un-freaking-believable," I mutter to myself, kicking off my shoes and removing my coat at the same time. I'm hanging my coat up in the closet when I hear a knock at my door. I quickly walk over and swing it open—and there he is.

Matt. His greens eyes are dark and low-lidded, gaze intense.

"I'm an asshole," he says, hands on either side of my doorframe.

I cross my arms in front of my chest. "Yeah, you are." I get ready to really give it to him, to ask him what happened, but he doesn't give me a second to say anything.

"I got nervous," he says with an awkward laugh.

"Screw that," I say simply, because I feel like we're way past all that crap.

He takes a deep breath and suddenly grabs me roughly by the waist, pulling me to him, his right hand cupping my face. My eyes are wide with shock as his lips crash over mine, leaving me breathless. He just went from day to night here, and I am absolutely here for it as he turns us and pushes me against the wall. The weight and feel of him on my body as he pushes against me is like nothing else. My eyes slide shut, and I finally get to feel what it's like to kiss him, to run my hands over his beard while I cup his face and angle his lips toward my neck, my hands in his hair. I tug at it, and his mouth moves back to mine, parting my lips with his tongue, biting my bottom lip gently.

The door to the apartment slams shut as his hands slide down my ass, squeezing a little before moving to the back of my thighs, and he pulls me up, wrapping my legs around his waist. I moan into his mouth. His tongue tastes like hops and heaven on mine, and I decide that this is what I want to do for the rest of my life. Just be pressed up against a wall by Matt Wilson, feeling every square inch of the wide expanse of his chest against mine, his scent filling my head, fogging my brain, making me dizzy.

His mouth moves back to my neck as I push the coat off his broad, strong shoulders, and I run my hands down his arms, feeling every curve of his muscles. He presses his hips into me with a groan, and I feel him hard against me, so I tighten my legs around him, doing my best to get some sort of friction, some sort of release. I squirm against him, wanting to climb him like a tree. I've never experienced this type of heat before, this type of passion. I don't ever want it to stop. I want to have this every day for the rest of my life.

How the hell did we go from nothing to *everything*? Because that's exactly what I'm feeling right now. His movements make me feel like no one's ever wanted me this much. The way he cups my face with one hand makes me feel cherished, and the fact that we're both still dressed is pissing me off. My skin is burning, completely on fire. I can feel the heat concentrated in between my thighs. I want him so bad, and by the feel of him, he wants me, too.

"*Fuck*," he says, his voice low in my ear, and I can't stand it any longer.

"Bedroom. Bed. Now," I demand. I sound desperate, but there's no time to act coy now—I'm about to spontaneously combust!

He leans back a little to look me in the eye. "Don't laugh at me, but...I've been building furniture all day."

"What does that mean?" I ask, confused. I'm so worked up I don't think I'd be able to make sense of anything right now.

"I want to fuck you so bad, Liza." An intense thrill like an electric shock runs through my body at his words. "But can we take a shower first?"

We're quiet for a beat, and then, we burst out laughing. He buries his face in my neck, his laughter reverberating all over my body.

"Seriously," he groans as I run my fingers through his hair. "You got to take a shower earlier, but I haven't, and I feel really fucking gross. It isn't fair."

I laugh again and press my forehead to his.

"Alright, take us to my bathroom," I say. "Let's get naked and shower. You can lather me up."

He laughs. "Now you're talking," he says, kissing me on the neck again. I love that we can laugh like this.

Matt kicks his shoes off and carries me to my bathroom, setting me in front of him with an anticipatory smile. I pull back the shower curtain, turn the hot water on, and turn back to Matt. I tug on the hem of his sweater and t-shirt, trying to pull them over his head, but he's too tall. He's like a giant oak tree, strong and steady. He smirks and bends over, helping me undress him, and I want to sigh in relief. I finally get to see him without a shirt on. And I'm staring quite intently.

"You okay there?" he asks, smirking.

"Shh...let me enjoy this moment," I say as I run my hands over his chest, my fingers bouncing over every ridge, every valley. I cannot believe his body looks like this from a little yoga and cycling. I might be drooling.

"I feel like licking you. Is that weird?" I say, completely serious, keeping my eyes on his chest and arms, trying to absorb how freaking *delicious* he looks.

Matt laughs. I think he runs his fingers through his hair, but I'm too distracted by his body to notice. "I mean, a little? Mostly because I'm disgusting right now." He shrugs.

"You look pretty damn good to me. I'm absolutely objectifying you right now, just so you know." I pull his lips down to mine, hands traveling down to his jeans.

"I am completely fine with that," he says around my lips. I unbutton his jeans with haste, and he helps me push them down his hips, along with his underwear. I do my best not to look down at him because I will 100% lose it if I do.

"Your turn," he whispers against my lips, pulling at my top. He undresses me with much more grace than I undressed him. He pulls me back into his arms in an intoxicating kiss as his hands travel to my bra clasp, unhooking it with ease. I dig my nails into his back when his hands travel down to my bottom, and he groans.

I want him. I want him. I want him.

I fucking need *him.*

"Turn around," he says gruffly, and I am so onboard with this rough, demanding Matt. I marvel at how he can be the sweetest man all day but rough and possessive in the bedroom— well, the bathroom—now.

I like it.

My eyes close again as he roughly pulls my back to his chest, and I feel him hard against me. One of Matt's arms wraps tightly around my waist, fingers digging into my skin, and he grinds his hips into me, showing me just how much he wants me, whispering promises about how he's gonna make it so good for me, *so fucking good, Liza,* and how badly he wants to taste me, how he wants to see what I feel like against his tongue when I come. I groan when he bites my neck and starts unbuttoning my jeans. He's caring and loving but primal and wild at the same time. His arm seems to tighten more and more around me by the second, and there's not a doubt in my mind that this is going to be incredible. My heart does backflips in my chest as the steam from the shower rises all around us, fogging up the bathroom in the same way Matt's hands and words are fogging my brain.

I reach one arm behind me, hooking it around his neck, holding his head to me, while my other hand wraps around him where he's hard and heavy, and I feel him, silk over steel. He groans against my skin when I squeeze and start to move my hand over his length.

"Open your eyes, Liza," he whispers in my ear, nibbling on my earlobe. "I want you to watch me while I make you feel *so good*."

"Oh, God," I moan in absolute delight. I look into his dark eyes in the foggy mirror as he roughly pushes my jeans down and kisses my neck.

I watch myself in the reflection, eyes clouded with lust, and suddenly, everything stops. My hand flies to my neck when I realize it's bare.

"Wait, Matt. Stop," I say urgently, my heart racing from fear now.

"What's wrong? What did I do?" he asks, concerned, loosening his hold around me.

"My—my necklace. Where is it?" I crouch on the bathroom floor and start going through our clothes, shaking them, hoping to God I hear the sound of metal hitting bathroom tile because I cannot have lost that necklace.

"Your necklace?" His confusion is irritating me. Rationally, I know that his mind is still on what we were doing, and he's probably wondering why I stopped suddenly over a piece of jewelry, but I need him to snap out of it.

"My necklace, Matt!" I say desperately, adrenaline flooding my body. "My dad gave it to me right before he died. Where is it? I never take it off!" I can feel the tears coming.

"Shit," he says quickly, pulling on his jeans while I crawl, topless, all over the bathroom floor, looking under the towel mat. "I don't remember seeing it tonight, Liza. Let me see if it's by the entrance." He walks away, and I sit on the bathroom floor, putting my hands in my face as I start to cry.

No.

Chapter Eleven

MATT

I PULL THE COLLAR OF MY JACKET UP TO COVER MY EARS from the biting October wind. It seems to be getting colder and colder every day now, but I can't say that I mind. Fall is my favorite season, and New York wears it incredibly well. *Almost* as nicely as Boston, in my opinion.

I probably should have taken a cab from work, but I thought I would give myself extra time to mentally prepare before seeing Vinny tonight for dinner at his house.

To be honest, I was surprised by the invite. Vinny and I are usually more *"Let's grab a beer somewhere"* kind of people—not the dinner-party type. But I guess that just goes to show how much we've changed, how much we've matured, since med school. Although, if I'm being 100% honest, it sometimes feels like I'm playing a game, like I'm pretending to be a grown-up.

Does everyone feel this way, or is it just me?

Maybe it's because I'm not settled yet—professionally or personally.

Professionally, I'm just starting my career trajectory, having only just recently finished my fellowship. This new job is great, but it still feels weird taking the lead on patients, making the final calls on treatment.

Personally...I'm into my friend's sister, and there's nothing I can do about it. I want to ask the universe why it wouldn't just let me fall for someone less complicated, but then again, when has love ever been simple for anyone?

As per usual, any thought of Liza makes my stomach churn from nerves, making me incredibly anxious. The last time I saw her was early Sunday morning when I left her apartment to go into the hospital for my shift. I wished I could've stayed longer, but there was no way I could skip work.

I had held her as she cried herself to sleep that night after spending hours upon hours looking for the necklace her dad gave her. She admitted to being too upset during her shower before we went out to dinner to notice if she still had it, so we had no idea *when* it had gone missing.

We tore her apartment apart, checked the U-Haul and the front of the building, called the restaurant to see if anyone had found it, and retraced our steps from there and back. And it was nowhere. At around three am, we called it quits, Liza in tears. We concluded that it must have fallen off at some point during the move, probably catching on something she was lifting and was too distracted to notice.

She said she would keep looking the next day, and I said I was sure it would turn up, but we both secretly knew it wouldn't —it was just too painful for her to admit out loud or have anyone say it.

I miss her and am dying to see her, but she's grown distant, replying to my texts with one- or two-word answers (*Yes, No, Not tonight, Maybe, I'm Okay*). It's been almost a week since that night, and I made the decision this morning that if I can't get a real response out of her or get her to call me back, I'm just going to show up at her place. I get that she needs space, and I'm trying to respect it, but honestly, I'm scared that she's isolating herself—not just from me, but from everyone around her, too. I want to see if Vinny mentions something first, though. If he's concerned about her, then I won't take it personally and will go check up on her. If he thinks she's fine, then...well, I guess it really would be about me.

Sigh.

I just need to get through this fucking dinner.

I reach Vinny's building and ask him to buzz me up. The building doesn't have a doorman, but the lobby is spacious, well-lit, and decorated with minimalistic modern touches—a far cry from the dump we used to live in six years ago.

I ride the elevator all the way up to the twelfth floor and ring the doorbell to his apartment. I start removing the scarf from around my neck, and make a mental note to start carrying a beanie with me as the temperature drops, when the door flies open.

My breath catches.

Fucking finally.

She looks so beautiful I could die a happy man right here, right now. Her dress is black and silver, flowy, held together at the waist by a wide black belt. She's also wearing high-heeled suede boots, adding at least three inches to her height, her lips closer to mine. I'm blessed with the fact that her dress shows a little cleavage—not too much to be considered inappropriate, but just enough to give me a nice reminder that I've seen her boobs, and they are *amazing*.

My initial reaction of pure joy at seeing her dissipates as soon as I take a second look at her face. Though still beautiful, Liza looks sad, tired—like she hasn't slept or had one thing to eat in days. Her normally wavy, full, and bouncy hair is a disheveled mess.

"What are you doing here?" she whispers at me, glaring.

Her reaction to my presence is hurtful and surprising. So what if I'm here? Is it really that bad? Does she hate me now or something?

"Hi, I'm doing great, Liza, thanks for asking," I say sarcastically.

"No, seriously, what are you doing here? You can't just show up here."

I roll my eyes at her, annoyed, but try not to push her away too much. "I was invited," I say.

"Invited? Why the hell would Vinny invite you? And why didn't you tell me you were coming?" Okay, so she's obviously not as happy to see me as I am to see her.

"First of all, Vinny is my friend, remember? Second of all, I didn't know you were coming!" I whisper-yell. "What's the big deal?"

"The big deal is that we almost slept together, and Vinny is going to freak if he ever finds out." She puts her hands on her hips like a school teacher about to send me to detention. Truthfully, I'd volunteer for detention if it meant she was the one doing the punishing.

Okay, get your head out of the gutter there.

"Yeah, *almost*. As in didn't," I say. She scoffs and rolls her eyes at me. It's like she's pushed me in the chest and kicked me in the balls. "Wait, are you mad at me?" I don't try to mask the shock on my face or in my voice.

"Yes. No." She shakes her head. "I don't know."

"Liza, what did I do?" I panic and sift through everything that happened that Saturday night and Sunday morning but can find nothing wrong. She cried. I held her. We looked for her necklace. I made her hot tea. I didn't use her vulnerability to take advantage of her or anything like that, so what happened? Maybe it's because I left in a hurry the following morning?

"Is it because I left early Sunday? Because that wasn't my

fault. I had work I had to get to." I reach for her hand, but she pushes mine away.

She frowns and takes a deep breath before saying, "I'm superstitious, okay? And the fact that I realized that my necklace was gone right before we...well, *you know*...makes me think that maybe it was a sign that we probably shouldn't be doing this," her voice cracks. She closes her eyes and takes another deep, steadying breath.

No.

This is so stupid.

I need to let her know how right we are for each other, how good this is. I can't let her just throw this away over a silly superstition. But I also don't want to push her when she's in a vulnerable position. I look down into her eyes and can't help myself. I run my fingers through her hair and down to her waist. I hold her gaze when I cup her face, and her breath stutters.

"Liza," I say as gently as possible. "I really care about you. I understand that what happened Saturday must have brought back a lot of grief—as you know, I lost a parent, too, so I know how it feels. But I don't think what happened was a sign that we aren't right for each other. If anything, it could be a sign that we are." I shake my head and exhale. "I don't know, Liza. I don't believe in any of that, but I respect that you do. If that's what you choose to believe, I want you to know that I'm not happy about it, because I really care about you." I take a deep breath before continuing.

"I've been going out of my mind this week wondering how you were, whether you were okay, why you weren't answering my calls and being so cold via texts. I want to be with you. I want to do what we talked about and see where this goes. But if this is really what you want, if you really want to stop..." I sigh deeply, feeling defeated. "Then I'll do it. I'll stop calling and texting, and I'll see you only on occasion, whenever our paths cross."

Her eyes water, and she sniffles but doesn't say anything. After a beat, she leans into me, placing her head on my chest, and I almost die from the relief. It's like my whole body has been tense for the past few days, bracing itself for impact, for this one deciding moment, and it's here, and the choice has been made, and...she chooses me. My arms wrap tightly around her, pulling her even closer, and I exhale. In this moment, I don't care if Vinny catches us.

"I'm so sorry," she mumbles against my coat. "I never meant to push you away like that."

"It's okay," I whisper. "It's been a really difficult week for you. Just know that you don't have to push me away. I'm here for support." She nods against my body, and I press my lips to the top of her head.

"Hey, guys. Watcha doing?" An amused Danielle stands beside us with her hands on her hips, a smile from ear to ear breaking across her face.

Oh, shit.

"Uhhhhh..." I see Liza's face flush as she scrambles for an excuse. She looks to me for help, but my mind is blank. There is nothing in this brain of mine right now. Suddenly, I know exactly what will happen. Danielle will tell Vinny what she saw, Vinny will lose it, and the whole thing will be so dramatic and problematic that Liza will decide it's too much to handle and will break things off with me.

"I was just telling Matt about the necklace and got upset, so he was comforting me," she says. Not a total lie.

"Uh, yeah," I say super convincingly. I should win an Oscar for my performance.

"*Riiiggghhhhtt,*" Danielle laughs. "Anyway, we were wondering where you went, Liza. The doorbell rang a few minutes ago, and you never came back. Would you mind helping Vinny put the twins to bed? I have to finish up with the sides."

She clears her throat and straightens. "Yup, absolutely. No problem," she says and walks away toward the hallway on the right.

My feet are made of stone. I cannot move. "Uhhh," I say intelligently.

"So," Danielle says, "you and Liza, huh?" She leans against the wall and smirks at me.

"I don't know what you're talking about," I say. I'm really a terrible liar—truly the worst.

"Right, right." She bobs her head. "Just so you know, I'm not gonna tell Vinny, if that's what you're worried about."

I narrow my eyes at her. Can I trust Danielle?

"Why wouldn't you tell him? I don't get it." I shake my head at her. "Vinny would flip if he found out that I have feelings for his little sister."

"Oh my god, you have *feelings* for her?!" She claps her hands excitedly.

"Shhh. Jesus!" I crane my neck to make sure no one is nearby to hear us. "What did you think this was?"

"Oh my God, this is so exciting! I thought it was just a crush, that maybe you would hang out, be her rebound or something, but I could totally tell from the moment she saw you that she was *so* into you, and you were into her. I hoped this would happen." Her smile is broad and genuine.

It annoys me that she automatically assumed that this thing was only about having a physical relationship, as if the thought of me being boyfriend material never crossed her mind. I hate that Vinny must have poisoned the well, and I shudder to think of the impression everyone in this family has of me because of it.

"I don't understand. Why are you okay with this? Isn't there a spouse code or something where you absolutely need to support every opinion and decision your partner makes?"

Danielle snorts. "*Puh-lease.* You've obviously never been married before." She rolls her eyes. "First of all, always agreeing on everything makes for a boring marriage with boring sex. You need to have some disagreements, some passion and spice in your life. Second of all, the wife is always right, and the husband's opinions don't matter as much." She points a finger at me. "Remember that when you get married. It will save you from a lot of headaches."

I laugh and run my fingers through my hair. "Okay, but I still don't get it. I thought Vinny would have ruined my reputation by telling you all of my worst college stories. Sometimes I wonder why the hell he keeps hanging out with me if he thinks I'm that much of an ass."

She sighs. "Vinny loves you. He just doesn't want you with his sister," she clarifies. "I want you to understand something, Matt. Liza isn't the only member of the Castelli family who has been struggling with the death of their father. Vinny has suddenly developed this new sense of responsibility and obligation to his family that no one asked him to take on, and he's taking it to extremes." She shrugs. "Most of the time, it's not a big deal. It's just dumb stuff like making his mom switch heating companies because the one she was using was ripping her off. Or riding Liza's ass to go to the doctor. Things like that. But other times, it's dumb stuff like this." She waves her hand up and down my body. "I knew you would be able to make her happy, but he just saw the opposite result, you know? I told him that you'd probably changed since school, since he had too, and that Liza needed someone who made her feel alive—which I'm hoping you do.

"When the time comes for you guys to tell him, I'll support it and try to talk him out of murdering you." She smiles.

"Danielle..." I breathe. "You don't know what this means to me."

She scoffs. "I'm not doing it for *you*," she says, rolling her eyes at me. "I'm doing it for *her*. She deserves so much better than some boring idiot who constantly put down her choices and tastes, who had no respect for her family values."

"She does," I say.

"I can tell she likes you, because every time your name comes up, she sits up a little straighter, like a dog sitting by his master's feet at the dinner table, waiting and begging for whatever scraps it can get. She's the dog waiting for any bits and pieces of information about your life. It's kind of cute in a gross way." She smirks. "Don't mess it up," she adds quickly with a menacing finger pointed at me.

"What about Vinny? Should I talk to him?"

"No! God no." She sighs. "You guys aren't there yet. Sure, he's gonna be mad that you didn't tell him earlier, but I wouldn't say anything until you are *both* one hundred percent sure of what you're doing. He needs to see her happy, certain in her decision. And I don't see that yet. She's still too hesitant. She for sure likes you—maybe even truly cares about you—but you have a ways to go."

I nod. "That's exactly what Liza said on Saturday."

Danielle smiles. "Good. So just do that. Go on dates, make out, flirt, you know..." She raises her eyebrows suggestively. "Just don't hurt her, because Vinny won't be the only person you'd be getting an ass-kicking from."

I laugh at the thought of Danielle kicking my butt, but I stop promptly as I realize that she's in pretty good shape. She might actually get some good punches in. "Don't worry, I have no intention of hurting Liza, and I definitely do not want to be on the other end of your ass-kicking."

"Me?" She laughs once. "I'm not the one you have to worry

about. Catterina is the one you should be scared of! We've both been hoping you'd get together since the vomit incident—I even purposefully stayed behind that day during the pumpkin patch to give you some time—but she'd beat you to death with a wooden spoon if you hurt her baby girl," she says with no trace of humor in her voice.

The fact that I have Catterina and Danielle's support means leaps and bounds for me and my relationship with Liza. Hopefully, if things go well, by December 1st we will be in a place stable enough to stop sneaking around and tell her family. And maybe with their support, Vinny will be able to see reason, and I won't have to lose a friend in order to gain a girlfriend.

Girlfriend...

I'm not particularly excited at the thought of being beaten with a cooking utensil, but I have no fear of that ever happening, so it's not a big deal to me.

"There will be no need for wooden-spoon beatings, I promise you." I stick out my hand for a handshake, but she doesn't take it.

"I don't want to offend you or anything, but I won't be touching your hands until you wash them in my guest bathroom over there." She points toward a door just before the hallway that leads to the bedrooms (or so I assume). "Remember, Matthew, this is a post-Covid world we're living in. You need to keep your hands clean and your mind dirty—not the other way around."

DINNER IS...INTERESTING. VINNY AND I ARE BACK TO BEING friends like he never warned me to stay away from his sister or called me to make sure I hadn't tried anything with her the day I helped her move into her apartment. We reminisce about the old days, but I try to steer him away from talking about the intense drinking and the girls—for everyone's sake. I don't want Vinny to keep associating me with that guy, I don't want Liza to get upset over other girls from my past, and I don't want Danielle to think less of me when I know I'm going to need her on my side. I need her to like me for whenever Liza feels comfortable enough to come clean or when December first rolls around—whichever comes first. And I *know* we'll still be together then because I can feel how right we are for each other.

So, I make sure that Vinny sticks to our academic shenanigans, like that time we pranked our anatomy professor by having each student dress up as a human organ for Halloween. Sure, it was weird as hell, but it was incredibly funny at the time.

I also learned all about how Danielle and he started dating, how he turned from annoying bro into doting boyfriend the second he met her, falling for her on their first date—at least according to Danielle. Vinny just blushed and huffed uncomfortably, which gave me hope. To me, that meant that he's actually much more of a softy than the man leads on.

"So, are you seeing anyone now?" he asks at a certain point during dinner as he shovels a huge bite of Danielle's Chinese chicken salad into his mouth.

Danielle chokes on her water, and Liza shifts uncomfortably in her seat.

Nice going, guys. Super subtle.

"Uh, yeah, actually." I look down at my plate, suddenly taking a huge interest in the food on it.

"No way." His eyes widen. "Is it serious?"

"I really want it to be," I say, and I see Liza's cheeks flush from the corner of my eye.

"Whoa, dude. Never thought I'd see the day."

I roll my eyes at him, hating that he's so surprised at my willingness to commit to someone.

"You know, I really don't get what your deal is," I snap at him. The whole table goes dead quiet.

Shit.

"What?" He frowns at me, and I see Danielle shaking her head at me, a warning not to push things.

"I just mean that..." I sigh. "I'm not twenty-five anymore, you know. Like, my hobbies do not include avoiding responsibilities and sleeping around anymore. I think I'm a pretty good guy, and you keep acting like I'm still this immature college student figuring shit out." I shrug.

No one says a fucking word at the table, and I swear I think this is where it all ends. This is where we get into an argument, and it all goes to hell.

Danielle kicks him under the table, and he grunts. He turns to look at her, and she gives him a meaningful glare.

Vinny sighs and looks at me. "I'm sorry, man. I guess it's just difficult to disassociate you from my partying days, you know? Just because we haven't really seen each other since then. But you know how glad I am that you're back in the city and that we're getting to know each other better. I like this guy too." He slaps me on the back.

What is happening? Are we having a moment?

He has just admitted that he's wrong.

The fact that *I'm* surprised by Vinny's apology means that he's not the only one still making assumptions based on who we used to be. Despite his crazy overprotectiveness, I guess it's evident that he's grown emotionally. Who would have thought?

This is good. This is really good.

"Thanks, man," I say.

We're all quiet for a bit until Liza breaks the awkward silence with, "Dinner's amazing, Dani."

"Yup, incredible," her husband says.

"Absolutely," I agree.

And with that, we catapult into a normal conversation, leaving behind any bitter memories of confrontations or uncomfortable moments at dinner.

Hope. There's hope.

Chapter Twelve

LIZA

"So the guy went all the way to the restaurant and back to look for your necklace and then spent the night holding you in bed while you cried because he didn't want to leave you alone?" Barbara asks over coffee the day after Vinny's dinner. She flips her long, blonde, stick-straight hair over her shoulder before leaning back into her chair.

"Yup." I take a sip from my cappuccino. We're sitting at a cafe near campus for our weekly hang. It's really easy in this city to get caught up with other things and lose touch with people, so Barbara and I make it a point to set time aside to sit down and catch each other up on our lives.

"You know not every guy would do that, right? Especially not one who hasn't even been on a date with you. *Especially* not someone who hasn't slept with you yet," she says seriously, narrowing her ice-blue eyes at me.

"I guess? I don't know. I really, *really* like him, but I'm still a little freaked out. It all kind of felt like a sign to me, with the whole necklace disappearing thing. Like my dad was telling me to stop or something."

She snorts. "Okay, Liza. I know you're superstitious, but this is next-level shit. Maybe you're just finding excuses because you're scared." She shakes her head in disapproval, and I can absolutely see where she's coming from, but I'm still a little freaked out.

"Are you trying to psychoanalyze me? I thought I was the therapist, and you were the dramatic actress here," I say jokingly, trying to lighten the mood.

"You're not a fully qualified therapist yet, so I feel comfortable enough overruling you here and taking the high ground."

I roll my eyes at her.

"Fine." She sits up straighter in her seat. "If you wanna be superstitious about the whole thing, how about this? How about the whole thing had to happen to show you that this guy is real and cares about you enough to drop everything just to help you? You guys have a connection and great chemistry, that's clear, but maybe this was just to show you how dependable and caring he can be." She shrugs and takes a sip of her matcha.

"You're just trying to adapt it to your opinion," I say.

"Aren't you doing the same thing?" She glares.

"Stop trying to be reasonable," I mutter under my breath.

Barbara sighs. "You know I love you, but I think you're just being a baby, honey. You're just scared because the last relationship you were in was with a passionless ass who thought he was better than you and everyone around you."

"Maybe you're a little right. Just a little," I concede, thinking about how different Matt is from Jeremy in a scary yet amazing way. "What if Vinny's right, though? What if he's still a player? I mean, *God*, Barbara, you need to see him. He's so hot. How can he not have women just throwing themselves at him all the time?"

"Vinny is way too overprotective for me to take him

completely at his word. I would take everything he says about Matt with a large grain of salt. Plus, it's not fair of you to make assumptions about Matt just because he's attractive."

"Ridiculously attractive," I correct her.

My phone vibrates in my pocket, and I pull it out.

MATT

Hey. You find it yet?

I bite my lip to stop a smile from spreading across my face—something that happens almost every time he sends me a message. I guess Barbara's right—he is incredibly caring. He's been so attentive with me.

"That him?" she asks with a knowing smirk.

"Yes," I say. "He's asking about the necklace." I reply back that I fear it's lost forever, but that it's fine-ish.

"Yeah, I don't know how you haven't ridden his face yet," she deadpans and oh-so-casually takes another sip from her drink.

"Jesus, Barbara!" I scoff and look around to see if anyone heard her. "That was a little loud," I whisper-yell, and she shrugs. "We haven't even been on a real date yet, you know. We kind of talked about things yesterday at my brother's and then after, while I waited for my Uber. We're good. I'm just waiting for him to ask me out."

She rolls her eyes at me. "Are you kidding me, Liza? Just ask *him* out. Ask him to my New York Icons party."

"You think he'd go? Isn't he a little too old for a Halloween party?"

"Um, it's not a Halloween party," she says, looking offended.

"It's on Halloween, and it's a costume party," I say flatly.

"It's a *New York Icons* party that just so happens to be on Halloween. It's a sophisticated soiree. No pumpkin costumes allowed." She smiles. "Only famous New Yorkers, real or fictional."

"I think I'm gonna go as Carrie Bradshaw." I shrug. "It'll give me an excuse to wear the shoes I splurged on for Vinny's wedding four years ago. I've literally only worn them the one time."

"Yes! Love that journey for you," Barbara says happily.

"You doing Barbra again?" I ask, doing my best to deflect. Barbara has an obsession with Barbra Streisand. So much so that she wants to change her first name to match the spelling of the legendary singer and actress'. She's been dressing up as her every Halloween since she first saw *Funny Girl* when she was nine years old.

"*Obvi*," she says with a massive smile. "I just need to pick which legendary outfit I'm gonna wear this year. I think I'm gonna pick one from *Funny Girl* again."

"Ooh," I say excitedly. "So many options!"

"I know. She's such a goddess." She claps her hands with a huge smile. "So, you gonna invite him or what? You can drunk-make-out in the coat room." She snorts.

"Fuck it." I sigh. "Worst thing that happens is he says no, right? And we can plan for something else." I take a deep breath and type out a message:

LIZA

> So I know it might be a little childish or whatever, but my friend is having a 'NY Icons' themed Halloween party this weekend, and I was wondering whether you'd like to go with me.

Barbara and I both stare anxiously at the three dots bouncing on my screen until his reply comes up.

MATT

Sure! What's a NY Icons party?

Barbara sits back in her seat and smiles. "Done and done," she says. "I'm proud of you. Now don't back out!"

Chapter Thirteen

MATT

IF YOU DON'T COUNT THE PUMPKIN PATCH, THE BRUNCH, or the dinner at the German place, this will be Liza's and my official first date, to which I just want to say *fucking finally.*

I look ridiculous in my fedora, striped suit, and plastic gun, but I think I'm rocking the mafia-boss look, right? *Right?*

God, I hope so, because I feel like a tool. I think I might be too old for costume parties, to be honest, but if this is what she wants us to do together as our first date, then I am 100% on board.

I reach her apartment and knock. When she finally opens the door, her dark hair is curled and big, she's in a white wife-beater and a pink tulle skirt, and she's wearing sparkly high heels.

"Hey!" I say, looking her up and down. An advantage of this costume thing is that I can take my time to ogle her, be obvious about it, and can pass it off as me just taking in her outfit. I decide right then and there that she should always wear that top—her breasts look freaking amazing in it. "Who are you supposed to be?" I ask as casually as possible, but really, my heart is racing at the prospect of tonight.

"Duh." She points at her shoes and skirt. "Carrie Bradshaw, obviously."

I laugh. "She's the chick from *Sex and the City*, right?"

Liza gasps, bringing a hand to her chest in mock horror. "How can you even ask that? It's one of SJP's most important roles." She twirls in front of me. "The outfit better be recognizable because I definitely do not look anything like her. My Italian curves make it really hard for me to pull it off."

"I don't know what you're talking about. I happen to *love* your Italian curves," I blurt.

Fuck. I don't know where that came from.

Use your filter, Matt!

"Thanks, I think." She smirks and bites her lip. "And who are you supposed to be?"

"Ah..." I look down at my outfit. "Al Capone? Honestly, I didn't know who to pick, and they had the gun and hat in the costume shop, so I just went with it."

"I love it. You look amazing in a suit." She bats her eyelashes at me.

Have mercy.

She points to the box in my hand. "What's that?"

I smile. "It's a first date/housewarming gift combo."

"Ooh, I love gifts. Gimme!" I hand her the box carefully, loving how excited and happy she looks.

"Whoa, it's surprisingly heavy." She walks to the kitchen's bar and places the box on it before opening it and pulling out the gift. It's a medium-sized white pumpkin with intricately carved flowers. I found it at a flower shop downtown, and it cost a fortune, but I thought she would like this better than a bouquet of roses or whatever. Liza is special, and I only ever want to make her feel that way. This isn't a game with her, and I don't want to treat this as a random hookup or date I met on an app. Liza means something to me, and I want her to know that.

"Instead of flowers, I thought it would be more appropriate to stay on-theme and get you a pumpkin, which also doubles as a decoration for your apartment—if you're into fall."

Also, I want this pumpkin to remind her of the amazing time we had together at the patch we visited together in Sag Harbor just a couple of weeks ago. It's dumb, but I kind of want her to start associating pumpkins with me the way I have with her.

She bites her lip and looks at me. "If I'm into fall? Matt, I'm a girl." She rolls her eyes at me like I'm stupid. "Women like me wait anxiously for nine months until the season comes around so that we can start wearing cozy sweaters and boots, buy the cheesiest decorations at Target, and ingest anything pumpkin-spiced. Of course I'm into fall. I freaking love it. This is amazing. Thank you." She walks over to me and wraps her arms around my neck, pulling me down for a soft, chaste kiss.

I try to stop myself, try to keep it light, but she knocks the breath out of me, and I have to wrap my arms around her waist to hold on for dear life. I inhale her coconut-scented shampoo as I lean down to kiss her neck, sliding one of my hands into her hair, pressing her to me.

We hold each other like this for a couple of minutes until I separate from her with one last peck on her lips.

"You really do look beautiful, Liza," I say as I look down into her eyes, willing her to understand how much she means to me, even if it's only been two weeks and change.

"Should we head out?" I ask.

She looks hesitant, like she wants to stay. I can see the lascivious gleam in her eyes, the playful, mischievous smile tugging at her lips. I laugh and push her away completely by the shoulders. "No way, champ. I know that look." It's the same one she had last week, up until she pushed me off her and started crying—a memory that unfortunately keeps replaying in my head several times a day. "We said we were going on a date, and we're going on a date." I grab her by the hand and drag her to the door, grabbing her coat on the way out.

"I AM SO, SO SORRY, MATT," SHE SAYS AS WE WALK THROUGH her friend Barbara's front door. "I didn't know it was going to be quite like this."

"Wow, yeah, this is..." I look around the apartment, speechless. It's like stepping into a time machine back to my freshman year in college. I don't know how her friend can afford to pay for an apartment this big in Manhattan as an actress, but she has enough room to be able to squeeze in *two* beer pong tables, an area for flip-cup, a keg, a full bar, and a table with snacks and desserts. Definitely looks and feels like a college party—the only difference being that it doesn't look like she's strapped for cash. Girl makes *bank*.

"What TV show did you say your friend was in again?" I ask.

"She was the older sister on a kid show for, like, four years," she says. "We went to school together until she had to drop out when she got that gig. After the show, she stopped acting and now just keeps cashing in her residuals, working only occasionally. Her residual checks are...large."

"I can see that." I nod, taking it all in.

"We can leave if you want," she says a little glumly.

I panic. I need to kick my ass into gear and not be a party pooper. This isn't my style anymore, but I don't want her to think I'm boring or a grouch. I remember the rules for beer pong, I can play a round of kings, and I can probably still kick ass at flip-cup. I'm sure my alcohol tolerance is much lower than when I was eighteen, but I can keep it to one game or two.

"No, let's stay. Plus, I want to meet your friend." I give her an encouraging smile.

"Yes, you're gonna love her! Barbara is *the best*. And we don't even have to stay the whole night. We can stay for, like, half an hour or an hour and then go back to my place." She smiles eagerly at me, and I melt. There is no way I will ever be able to compete with those big brown eyes of hers. One look and she has the ability to bring me down to my knees. I'll do anything she asks me to.

Liza drags me by the hand through the crowd, spotting her friend playing—and losing, by the looks of it—a round of beer pong with a tall dude dressed like Andy Warhol. She's dressed in head-to-toe leopard print, hair pulled up under a turban in the same material.

"Ohmigod, *Liiizaaa*," she slurs, abandoning her game and coming to meet us. She wraps herself around my date and stumbles a little. "I am *soooo* happy you came. What do you think?" She twirls in front of us to show off her outfit.

Liza laughs and says, "Best Fanny Brice costume ever."

"Yes, girl! Except these nails are *killing* me. I totally bombed the last three beer pong games I played because I can't even hold the ball right." She twirls her fingers in front of us, showing off her longer-than-Kylie's acrylic nails. "I can't even text." We all laugh, and she turns to me. "You must be Vinny's hot friend. Ohmigod, you were right, Liza—he's hot. Vinny is such a dick for not letting you guys bump uglies."

"Okaaaay." Liza grabs her by the shoulders. "Let's get you some water, yeah?"

We walk over to the bar and get her to chug a couple of

glasses of water while people approach both the girls to say hi. I don't mind being left out while they socialize—it's their crowd, after all. I can happily sit here and just enjoy having my arm wrapped around Liza's waist, feeling her against me for the rest of the night.

At one point in the middle of a conversation with one of her friends, I place a kiss on her head, staring absentmindedly into the crowd until my eyes lock with a woman with a black bob, white button-down shirt, and black skirt.

Kelly.

Fuck.

I haven't seen her since she kicked me out of her house over two weeks ago for not wanting to sleep with her again. I stand up straight, and Liza turns to look at me, seeing the panic spread all across my face.

"Hey, what's wrong?" She places a palm on my face, and I know she's just made it worse, because Kelly is territorial, a predator. Kelly will see the fact that I'm here with another woman as a challenge, and it will be a massive fucking problem.

I clear my throat. "Nothing, I'm good." I check my watch, and—fuck—it's only been half an hour since we got here. Too early to go. Should I just fake being sick? Pretend like I caught a bug? But I really wanted to spend time with her tonight. If I tell her I'm sick, I'm going to have to go home and ruin our first date. Maybe if I just ignore Kelly's presence, act like I didn't see her, everything will be—

"Matt?"

Fuuuckkkkk.

"Kelly," I say, back ramrod straight. "How are you?"

"Good, good," she says. I feel Liza tense beside me, so I tighten my arm around her, trying to communicate to her that everything's fine. "So how do you know Liza?"

Fuck. Me.

"Wh—what? You guys know each other?" I look quickly between Liza and Kelly, about to lose it when I see the expression on my date's face. It's murderous.

"We went to high school together," Liza says coldly, pressing herself closer into me, taking a sip from her beer.

"Yes, we did." Kelly presses her lips together into a tight line. "So, you guys are dating now?" I can see the intent clear in her eyes. She wants to stir shit up.

I want to drag my hand down my face in frustration. Why are some people like this? Why do they like to stir up trouble? Jesus. They just want to see the world burn.

"Yup," Liza says, her lips popping.

Kelly narrows her eyes at her but throws her a fake smile. "How nice," she says. "So interesting, I thought you were single when you came over the other day to my place, Matt."

Liza pushes off me.

Fucking. Kelly.

"That was before I met Liza," I say, trying to keep my voice level, reaching for Liza's hand again, but she casually pulls it away to reach for some more beer behind her.

"You know what, I'll let you guys catch up," she says as she starts to walk away.

"Liza!" I leave Kelly standing there and follow my date through the crowd. I catch her hand and pull her to me. "Hey, stop. Where are you going?"

"Did you sleep with her?" she asks, eyes wide with panic.

"Yes, but—"

"Oh my God!" She starts walking away.

"But this was *way* before we started seeing each other," I will her to understand, hoping she hears me over the music. I follow closely behind, weaving through the other guests. "Liza!"

She turns, her eyes watering. "You don't get it. She's the *worst* type of person, Matt. She made my life a living hell in high school. And you *slept* with her. You're the kind of guy who sleeps with the Kellys of the world. And—" She gasps. "Is she the girl who kicked you out of her house? Is she the one who was pissed you wouldn't sleep with her again? Is that how you ended up at my house that day? Is that why you were in Sag Harbor?"

My stomach drops, and I try to swallow the knot in my throat. "Yes." I nod.

"Oh, God." She puts her head in her hands. "I need some space, Matt. Just give me a little space. I'll find you in a bit."

Liza turns and walks away, leaving me standing there surrounded by sweaty, drunk people dressed as famous New Yorkers. I will my feet to move, to follow, but they understand what Liza needs more than my brain does. They get that she needs a minute or two to process this. So I stay still, dumbfounded, staring after her as she disappears into the crowd of people.

I heave a sigh and walk back toward the bar. I need a fucking drink—a real one this time.

I dump some ice in a red Solo cup and pour myself some whiskey, impressed by Barbara's selection of spirits. Girl's got great taste.

"Hey." I turn around to find Kelly standing behind me, looking apologetic.

I groan and roll my eyes at her. "*What?*"

"I know, I'm sorry." She grimaces. "What I did was really petty."

"Yeah," I reply flatly and take a long sip of my drink, wincing. "Really fucking petty."

She smiles sadly at me and places a hand on my shoulder, softly bringing her hand down my arm, staring up at me through her lashes. Oh no, where is she going with this? "I just saw you standing there and remembered how good it was," she says with a lascivious smile. "Don't you remember how good it was? I was hoping we could revisit the past for a night."

I stare at her hand for a second in shock. Is she kidding me right now? I told her that sleeping together was a one-time thing, something I reminded her of two weeks ago, which caused her to promptly kick me out of her house, and now she sees me with another woman at a party, and she still wants to hook up? I think that kicking me out of her house was about her being embarrassed more than anything else, but I think that the come-on tonight is a competitive thing with Liza. Like she's got to prove that she can get whomever she wants, that she's better than the girl she used to bully in high school.

I push her hand off my arm as gently as possible and stare her down. "Kelly, I appreciate your interest, but it is not reciprocated. Now, if you'll excuse me, I'm going to find my date."

I walk away, frustrated. How the hell am I supposed to find her in this fucking party? This was supposed to be an awesome night. We were going to play games. I was going to meet her friends. We were going to dance, make out, and then end up at her place. We didn't even have to have sex yet. I just wanted to sleep over, wanted to wake up next to her again.

I walk around the party twice, checking every room, every bathroom, looking for her, but I come up short. Eventually, I find Barbara and ask her if she's seen Liza.

"Hey, *diiiiiicccckkkk,*" she hisses at me. "She left because you're a *dick.* She saw you with Kelly, all cozy. You DICK."

Jesus.

I exhale and run my fingers through my hair. "I wasn't *cozy* with her, for fuck's sake! I pushed her away. Did she go home?" Please don't tell me she went home with another guy. I'll lose my damn mind.

She narrows her eyes at me. "You like her?"

"Yes!" I groan. "Please just tell me whether she went home or not. I need to see her."

She takes a beat and sways a little. Slapping me on the back, she says, "Go forth and find her, my son. She is woman. You are man."

"Huh?" I ask.

She rolls her eyes at me and smacks me on the arm. "'*You are Woman, I am Man*'? Fanny and Nicky! *Funny Girl?*" She exhales. "Just go find your woman—she went home."

"*Thank you!*" I say, turning quickly.

"But don't be a Nicky!" I hear her call out to me.

I tell her I have no idea what that means but that I promise to be good to Liza before I then run out Barbara's front door and into the New York City night.

Chapter Fourteen

LIZA

I huff as I push open my apartment door and double-lock it behind me, adding the chain. I'm so happy to be home. I just had to get out of that party. As soon as I saw Kelly's hand on Matt, I knew that I was about to lose it, so I thought it would be best for me to leave in order to avoid a scene.

I cannot believe how dumb I was. I cannot believe that I actually thought that Matt was different, but I guess my brother was right all along.

To be clear, I'm not necessarily mad because he slept with someone else, because everyone has a past, and it wouldn't be fair to hold it against him. I'm mad because of *who* he slept with, and I'm especially mad because I caught them being a little too friendly with each other when I came back from the bathroom. And I just *know* Kelly. I know her reputation for being a man-eater, for breaking up relationships, for being an absolute bully with no regard whatsoever for anyone else's feelings.

She's the worst type of person.

And Matt slept with her.

Which means he's into those types of girls, the kind that

loves to hurt other women just to prove that they can, to prove that they're somehow better than everyone else.

Honestly, I was ready to get over the initial shock of finding out that they were a thing and that she was the one who kicked him out of her house, but then I saw them together, and it just triggered something in me. It took me back to my high school days when she would start mean rumors about me, make fun of me in front of my boyfriend, and then ultimately hook up with him at a party while in my direct line of sight. I don't know what I ever did to her, but she targeted me in school and made my life a living hell up until graduation.

When I showed up to my brother's apartment in New York after I had broken up with my then boyfriend (the first time I met Matt), it was because he had publicly cheated on me with Kelly. I caught them at the back of a party, where my ex had her pressed against a tree, and they were mauling each other. He was an ass for cheating on me, of course, but what she did was equally as bad, because it wasn't like she was some random girl he met who didn't know I existed. Nope. She *knew* he was my boyfriend and went for him just to hurt me. And I know it was a deliberate thing, because she made eye contact with me while he kissed her neck, and she smiled victoriously.

She *smiled*.

She's pure evil, and I can't process how anyone would ever want to be with someone like that. I mean, what does that say about me if Matt liked us both? I'm not sure I feel so comfortable with that idea either—it irks me. Does it put me on her same level? Do we have similar personalities? I would *never* knowingly hook up with someone in a relationship, so we definitely don't have that in common, and I really doubt that we're similar in any other regard.

I kick my shoes off by the bed and undress, pulling on some leggings and a tank top. I brush my hair, my Carrie Bradshaw curls disappearing with each stroke, and wash my face, making sure I remove all traces of makeup. Yes, I'm definitely one of those girls who *has* to wash her face and do her entire skincare routine before going to bed—don't hate me 'cause you ain't me. I'm just about ready to put on my first night cream when there's a knock on the door.

I grab my phone from my purse and dial 911 but don't press send.

Hey, don't make fun of me for being paranoid. I'm a single woman living in New York. I need to be careful.

I walk over to the door and peek through the peephole.

Matt.

"What are you doing here?" I ask through the door. "Also, how did you even get into the building?"

"One of your neighbors let me in. Can you please open the door?" It's in the form of a question but not really a request. He practically barks the order at me. Matt does not sound happy *at all*—angry is more like it.

Why does he get to be mad? I'm the only one who gets to be angry here! I'm the one who saw him being felt up by another woman while he was on a date with me. I'm the one whose date got real chummy with her childhood bully. Honestly, I was planning on completely ghosting him after tonight, but I may as well take advantage of the fact that he showed up here, while I'm still seething in anger, and really let him have it.

So, I unlock the top and bottom locks, slide off the chain, and swing the door open to see him standing there, glaring at me, looking glorious. I open my mouth to start to say something, ready to give him a piece of my mind, but he cuts me off before I can even open my mouth to get a word in.

"No," he says, shaking his head. It comes out with such authority that I feel it all the way down to my toes. Matt's hair looks sexy and disheveled, like he's been running his fingers through it all the way here, his mafia-boss hat forgotten at the party. "No way. You're gonna let me talk first."

I laugh dryly once. "Excuse me, what?" I raise an eyebrow at him. Who the hell does he think he is? "I—"

"*No.* I said *I* get to talk first, because you walked away, so you don't get to say anything right now." He pushes by me into my apartment, leaving me speechless. I reluctantly close the door and place my phone on the table by the door. I don't need it anymore. He's not here to kill me—though I might end up killing him.

He stands in front of me with his hands on his hips, exhales once, and looks me straight in the eye.

"I'm not gonna sugarcoat anything or waste any more of our time here," he says, and I gulp nervously. "I want to be clear about what I think and how I feel, so here goes." He squares his shoulders in front of me as if preparing for battle. His green eyes blaze, looking determined, showing me that he is a man on a mission, a man who doesn't want to give up but knows it's time to do or die.

"You're a runner, Liza," he says simply. "You freak out, and you run to avoid getting hurt, and you end up never giving anyone a real, honest-to-God shot. And it needs to stop because I don't play like that anymore. Contrary to what your brother believes, I am not a player. I haven't been one in a while, and to be honest, I never really liked the games.

"I care about you a lot—I've made that really fucking clear to you on several occasions. I don't want anyone else. I don't want to hook up with other women. I want to be with you and only you." I feel a thrill like electricity shoot through my entire body at his words, the sensation lingering in my chest and the tips of my fingers, making me want to desperately reach out and touch him, just a little bit, just for a while.

"I *told* you I was ready to commit to this and come out to

everyone, and you said you wanted to chase this first, to make sure it was real before telling anyone. And I respected it. I understood because I thought it was about your brother and wanting to avoid a fight with him in the event that none of this led to anything. Then, we went through the whole necklace thing, and you said it was because you were superstitious." He scoffs and shakes his head. "You kept making excuses, and I bought them, taking your word. But now, after what happened tonight, I realize that your whole problem with us has been about *you* and how you feel." He points at me. "Your whole deal is that you can't handle what this is."

"My *deal*?" I scoff, trying to distract myself from how having him here in my apartment makes me want and feel. I think about when he pulled me into his arms and held me as we swayed gently in my bedroom to soft music. "This has nothing to do with me being *scared* or with being a *runner*, because I'm not. It has everything to do with the fact that I caught you and Kelly cozying up to each other while you thought I was still in the bathroom." I feel my skin flush, heat crawling up my neck to my ears. The thought of her hand on his arm fills me with a jealous rage that I've never experienced in my life, *and I fucking hate it.* I hate that he makes me feel so...so... *so much.*

He shakes his head and takes a step closer to me. "No, no, no. Because if you weren't scared shitless, you would have at least walked up to me and told me off, and I could have explained to you that *she* was coming on to *me* and that I brushed her off. I would have explained how I told her that I was there with you, and I was not interested in her at all. We would have cleared up this entire misunderstanding in a couple of minutes, and then we would have been able to continue to enjoy the party. Instead, you decided to walk away without even saying goodbye."

I cross my arms in front of my chest and shrug. "I just

wanted to avoid a public confrontation," I say nonchalantly, as if everything he's said so far has left me unaffected. But there is some truth to his claims. We haven't known each other that long, and already I feel really strongly for him, which really scares me sometimes. It makes me fearful of how much it would hurt months down the line if he ever really did cheat on me or leave me. "I realized that I was wrong and that you're still that same guy from six years ago, walking a different girl out of your apartment every morning."

"You're just making excuses," he says, narrowing his eyes at me. "You know I'm not like that anymore. You know it's different with you, and it always has been since day fucking one!" He stomps his foot in frustration. I know he's right. Matt has only ever shown me kindness and understanding. He's never once treated me like a hook-up—not even during his darkest days in med school. "I *know* you care about me, and I *know* you're freaking out because of it. Because you never once felt this way before about anyone. Because your stupid professor never made you feel the same way. Never made your skin ache, fucking *burn* for anyone like this." He runs his fingertips over my arm, barely grazing my skin, sending shivers up and down my spine. "Never made you feel crazy but like everything finally made sense at the same time. No other person in your life has ever made you feel so fucking *unhinged*." My breath stutters, and I shut my eyes. His cedar scent is overpowering, and I feel myself losing the will to resist him. He's so close I can feel the heat of his body on mine. I dig my nails into my arms, doing my absolute best to keep myself from reaching out and running them down his chest.

"And do you know how I know that you feel all of this, Liza?" His lips are at my ear now, beard tickling the delicate skin of my neck, whispering in a low gravelly voice. "I know because I feel the exact same way about you." He places a hand on my waist. "All I ever fucking think about anymore is *you*. All I want is you, Liza." He grips me tighter. "I've never felt so physically, emotionally, or intellectually attracted to someone." I let out an involuntary whimper, and I pray to God he didn't hear.

"I fucking *want* this. More than I have ever wanted anything in my entire life."

I swallow the knot forming in the back of my throat and shake my head. He lets go of my waist and loosens my hands from across my body, taking them gently into his own.

"Fine. So I'm scared," my voice cracks. "So what? It's all your fault! Before, I thought that being in a relationship meant being with someone like Jeremy. We would go out to dinner, he would say I looked nice, we'd eat, and then go home. There was no passion, no can't-get-you-out-of-my-head, thinking-about-you-nonstop. It was stable and calm—but not in a good way. Honestly, I thought that's what a relationship looked like, because it was all I had ever experienced.

"And then *you* show up with your stupid pulling out my chair for me all the time, and bringing me water before I even ask, and being so fucking thoughtful with your cute pumpkin flowers, and building my furniture, and the dancing, and standing up for me, and..." I exhale, trying to relieve some of the pressure building up in my chest. "It's just too much, too fast, Matt. It's just...*so much*," I say in a small voice, overwhelmed by the sudden flood of emotions I feel coming on. My heart is racing in my chest, my breathing already ragged, because he's right. Matt is completely right. I'm scared—terrified, even—because I know what true loss is, and I don't want to ever have to relive it. I know now that losing him would be nothing like losing Jeremy. What I felt for my ex isn't even a small fraction of what I feel for Matt. Not having him in my life anymore would be devastating, soul-crushing, and I think that I've had enough of grief for now, thanks.

My words hang between us for a few moments as he gauges my body language. I can see his mind racing, see him trying to solve me like a puzzle, see him trying to find a way to salvage this and come out winning, making me fall for him just a little more.

"I don't know what to say," I say finally.

He lifts a shoulder. "You need to tell me whether you want this or not."

I take a deep breath. "It's not that simple."

"It really is." He stares me down. Eventually, he groans and runs a hand down his face before saying, "I'm willing to stick to our earlier agreement of not telling your brother yet. *That* I totally understand. But when it comes to this"—he points back and forth between the two of us—"I want full commitment. I want to know whether you're in or you're out. Because I am in. I am so fucking in, Liza. There is no doubt in my mind that I want you—mind, body, and soul. It all just comes down to whether or not you think you're brave enough to handle it."

He stares back at me, wide-eyed, and I don't know what to say, what to answer. I want to be with him—I do. But what if it hurts? What if he gets tired of all my little idiosyncrasies and leaves me? Or what if we spend a lifetime together, and then I'm left a vacuous being, desperately alone because the person I loved the most is gone? Am I strong enough to take a chance on love? Either way, I'm going to lose him—whether it's in a couple of months because it doesn't work out or in fifty years after having grown old together.

Matt looks like a man balancing on the edge of a building, so close to falling into the abyss, trying desperately to find his way back to safety. I can tell he's trying so hard not to push me harder, not to beg and ask me to take this chance. I realize how big of an idiot I've been tonight, pushing him away, when he's shown me time and time again that I can count on him, even during his darkest days.

It really is about me being scared, about me being afraid of losing him and being left heartbroken, alone. But he's here, taking a chance, putting everything on the line and being so brave it makes me melt, taking on the same fears. If he can do this for me, I can do it for him, too? Right?

"Will you help me? Will you help me through any freak-outs and not get frustrated with me when I get insecure and neurotic?" I feel my bottom lip tremble, so I bite down on it.

Matt gives me a hopeful smile and squeezes my hands in encouragement. "I can't promise you that I won't get frustrated by your insecurities or neuroses, because that's just unrealistic. But I can promise you that I will be there, every damn day, reminding you just how much you mean to me." He raises his hands to cup my face. "Because you mean *everything* to me, Liza."

His lips come crashing down on mine, and the wave of relief I feel at the contact is instant and visceral. "Everything," he whispers against them just before he slips his tongue inside, tasting me, claiming me, showing me how much I can depend on him.

He lets out a groan, deep in his chest, as he brings one arm tightly around my waist while his other hand slides into my hair, holding me to him. I moan, clutching the lapels of his jacket, holding on as I literally go weak in the knees. The heat in my belly is back, the ache, the need between my legs crying out, urging me to get this man naked and to do it now. My heart feels full, feels like it's about to explode.

I want him. I need him. I *love* him.

The reality of the depth of my feelings for him hits me like a truck. How can I feel so much so quickly?

"You're so beautiful," he whispers in my ear before kissing a trail down my neck to my collarbone. "So fucking beautiful."

My heart starts doing Olympic-level backflips, and I ask myself how the hell I got so lucky to find someone as incredible as Matt as I pull his mouth back to mine and push his jacket off his shoulders, tossing it aside. He slips my tank top off and groans at the sight of my bare chest.

"*Fuck*," he exhales.

"C'mere," I beg, pulling him to me. I frantically start to unbutton his shirt, starting from the top, as he pulls its tails from his pants and starts unbuttoning it from the bottom. Our hands meet, and he takes his shirt off in one fell swoop, moving his hands to quickly unbuckle and unzip his pants. I help work his pants and underwear down, breathless, but they get stuck at his feet. "Shoes," I say against his chest as I kiss it. "Shoes, shoes."

"Fuck," he says again, panting, and pushes me softly away so he can bend over and remove them, but I press a hand against his chest.

"Let me," I say, kissing down his chest, his stomach, until I'm kneeling in front of him, taking him in my mouth. Matt lets out a primal groan, his head snapping back, hands falling on the wall for support. I'm on my knees, but he's the one at my mercy —and I'm drunk on the power. His hands slip into my hair but just enough to pull it away so he can see me. He doesn't push down or try to control the speed or depth. He's letting me run this show for now. When I feel his body start to tense, and his moans get louder, I release him and untie his shoes, remove his socks, and finally relieve him of his pants.

Matt pulls me up by the shoulders and pushes me against the wall. "Want you so bad," I say against his lips. "Need you now," I moan. I do my best to quickly peel my leggings off my legs and look graceful while doing it, but it's impossible. We both laugh a little as I stumble and almost knock over the table by the entrance. "Sorry," I chuckle.

"Don't be," he says with a smile, standing naked in front of me in more ways than one. "Come here," he says softly, sticking out his hand. I take it, and he pulls me into him softly, and I lay my head against his chest, inhaling his signature scent.

He holds me for a moment, our naked bodies intertwined, before bringing his lips back down to mine.

We seem to slow down now, our kisses deeper, more intense, as the reality that we're about to have sex for the first time sinks in. We've both just realized that, however much we've been wanting this, however much we've been thinking about it, we want to savor it and not have it wasted on a quick fuck against the wall by my front door. We both deserve better, and so does our relationship.

You mean something to me, his kisses tell me.

This is important to me, my moans assure him.

Suddenly, Matt's hands glide to the backs of my thighs, and he lifts me, wrapping my legs around his hard, muscular body. He walks us toward my bedroom, toward the bed that he unknowingly built for *us,* where he lays me down gently on my back and proceeds to lie down next to me.

I look up into his eyes and press a hand to his cheek, his beard soft against my palm. "What's wrong?" I ask when I see his brows furrow, his lips part as if about to say something.

"Nothing." He shakes his head at me. "I just can't believe this is finally happening."

He looks like he wants to say more but decides to kiss my neck and roll on top of me instead, distracting me from any further line of questioning I want to throw at him.

"I need you," I say again. He sucks a nipple into his mouth and tugs with his teeth, and I squirm and gasp at the mixture of pleasure and pain. I can feel him smile against me before he starts to kiss down my chest and stomach, his destination clear, but I stop him. All this buildup has made me feel crazy with need, my skin tingling, hands shaking. "No." I shake my head. "I need you inside me *now*." He looks like he wants to fight me on this, but ultimately, with my permission, his own hunger overpowers his need to please me with his mouth. "You make me so crazy," I confess. "I feel electric."

His lips crash over mine as I feel his weight on top of my body, pressing me down into the mattress, *and it feels amazing*. "Condom?" he whispers against my lips.

"You didn't bring one?" I ask, panicking.

"I—I didn't want to assume," he says. "I didn't want to jinx it, either."

I groan. "I thought you weren't superstitious."

"I wasn't gonna take any chances with you," he grunts out.

"Ugh, Matt. I don't have any condoms, either." I whine.

We stare at each other, eyes wide, and he frowns when he sees my pleading expression. "*No way*," Matt says. He tries to push off me, but I wrap my arms and legs tightly around him, holding him to me, feeling him *just there*, just at my entrance. "No way, Liza." He shakes his head in a panic.

"But Matt," I say, kissing down his neck and licking him from his collarbone to just below his ear. He groans like he's in pain and presses his forehead to the side of my face. "I immediately got tested after I found out about Jeremy and the redhead. Plus, I'm on the pill." He's quiet, but his hips start involuntarily thrusting lightly, teasing me.

"I mean, I've been tested since the last time I had sex, but..." He groans when I bite his earlobe and tug. "Fuck, Liza."

He places one forearm on either side of my face, caging me in. "You really want this?"

"I've never wanted anything more in my life," I say,

repeating his words back to him with the same intensity. "I want to feel you, skin on skin."

"Oh, Jesus," he says as he sinks slowly into me, little by little, as my body adjusts to his, stretching. He starts with slow, small thrusts, and we get lost in each other when I finally get used to his size. We're a blur of arms and legs, a symphony of moans and whispered words of devotion and promises. It's a constant struggle to try and slow down and enjoy the moment while wanting to speed up at the same time, but we manage it.

At a certain point, he rolls us over, me on top of him. Matt sits up, wrapping his arms around my waist and kissing my neck as he thrusts from below me. My eyes roll in the back of my head as I start to meet his rhythm.

"...*everything*..." he says over and over again in my ear. He tells me I'm *fucking everything*.

One of his hands slides in between us, and he touches me right *there*. I gasp and throw my head back, looking up at the ceiling.

"Like that," I say desperately. "Don't stop."

He grunts against my neck, squeezing my bottom with one hand and touching me with the other, his movements below me growing frantic, faster, as I feel him as close as I am. He tells me he needs me to come with him, that he needs to come inside me, and with a final thrust, I fall with him, holding each other tightly as the final bursts of pleasure run through our bodies.

Chapter Fifteen

MATT

THE LATE-MORNING LIGHT SPILLS INTO LIZA'S BEDROOM AS I wake to the incredibly hate-inducing sound of my alarm. It almost ruins arguably one of the most perfect mornings I have had in years—or ever, if I'm being honest.

My arm is wrapped lightly around her waist while she sleeps soundly. Her naked back is pressed against my chest, and I marvel at how small yet so strong she feels in my arms. My nose is pressed into Liza's hair, inhaling her sweet coconut scent, feeling it reach every corner of my body, soothing any previous concerns I ever had about us. Last night was the defining moment in our relationship, where we both cut the shit and decided to commit, to stop doing it halfway. Sure, it still meant that we weren't ready to announce it in the family newsletter or anything, but it was enough for us to determine that we're committed, that the feelings we have for each other aren't lukewarm—they mean something.

I told her she meant everything to me.

I flush as I realize just how close I came last night to actually telling her that I am in love with her. I'm glad I had the sense and self-restraint to be able to silence the urge—though, it wasn't easy. I definitely feel it, but I don't want her to freak out. Last night, she said that what we had was a lot for her—*too much*, even—so I want to keep the confessions to a minimum for the time being.

I don't want to move, to ruin this moment, but I need to stop that horrible sound before it drives me insane. I make a move to remove my arm from around her waist but am met with a groan and a hand that pulls me back to her. I chuckle at her resistance.

"What *is* that?" she asks. Her breathy voice brings back memories from last night, from when she begged me not to stop, when she told me how much she liked it. My stomach tightens, skin heats, fingers aching to touch every inch of her soft skin.

"My alarm," I croak. I sigh and reluctantly start to get up, but she pulls me back in once more, rolling me onto my back, burrowing her face in my neck.

"Mmm, you smell so good. Like Matt and cedar and sex," she says, and I laugh and dig my fingers into her hair, holding her to me as I kiss the top of her head. I want to grab her by the hips, have her straddle me and ride my cock, but the screeching coming from my phone is keeping me from fully enjoying this moment.

"Leave it," Liza says, reading my mind as her hands trace my collarbone.

I kiss her bare shoulder with an open mouth, feeling how soft she is, tasting her, one hand skirting down her stomach, reacquainting myself with her body after last night. She bites down on my shoulder to stifle a moan as I reach the apex of her thighs, and I wish she would just let me hear her. I love her sounds. I remember them as they bounced off her bedroom walls last night, driving me crazy, egging me on, making me harder with every single one until I couldn't handle it any longer.

She arches against me, thoroughly enjoying the movements of my fingers on her, and I smile mischievously. I remove my hand from her just as she starts to build, and I get up from the bed.

"What the hell?" she asks, sitting up.

I laugh and run a hand through my hair. I love seeing her frustrated, needing me. "I'll be back. Just need to turn this stupid thing off."

She whines and looks up at me in frustration with pleading eyes. Her hair is disheveled, but she looks like a goddess, hair wild, curling just below her breasts at her waist. It is a serious case of sex hair, but it suits her.

So tempting.

"One second," I say, chuckling. "I'll be right back."

I kiss her lightly on the lips, as if we've been doing it for years, running my knuckles over her cheek. She grabs my hand by the wrist and turns her face to kiss my palm softly. Warmth spreads through my chest, and I want to shake her for making it so goddamn hard for me to walk away from her, even if it's just a few feet to turn off my alarm. The tenderness of the moment causes something to catch in my throat, and I try unsuccessfully to swallow it down with a gulp.

Finally, I manage to pull myself away from her and walk to where I left my clothes by the entrance, in search of the cock-blocker extraordinaire—my phone. The floor is in complete disarray, littered with clothes and shoes, both hers and mine, memories of last night's frantic undressing flooding my mind. I smile as I rifle through my pockets and find my phone, finally turning the culprit of the sound off. I scoop all our clothes up in one go, leaving my shoes by the door, and carry them with me.

When I reach her bedroom, the knot in my throat comes back as I see her lying there, eyes closed, looking angelic. Her dark-brown hair is spread across her pillow, and she's lying on her stomach, sheet low on her back. She hears me approach the bed, and her eyes fly open. I dump our clothes on the chair by the door and crawl back into bed, hypnotized by her broad smile.

"You're back," she says, craning her neck up, lips searching for mine. I press a chaste kiss on her lips and smile, my chest tightening with happiness over the fact that I get to do this with her all the time now. I slide under the covers next to her and spin Liza in my arms to face away from me. I want to get back to those first few minutes of absolute bliss I felt when I first woke up this morning, when I was barely conscious, only the thought of her skin and her scent on my mind. I wrap her in my arms again, pressing her close to me, and kiss her bare shoulder, dragging my nose back to her neck where I place another kiss. She sighs and looks over her shoulder at me, eyes flickering to my lips. I laugh softly and oblige her wordless request, kissing her, slowly parting her lips, dragging my tongue against hers, and it's like a spark to tinder. My grip tightens around her, and she moans in my mouth, nipping at my bottom lip. I was at a half-mast before, but I'm rock solid now, my hunger for her seemingly insatiable even after the three rounds of sex from last night.

Liza's hand reaches behind her to hold me, squeeze me, and I thrust into it as I continue to kiss her, her body twisted in my arms, my right hand playing with her nipples, tugging, pulling, twisting. Her head snaps back, pushing her breasts harder into my hand, and I love how much she enjoys a little pain with her pleasure.

She squeezes me a little too hard for comfort, and just as I'm about to roll her on her stomach to teach her a lesson, there's a knock at the door followed by the doorbell.

I freeze.

"What are you doing?" she asks. "Don't stop."

"There's someone at your door," I say, stating the obvious.

She looks at me again with the same expression she's used so many times before, the one that tells me she's questioning my level of intelligence. "Just keep going. Who cares? Ignore them," she says, reading my mind from before and rolling herself onto her hands and knees.

"Aw, fuck," I say, climbing onto my knees behind her. I can't resist her in this position, giving me all the power and control, her ass in the air. I settle myself behind her, positioning myself *just there*. My hands are on her hips, holding her, and I'm about to thrust into her when the doorbell rings again. This time, however, it's followed by a very familiar voice.

"Liza! You awake? We said noon!" Vinny's voice sounds far away as Liza looks up at me with horrified eyes, and I freeze.

"Oh my god, you need to *hide*. I completely forgot I had plans with them today," she whisper-yells. "Coming!" she yells. "Just getting dressed."

"What the fuck, Liza?" I say in a low voice, adrenaline coursing through my veins. I'm rooted to the bed, unable to move. Meanwhile, she's pulling on an entire outfit in less time than it takes for a Formula 1 car to get its wheels changed mid-race (I make a mental note to commit this moment to memory so I can bring it up next time she tells me she needs a couple of more minutes to get ready).

The doorbell rings incessantly now, and I hear Danielle say, *"Vinny, stop. You're acting like a child."*

I jump off the bed and step on something sharp and painful. I bite my lip to stifle a yelp and inspect my foot. I just stepped on the spikiest heel I've ever seen in my life.

"Careful!" she hisses. "Those are Manolos!" Like it's supposed to mean something to me. What the hell is she talking about?

"Stay here," she says. "Don't make a sound once I open the

front door." She walks out of the bedroom, shutting the door behind her, giving me a nice final view of her denim-clad ass.

I drag my pants on as I hear her open the door and greet her brother, sister-in-law, and niece and nephew. I hear Vinny's kids through the door, throwing themselves at their aunt, so happy to see her.

"*What took you so long?*" Vinny asks her, irritated. "*You were supposed to be ready by now to go to the zoo with us.*"

"*Hey, guys,*" I hear her greet the twins, completely ignoring her brother. "*I missed you.*"

My stomach drops when I realize I left my shoes out there. *FUUUUUCK.*

I pray Liza saw them before opening the door and had the good sense to hide them somewhere just in time.

"*So, we gonna see this new apartment of yours now or what?*" Vinny asks. "*I think the only person who's seen it is Matt,*" he mutters. "*You need to give us a tour.*"

Liza laughs awkwardly. "*How about we do it when we come back? I'm starving. Let's have lunch before we go to the zoo.*"

I need Liza to get them out of the house ASAP. If Vinny catches me here, I'm a dead man. If he catches me half-naked... well, I don't even want to think about that. "*Seriously, Vinny. Don't.*" She sounds nervous now, like she's on death row. It dawns on me that they must be ignoring her request and taking a look around the apartment. Suddenly, I hear her high-pitched voice yell, "*No! Don't go into my bedroom, please! It's too messy!*" I hide quickly in her closet as quietly as possible, taking the rest of my clothes with me. The space is small and packed with her clothes and shoes, making it impossible for me to stand here comfortably. I'm standing on my toes, supporting myself on the door frame with one hand and holding my jacket and shirt in the other. I think I may be having a heart attack, but at least I'll be surrounded by her comforting signature scent when I die.

"It's not so disorganized," I hear Danielle's voice in the bedroom. I'm sweating bullets now, panicking. Maybe it really is best to just fucking own up to this. This seems so childish.

"Seriously, it is. I'll show you another day." She sounds so anxious, and I wish I could ask her to try and do a better job at keeping her cool.

"Liza," I hear Vinny call her from far away. *"Can you come here? I need to ask you something about the kitchen."* I sigh as I hear steps retreat away, thinking they've both left the bedroom, but the closet door immediately flies open. I freeze at the sight of Danielle, and she gasps in shock.

"What is it?" I hear Vinny ask her.

"Shh, please," I beg.

"Uh, nothing, nothing! Just shocked by the small amount of closet space Liza has, is all."

This is horrible. I'm shirtless, shoeless, and hiding in a closet. This is definitely not a good look for me.

"Whatever, she has too much shit, anyway," he says in response with a snort. I hear him say something to Liza, but my focus shifts exclusively to the woman in front of me—the one with the ability to rat me out and blow my cover.

"I *knew* it," she whispers with a smile. "I saw some men's shoes by the door, and then I freaked when I walked into the bedroom and noticed that this entire room smells like sex. Which is absolutely gross, by the way. I mean, how many times did you do it last night? Don't answer that. But also, good job." She smiles.

I groan. "He didn't see the shoes, did he?"

"No, I kicked them over behind the door without him noticing," she says with a proud smile. The gratitude I feel for Liza's sister-in-law in this moment is immeasurable.

"Thank you," I mouth.

"You're welcome. Now get back into the closet. I'll try to get us out of here as fast as possible." She gently closes the door in my face.

"*Vincenzo Castelli, I swear to God, if you don't get me to a restaurant right now to have some lunch, I'm going to lose my freaking mind,*" Danielle says in an admonishing tone I've only ever heard her use with her children before.

"*But, babe, I haven't even seen her room yet. I was checking out the stove. It's a Viking, like the ones on the Food Network,*" he whines.

"*No, let's go,*" she says with finality as she opens the door. "*Come on, kids,*" she calls the twins, and I hear them run to her. Vinny grunts something back that I can't make out, to which she replies that she doesn't care.

"*One sec, guys. I need to get my purse,*" I hear Liza say. After only a few moments, the door to the closet opens again, and she brings a finger to her lips, warning me not to say anything. She smiles and stretches up to give me a slow, deep, quiet kiss before turning around, closing the door, and walking out, leaving me half naked in her apartment.

That was a really close call. Way too fucking close for comfort.

Chapter Sixteen

MATT

"Can you pass me that brush?" she says, looking at me in the mirror as we both ready ourselves for tonight's event. I'm taking Liza out to a fundraising dinner for my hospital at the New York Public Library, and we're both getting ready at her apartment. I didn't think I'd have time to go home, change, and pick her up, so I decided to bring my things with me and go straight from work to her place.

The event is black tie, which should be a fun change after an entire week of spending every night on the couch, me in my sweatpants, Liza in her leggings, eating whatever delivery we felt like that night—and I have loved every fucking second of it. I could spend the rest of my days coming home to her dressed just like that, ordering take-out because we're too tired to cook, talking about our day while the TV plays reruns of whatever show she's into that week in the background.

But I know balance is important, and we can't turn into complete recluses, locking ourselves up in an apartment without talking to anyone else ever again. Plus, I'm dying to see her in the sexy dress she says she bought especially for tonight. She's a little insecure about her curves, which drives me nuts because I would start a religion just to idolize them if I could, so if she says she looks sexy in this dress, I can't even begin to imagine how incredibly hot she'll look.

So yes, I'm really excited. I get to take my girl out on a really nice date tonight, get to show her off to all my work colleagues, get to do something different. It will be the first time we go somewhere with other people, where we'll be able to walk in together, arm in arm.

I'm nervous, though, too, because I did something a little out there, something that she may consider to fall under the "*too much*" category, and I'm scared that it will set back all the progress we've made this past week—which has pretty much been the most uneventful yet best week of my life. We've been practically living together, spending every night since Halloween at her place—she just hasn't noticed it yet, and I sure as hell am not going to risk losing this by pointing it out.

For the first time in a really long time, I think I might actually be happy. No, I *know* I'm happy, and I also know that a huge part of it is because of her, which is why I have to be really careful tonight. I just need to ease into it, even if I'm sure that she's going to like what I did.

"Sure," I say and pass her the requested brush. She runs it through her hair before wrapping a strand around a curling iron —which looks more like a dangerous weapon than a styling implement. I've already burned my hand on it once tonight and decided to never go near it again.

While maneuvering the curling wand, her robe slips off one shoulder, and I nearly start to drool. She's so beautiful. I'll make sure to remember to kiss her when she's done—it's just too dangerous now.

"I'm done," I say as I finish spreading the last of my after-shave on my face. "I'll wait for you out in the living room, okay?"

"Okay," she says softly, setting the wand on the counter before stretching up on her toes to kiss me. I try to pull away from her, but kissing Liza is like drowning and never wanting to come up. I pull her closer to me and play with the belt of her robe, wanting to tug it open in one fell swoop. She smiles knowingly against my lips and pushes me away gently with a smirk. "I have to finish getting ready, and we don't have time for any of that," she admonishes me.

I groan and take a deep breath. "Fine," I say like a petulant teenager. "But I'll remember this moment, Liza Castelli." I point a menacing finger in her direction.

She laughs, and I reluctantly abandon my post in the bathroom and walk out to the living room to pull the gift I got her out of the overnight bag I packed for tonight. I take it with me to the couch where I turn on Netflix to whatever was playing last —a dating show about a bunch of people on an island "looking for love" (aka a $100,000 cash prize and a sponsorship deal with a gummy bear multivitamin brand)—one of Liza's guilty pleasures. I don't pay attention to the sounds of three women arguing over the same guy (who I think is actually hooking up behind all their backs with one of the guys—jeez, what is going on in this show?). Instead, I open and shut the box in my hand, fidgeting with its contents, trying not to get any smudge marks on it.

I hope to God she likes it.

"Oh no, you're watching this without me?" I turn in my seat to look at her, and my jaw drops. "I haven't seen this episode!" she complains, walking farther into the living room like she doesn't look like a complete fox, like the sight of her in the long, black, sparkly dress didn't just literally make my heart skip a beat. "I thought you hated this show."

"Liza..." I manage to say, my voice cracking. "You...that *dress*...holy shit."

She flushes. "Yeah? You think?" She runs her hands up and down her thighs, smoothing down the material, but there's no need—she's perfect.

I nod vigorously as I stand and walk over to her, taking her hands in mine.

"It's a little tight, and it makes my butt look—"

"It enhances just how beautiful you already are," I say, 100% serious. "You look absolutely perfect." Her hair is up in an intricate hairstyle, braided on the sides and all tied together in a low bun with loose tendrils delicately framing her face. Her dress is black and strapless, tight all throughout her torso and just below where her ass ends, emphasizing her curves—my favorite part of her body. From there, the dress flares out into a mini-train, trailing gracefully behind Liza with every move she makes.

She looks like a movie star stepping onto the red carpet. She should be surrounded by a crowd of screaming fans and paparazzi asking who she's wearing and screaming at her to *Look here! No, look here!* as they take a million pictures of her.

I can't believe my luck to have been able to find a woman like her—the whole fucking package. She's smart, sexy, and funny, and I'm suddenly so overcome by the depth of my feelings for her that my chest starts to tighten.

She smiles sheepishly at me. "Thank you," she says, biting her lip.

I want to pull her into my arms, carry her into the bedroom, and have my way with her, but that's not really an option that's on the table right now. If tonight weren't a work event, I'd suggest we skip it altogether and just jump back into bed. I do my best to distract myself from these wayward thoughts by deciding that it suddenly feels like the best time for me to give her the gift I picked out especially for her.

"So," I say after giving her a long, slow kiss. "I actually got you something."

"Another gift?" She smiles excitedly. "You shouldn't have! I already have the pumpkin. And it's hasn't even rotted yet!" She points at the pristine white pumpkin sitting in the middle of her coffee table and laughs a little.

"No," I shake my head. "This is something...different. A real present." I pick up the rectangular velvet box from where I left it on the couch cushion, and she gasps.

"Matt, a velvet box almost always means jewelry," she says carefully, eyes widening.

I need to tread lightly, make it sound like I was thinking about her but that it wasn't necessarily a big deal—although, it kind of was a little bit. Liza pinches the lid of the box, but doesn't open it, hesitating, as if there were a chance that something could jump out of there and attack her.

It kind of stings.

"It's nothing huge." I shrug as casually as possible. "I just know you were really upset when you lost the necklace your dad gave you, so I asked my mom if she had anything similar to it—you know, since she's a jeweler," I lie. It was actually kind of a whole process. I couldn't remember exactly what it looked like, so I had Danielle describe the medal on the necklace in as much detail as possible in an email, which I then forwarded to my mother so she could custom-make a replica of the original. Plus, I had to rush order it and everything.

Explaining why I needed my mother to do this for me was also a whole trip. She and I don't really have that much of a communicative relationship, so it was difficult to open up and tell her about my relationship with Liza. We're still so new—I don't want to jinx us.

Liza's eyes start to water, and she carefully—and may I add

slowly—opens the box. She gasps and brings the fingers of her right hand to her mouth.

"*Matt...*" she says, her voice breaking. "I don't know what to say."

"You can say you'll wear it tonight," I say hopefully. "Only if you like it, of course. It's okay if you don't."

"Are you kidding? I *love* it." A tear slips from her eye, and she pats it dry. My heart squeezes in my chest, and I smile down into her beautiful dark-brown eyes, a swirl of browns and golds. "Oh crap, you couldn't have given this to me before I did my make-up?" she jokes with a sniffle as she lifts her face to the ceiling. "I'm gonna ruin an hour's worth of work here."

I laugh and cup her face in my hands, tilting her face so I can lay a sweet kiss on her lips.

"Here, put it on for me," Liza says, handing me the box. She turns her back to me and lowers her head so I can place the necklace around her neck and easily secure the clasp shut. I place a soft, open-mouthed kiss on her shoulder and wrap my arms around her waist, breathing her in.

"Mmm, I love it when you kiss my shoulder like that, even if your beard tickles a little," she sighs.

"Yeah?" I smile against her skin, kissing her the same way again, feeling how good she feels. Liza turns in my arms and clasps her hands behind my neck.

"Matt, this is so sweet. I can't believe you did this."

"It was nothing," I say against her lips. "I'm so happy you like it."

I love you.

I guess I shouldn't be surprised by how amazing Liza is with complete strangers, but honestly, she's been a dream. In the past, whenever I've taken a date to one of these things, it's been difficult to get them to mingle with other doctors and hospital administrators. I don't know whether it's because she's used to doctors because of her brother or whether it's her natural people skills, but she's become every person at our table's favorite guest. She doesn't just participate in conversation, she makes sure everyone is included. She's charming and funny and smart, and the head of cardiology, Dr. Parker—my boss—is absolutely smitten with her.

I wrap an arm around her shoulder, lightly tracing patterns on her skin as she talks to him about future hospital renovations. I smile when I see my touch raise goosebumps on her skin.

"She really is something," Parker says at one point in the conversation after she makes him laugh.

I smile proudly at her and bring her left hand to my mouth to kiss. "She definitely is." I don't let go of her hand as they ease comfortably back into their conversation, and I marvel at how easily people open up to her. She's going to be an amazing therapist, getting to help people every day.

At one point in the night, they open up the dance floor for guests—an opportunity I make sure I don't pass on. I pull her into my arms, where she lays her head on my chest, and we sway to Sinatra.

"You having fun?" I ask in her ear. "I know these things can get really boring—especially when you don't know anyone except for your date."

"Are you kidding? Your boss is a trip. Did you know he collects backgammon sets? He's also part of a club where they meet up twice a month to drink and play all day. The stories he told me about the guys who are part of that group were hilarious!" She laughs.

"I think you now know more about Parker than I do, and I've been working at the hospital for months," I say, shaking my head at her in disbelief.

"Oh my god, he's so nice. You're so lucky to have a boss like that—seriously."

Now I really laugh. "Parker is known to be a hardass with a short fuse," I tell her in a whisper, looking around to make sure no one can hear. "Tonight is the first time I've ever seen him smile. I think he just fell in love with you, and you brought out his nice side."

She snorts, like the thought of anyone loving her is completely ridiculous. "No such thing as love at first sight."

I smile, deciding to take a risk. "I can't say I agree with that statement," I say, my lips at her ear, pulling her closer to me. Not quite those three little words, but close to them. Her skin erupts in goosebumps again, and I feel like I've been hit by lightning. She liked it.

Liza reaches up to kiss my neck, and I swear I don't think I've ever been happier than I am now.

"Can we go home now?" she asks in a breathy voice.

I look down into her hungry eyes and reply with, *"Fuck. Yes."*

She laughs at my eagerness and tells me she needs to use the restroom first. We walk back to our table to pick up her purse and wrap and say goodnight to our friends from the table. Dr. Parker looks truly disappointed by our—more specifically, Liza's —departure, but he tells her that he's happy he got to meet her.

I kiss her on the cheek before she disappears through the restroom doors, and I stand a few feet away to wait for her.

"Matt?" I turn to a voice behind me and see Gurash, an old buddy of mine from med school.

"Guru! Dude! I haven't seen you in forever!" We hug in an

unexpected burst of emotion (must be all the time I've been spending with Liza). "Where've you been?"

"Man, I stayed in New York after graduation. Did my residency at Cornell-Weill and am working at a practice there, too, but my girlfriend works for NYU, so that's why I'm here tonight," he says excitedly.

"Whoa, awesome, man. I, for sure, thought you'd end up going back to California," I say. Guru was one of my really close friends while studying at Columbia. I haven't seen him in ages, but he doesn't look like he's changed much—just that he's been to the gym a lot.

"Naw," he says, scratching the back of his head. "My girlfriend convinced me to stay in the city." He laughs sheepishly. "But it's fine. I mean, I don't regret it. Plus, I get to see Vinny every day again."

My stomach drops. "What do you mean?" My heart starts racing because I just *know* what the next words out of his mouth are going to be, and I'm here on a date with the last person I should be seen with. I need to get out of here and text Liza to meet me in front of the building ASAP.

"I mean Vinny and I now work at the same practice. Isn't that cool?" He smiles and smacks me on the shoulder. "So, who are you here with anyway?"

Chapter Seventeen

LIZA

I fix my hair in the mirror of the bathroom, tucking some strands that have come out of my braid back into place. I take a minute to inspect the woman in the reflection, having a hard time recognizing her. She's smiling, cheeks flushed, a sparkle dancing in her dark eyes. She looks *happy*.

I sigh deeply, bringing my hands to touch the new necklace around my neck. Sure, it's not the one my dad gave me, but it's important to me, too, given to me by the man currently waiting for me outside, waiting patiently as he has been for about a month since we first reconnected in Sag Harbor during that Columbus Day weekend at my mother's house.

He's so good to me.

This week with Matt has been pure bliss—and not in a *The Bachelor* type of way, where you go zip-lining on dates and end your nights with a dinner on a boat and a live band no one has heard of playing in the background just for the two of you. Nope. I mean it in the real way. Like I told Matt, I thought love and being in a relationship was just dinners, flowers, telling me I'm pretty—cliché stuff.

Now I know that, even though those things are fun and nice, love is also about the real things. Like remembering to bring home your favorite Indian food without even having to ask. Or coming over to your apartment and just sitting quietly next to each other while you both work just so you can be in the same room together, just so you can feel close. I realize now that true love is in the little things as much as it is in the big things. Big things like having your mother make the girl you're dating a similar necklace for her after she loses it.

I definitely love him.

I'm not 100% sure that I'm ready to say it out loud—I don't think I'm brave enough to yet—but I think I understand what Vinny meant that day in Mom's kitchen when he said I had never been in love. I think he was right. I've never felt this way before.

I love him when he massages my feet. I love him when I run my fingers through his beard. I love him when he comes over, exhausted after a long day of work, and falls asleep on my couch with his neck snapped back, mouth gaping open, drooling. I love him when he makes me laugh. And I love him when he makes love to me.

I'm totally gone here.

I may not be able to tell him how much I care about him yet because I'm a little coward, but I make a promise to myself right here, right now that I will always, from this day forth, not let a second go by without him feeling absolutely loved.

With my new mission in mind, I wash and dry my hands and, with a final glance in the mirror, exit the bathroom to meet the man that's changed me for good—for the better.

I spy Matt a few feet from the bathroom door, his back to me, and I smile, excited that I get to go home with him now, not really caring whether it's to have some sexy time or just cuddle up on the couch—I swear both activities are fine by me at the moment. He's talking to someone, but I can't really make out his face. As I get closer, though, I see who it is and come to a screeching halt, almost falling flat on my face as the heel of my shoe tangles in the train of my dress, and I nearly knock over a very nice waiter with a tray full of stuffed mushroom caps.

"Liza? Is that you?" my brother's friend and business partner asks. "It's so weird to see you here!"

"Guru! Hi!" I'm totally not freaking out right now, and it's definitely not showing on my face or in the sound of my voice. "How's it going?"

Guru's arms wrap around me, and I look at Matt over his shoulder, eyes wide with panic, trying to communicate with him that we need to get out of this situation as quickly and as delicately as possible.

He stares back, his expression resembling what I imagine mine looks like, telling me he understands and that he'll let me take the lead here.

I totally get the whole couples' mind-reading thing now, and he and I have it down to near perfection—even if it hasn't been that long.

"Good, everything's good! You remember Matt? He went to school with your brother and me," Guru introduces Matt to me, and I stick out my hand to him.

"Yeah, I think I remember you. Nice to see you again." I

smile. Matt takes my hand and shakes it, but his expression is cold, lips thin. He is definitely not happy right now.

Guru coughs uncomfortably at the awkward exchange between us and asks, "What are you doing at a hospital event?"

"Oh, I came here with a date," I say in a low voice, glancing nervously at Matt who takes a deep, sharp breath.

"Yeah, Vinny told me you and that professor broke up. Is this guy your new boyfriend? Is he a doctor?" He elbows me in the ribs, teasing me. "I need to meet him."

Shit.

"He's a donor, actually," I lie smoothly. If I say he's a doctor or a hospital administrator, I have a higher chance of getting caught up in a lie, whereas a donor could be someone completely random.

"Oh, wow. He must have some deep pockets then. Is he around? I'd love to meet him and report back to Vinny." He winks at me.

Oh my God, no.

"Actually..." I lean a little closer to Guru like I'm telling him a secret. "Would you mind not saying anything? You know how Vinny can get, and I *just* started seeing this guy. I don't want to scare him away." I try to smile my most convincing and alluring smile, hoping it works.

"Of course. I totally get it. I've heard how protective he is," he laughs.

I force a smile and chance a look at Matt, still quiet. He's unmoving, arms behind his back, staring off over my shoulder. "Well, I'm gonna head off. He's waiting for me outside. Good to see the both of you."

"Bye." Guru kisses me on the cheek, and Matt shakes my hand (???), grunting out a pathetic goodbye.

Great. This is just great. I can just imagine what tonight is gonna be like.

I turn around and make my way out of the building, wondering whether I should wait for him to come outside or meet him at my place. I get my coat from coat check and wait by the line of taxis in front of the building. I wait a couple of minutes before texting Matt that I'm here and asking him whether I should just head home or whether I should wait for him a little longer.

Just as I'm about to press send, I hear him behind me. "Hey." His voice is low, his brows furrowed. "Let's get a taxi," he says quietly as he raises his hand in the air, calling a yellow cab to him without making any sort of eye contact with me.

He's trying to rein it in, but I can tell that he's fuming, frustrated that, once again, we had to pretend we were nothing to each other. He's angry—at me, at the situation. I know that he'll push again tonight, that he'll plead with me to come out to my family. And I know I'll say no. I'll end up hurting him even though I don't want to. He'll say it's not fair to him—and he's absolutely right. And then he'll get tired and leave me for it.

As upset as I can tell he is by this whole situation, he's still gentleman enough that he holds the door open for me, shutting it softly behind me. He walks around the car to the other side to get in so I don't have to scoot in farther. I want to thank him but am scared of being the first one to talk, wanting to save the fight for when we're at my place.

I reach out to grab his hand in the cab, and he lets me take it but looks out the window at the city, bright lights flashing by as we make our way to the Upper West Side. We say nothing the entire way to my apartment, remaining quiet even throughout the elevator ride. He says nothing, avoids my gaze, and is stiff-cold while still being polite and gentlemanlike. I hate it.

I finally lose it when we get home, and he removes his jacket as he walks into the kitchen.

"Aren't you going to say something?" The tone of my voice

is pretty abrasive, and I know I'm playing with fire here, but fuck it. If I need to provoke him to get him to talk to me, then I will.

"What would you like me to say?" His eyes are like daggers when they finally meet mine. He serves himself a glass of water and takes a sip from it, looking fierce.

"I'd like to at least discuss this." I follow him into the bedroom and watch him sit on the edge of the bed as he unlaces his shoes.

"Discuss what? How I'm fucking tired of this lying and sneaking around? How we just narrowly avoided getting caught by your brother's business partner?" He throws his hands in the air in frustration. "This whole thing is fucking ridiculous, Liza. I'm tired of hiding and holding back."

"You know why it has to be like this. It's only while we figure stuff out."

"Well, I've figured my shit out. I know how I feel about you. *I'm* ready for this. And I'm tired of the fact that I can't have one fucking night with my girlfriend where I don't feel like a fucking criminal. *Jesus*, Liza!" he says, tossing a shoe at the chair in my room. I wince. He exhales and puts his elbows on his knees, face in his hands. "I don't know what to say."

"It's the first time you've called me that—out loud," I say, both sidetracking but actually wanting to talk about it.

It works, because Matt stops to look up at me, confused. "Sure I have."

"No." I shake my head, crouching in front of him, sliding my hands up his arms to his wrists. "You introduced me as your date tonight, not your girlfriend. You've never called me your girlfriend before."

He drops his hands. "Well, isn't that what you are?"

"I hope so." I smile. "I really liked you saying it." It's true. He makes me feel like I've been hit by lightning in the most incredible way, skin electric, mind racing, heart beating out of my chest.

He cups my face with a hand and kisses me softly. "Good. I like it too." I press my forehead to his and smile. "I'm sorry I'm upset," he sighs. "We were just having such a good time, and then I was reminded about this whole stupid thing." He exhales, and I brace myself for the inevitable ultimatum that I feel coming my way. He's going to tell me that it's time to come clean, that he's tired of me being scared and that I'm just going to have to deal with it, that he doesn't like ultimatums but it's just what needs to be done.

But it never comes.

"Please don't think that I'm pressuring you," he says with another deep sigh. "I'm just really happy, and I hate having to hide why. But I told you I would wait and that I would be patient, so that's what I'm gonna do. It's just...some days are harder than others." Matt smiles sheepishly at me.

"Matt, thank you," I say simply, following it with a kiss. It builds, as most of them tend to do between the two of us, his tongue parting my lips, breath quickening, heart racing, and I remember the promise I made to myself earlier tonight. I need to make sure he knows that he's loved. And tonight, there's one way I could show him.

I stand up and unzip my dress in front of him, left only in my lingerie and high heels. He inhales a sharp gasp, making my heart do backflips in my chest.

"Jesus," he whispers, pulling me closer by the hips until I straddle him. I kiss him again, getting lost in the feel of him, in his scent, in the way he says my name against my neck, and he pulls me down onto the mattress with him so that I can show him just how much he means to me, how much I care.

Chapter Eighteen

LIZA

"DANIELLE, YOU HAVE TO ROLL IT *GENTLY* WITH YOUR thumb on the fork, not like a brute," my mother says, exasperated with my sister-in-law. Danielle frowns, trying her hardest to follow directions, but she's still unable to get the shape of the gnocchi right.

We're in my mother's kitchen, preparing lunch for the family, and Mom is trying to teach Danielle another one of her Italian dishes. She says that if she and my brother refuse teach their children the Italian language, they at least need to learn how to eat proper Italian food.

"Like this?" She holds up the small dumpling with an eager smile. My mother looks at me and rolls her eyes. I give her a look, asking her to cut her some slack, and she exhales.

"Better, but not good."

Danielle takes it as a win. Smiling, she drops her sweet potato gnocchi on the tray next to the others we've prepared so far. After we've rolled all the dough into little pieces, we'll boil them until they float to the top of the pot and enjoy one of my favorite dishes. "Do these go with your red sauce?"

"*Ovviamente no, Danielle,*" my Mom tells her in Italian and shakes her head. "Obviously not. The flavor profiles don't match. With this, we do *burro fuso e salvia*. Brown butter and sage." Danielle blushes and looks down, embarrassed that she got that one wrong, grabbing another piece of dough and rolling it onto the fork.

Normally, my mother and Danielle get along swimmingly, but when it comes to the kitchen, Catterina Castelli is unforgiving and relentless. That, combined with Danielle's subpar cooking skills, type-A personality, and eagerness to please, just makes for a tense situation all around. I gotta give them both props, though, because cooking together has always been and always will be a horribly tense situation, but they always make the effort for the twins. Danielle and Vinny may have not made any effort to have their kids learn Italian, but they definitely try their hardest to make sure that their children grow up with the same traditions we did, and food is a huge part of that.

"*Maaaahhhh!!*" we hear Vinny bellow from the living room. "*I need you!!*" My mother sighs, wipes her hands on a kitchen towel, and tells him, "*Vengo! I'm coming,*" muttering the occasional Italian expletive under her breath.

"*So,*" Danielle doesn't waste a minute. "Are you still seeing Matt?"

"*Shhhh!!*" I hiss, looking over my shoulder in case anyone is around to hear her. "Are you crazy? Vinny could hear you. We can't talk about this here."

Danielle rolls her eyes at me. "Don't worry about Vinny. He's not coming in here anytime soon. Tell me. I need to know! I *deserve* to know."

"Ugh," I say, rolling another bit of dough into a snake-like shape before cutting it into more pieces to be rolled and shaped.

"Girl, I caught him naked in your closet, and I didn't say anything," she points out. It's annoying, but I do have to give her credit where credit is due. Without her help, things would have definitely exploded into a cataclysmic event—not to be dramatic or anything. "You owe me."

"He was only *half*-naked," I clarify. She really did save my ass that day—and the day she invited him for dinner at her house. I guess she deserves a little info. "Fine." I wipe my hands on a kitchen towel and serve us both a glass of wine—I feel like the situation calls for it. Girl talk is always better with a good glass of red. "We're great. He's great." I try to stop a huge smile from breaking out all over my face, but I can't help it. It's something that happens every time I think or talk about him.

I'm gross and annoying, I know. I love it.

"Did he give you anything special?" she asks eagerly, wiggling her eyebrows as I pass her one of the glasses.

"Ew, Danielle. You already know we had sex! There's no need to get specific about it."

She snorts. "No, silly. I mean the necklace. Did he give you the necklace?"

My hand flies to the gold necklace under my sweater. I haven't taken it off since last week when Matt so sweetly gave it to me before the fundraiser. "How did you know about that?"

She smiles proudly at herself and takes a swig from her glass of wine. "The guy *called* me to ask if I could help him find a picture or remember the design or something so he could send it to his jeweler and *have it made*."

"Wait." I take a deep breath. "So, it wasn't just a coincidence that his mom had something similar to it in her collection? He actually asked her to make it for him?" My heart squeezes in my chest at what it must have taken for Matt to talk to his mother about us. I know he's not close with her and that they have their issues, so I understand how even bigger of a deal it is that he called her to help.

"Yup. And I don't even know how he managed that. I

thought it took ages to get custom shit done," Danielle says, and I nod in agreement.

"His mom owns her own jewelry line. But still."

"He's so sweet," she says simply with a sigh.

"The sweetest. He makes me really happy, Dani. Like, I don't think I've ever been this happy, and that kind of makes me sad. Because *how* could I have wasted my time with other men, you know?" I can't even begin to wrap my mind around the fact that I dated all the losers and assholes that came before him. "But whatever. I mean, I wouldn't change anything because this road led me to him, but still... I've just never felt this way before."

She squeals in excitement, clapping her hands and jumping up and down in place like a teenage girl. "Ohmigod, this is so crazy. I *knew* it."

"Yeah, yeah, okay, you knew it." I roll my eyes at her. Omniscient Danielle.

"God, I'm so happy for you," she says genuinely with a huge smile on her face. "You look so glowy and in love."

I can't keep the smile off my face when I blush. "I feel it."

She squeals even louder, but I cover my ears just in time.

"Jeez, Dani! Keep it down," I say, but I laugh because I really am so happy to be with Matt. "We really are way too involved in each other's lives as a family, you know."

"This is an Italian family. It comes with the territory," she says as if I'm new here and haven't been part of it my entire life. "So, what's the deal, then? When are you guys going public?"

"I wanted to chase this a little bit to make sure it was something real, and he agreed. But I think we're pretty much on the same page that we're committed to each other. I just have a lot of mental paperwork to do—it's not just about my brother."

Danielle frowns but doesn't say anything.

"What?" My stomach flips, suddenly nervous.

"I thought it wouldn't be as difficult to get your brother on board, but he keeps talking about how happy he is to have 'his bro back,'" she says with air-quotes. Danielle shakes her head and then takes another sip of her wine. "I guess I underestimated how much Vinny needed a friend."

It's true. Vinny and Matt have been spending quite a lot of time together recently. It seems like whenever he isn't with me or at work, Matt is at my brother's house, playing video games or watching sports. It has gotten to the point where the twins are already calling him "Uncle Matt" (I will not put into words what hearing that did to my heart—or my ovaries, for that matter —but I think you can guess). The two of them have really rekindled their friendship, which has made Matt feel even worse about lying to him every time he comes over.

It's been tough, but he's been really good about not pushing me now that he understands it's not just about my brother but about giving me the chance to learn how I can let myself be happy with him.

"No, I know they've gotten really close," I say. "I think closer than when they were in college, actually, since they're real adults now and their relationship is not based just around partying. But still. I think, once he figures out how serious we are about each other, he won't be that mad."

"How serious?" Danielle narrows her eyes at me. "Because you obviously have to be sure."

"Dani, I am definitely sure about my feelings." I take a deep breath, ready to say it out loud to someone for the first time. "I think I might actually lo—"

"*Elisabetta*." My mother walks into the kitchen with my brother in tow. That was a close one. "Is your friend Barbara coming for Thanksgiving this year again?" she asks.

Barbara's parents refuse to celebrate Thanksgiving, so she's spent it almost every year since I've known her at our house. My mother has always loved Babs's eccentricity and sense of humor, which she especially brings to dinner with the family by making a crazy centerpiece for the table.

"No, Ma. She's shooting a commercial in Japan," I reply, finishing off the rest of my wine. It's actually kind of ridiculous —a cat shampoo commercial where she's dressed as a cat, and a bottle of shampoo is chasing her all over Tokyo. I really don't get it, but whatever. Not my problem.

"What a shame! She always brought such a fun twist to the holiday weekend, especially when she would have a little too much wine and start to sing some of her favorite show tunes." She sighs. Mom loves Barbara. "Vincenzo, what about you? Do you have a friend you can bring?"

No, no, no, no.

"Actually..." *NO!* "I'm pretty sure Matt doesn't have plans that day. I think he mentioned his mother bailed on him last minute."

This is true. Matt was supposed to go down to Florida to spend the holidays with his mother, but she decided to go to Europe with her husband and their friends instead, leaving him alone for the holiday weekend. I hated the thought of him spending Thanksgiving by himself in his apartment, but there was no way I could invite him to our family dinner even if I wanted to (which I don't). He told me he would be fine, that he would just order Chinese food and watch a bunch of bloody movies—the kind that he doesn't get to watch when he's with me because I can't stand them. I thought about skipping, making up an excuse about a paper I had to finish or something, but I couldn't do that to my mom. She spends almost every day alone in that house. The holidays are what she looks forward to the most, especially since my dad died.

"Oh, yes. He's such a nice boy. Call him!" Her eyes flash to mine and then back to Vinny.

Whoa, wait. What the hell was that?

Vinny pulls his phone out and starts to scroll through it. "'Kay, let me give him a call."

I jump out of my chair, tripping over my feet, and make it to my purse. The three of them look at me like I've gone absolutely insane, but I ignore them. I'm a woman on a mission to stop my secret boyfriend from accepting a friendly invitation to dinner at my mother's house. "Sorry, just forgot I had to reply to an email ASAP."

I pull my phone out of my bag and quickly type out a text to Matt.

DO NOT ACCEPT THE INVITATION.

Vinny puts the phone on speaker so he can make himself a sandwich while it rings. I pray to God Matt sees the message before he picks up or at least realizes how completely horrible it would be if he were to spend the holidays with us. We would be too obvious. They'd find us out in the first five minutes. I'd want to touch him constantly, want to steal kisses. I'd lose my mind, trying to pretend like I wasn't into him, least of all *in love with him*.

"Hello?" I hear his voice come through the other line. As per usual, his voice makes me feel like butter melting on a warm piece of bread. Will I ever get over this feeling? God, I hope not.

"Yooooooooo, Matt!" Vinny says in his bro voice as he slaps some pastrami onto a slice of bread. "What's good?"

My mother whispers something about how we're about to have lunch and maybe he shouldn't be eating right now.

"I'm a growing boy, Ma," he whispers in frustration.

I hear Matt chuckle on the other end of the line at their exchange. "Nothing much. You in Sag Harbor?"

"Yeah, how'd you know?" Vinny raises an eyebrow at his phone, squirting some mustard on another slice of bread.

There's a brief pause on the other end of the line. "You told me, man."

"Huh, I don't remember that."

"Yeah, you did. Plus, I just heard you have a conversation with your mom." Awkward silence... Danielle and I look nervously at each other. "So, what's up?" he changes the topic quickly.

"Right, so do you have plans for Thanksgiving?" Vinny gets to the point quickly.

"Yes. I'm going to watch TV and eat Chinese food," he says without humor. He's not saying it to be pitied—that's not the type of guy Matt is. He's just accepted the fact that he's alone over the holidays and going to take it in stride, which, to be honest, hurts my heart. I don't want him to be alone. And I really don't want him to feel like that's okay.

I realize immediately that, by sending Matt that text asking him not to come, I may have inadvertently broken the one rule I promised myself I wouldn't ever break. I'm scared I made him feel unloved or unwanted when all I wanted to communicate was that it might not be a great idea for us to spend a whole long weekend together at my mother's, pretending like we're not dating.

Luckily, my brother makes sure to let his friend know that he's welcome at our family home. "No way, man. You're coming back out to Long Island and spending it with us. You can stay the whole weekend, right? You're off?"

Silence. "Yeah, I mean, I'm not scheduled for any shifts at the hospital, and our office is closed," he says with hesitation. He sounds like he wants to be excited but knows he should be careful.

"Awesome! Can you come in Wednesday night? I'd give you

a ride, but Dani and I decided to take the whole week off since we're spending Christmas with her parents, and we want to spend more time with my mom."

"No, it's cool. I can drive in by myself Wednesday night after work."

"One sec, Matt." Vinny looks at me and asks, "When are you coming in?"

"Uh, I have a presentation Wednesday morning, so probably that afternoon or night?" I say in a low voice.

"Uh...hey, Liza," Matt says nervously over the phone. What the hell does he expect me to say?

Danielle starts to laugh but tries to cover it up immediately with a cough, and I want to murder her. Her inability to be subtle is killing me.

"Uh, hey," I parrot.

"Right, so it's settled. You guys can come in together. Otherwise, Liza will have to take the bus or the train in, and that shit's gonna be packed. You don't mind, do you?"

"No." I hear Matt's smile on the other end of the line. "I really don't." I blush.

"Cool," Vinny says as he finishes making his sandwich and stuffs it into his mouth. "I'll send you her contact info so you guys can coordinate." His mouth is full, and what came out was barely understandable, but it was clear enough to finally make Danielle's self-control evaporate and burst out into a full laugh.

Fucking wine.

Should not have given any to her. She's such a lightweight.

Vinny and my mother look at her quizzically, but she just shakes her head, apologizes, and says she just remembered a joke someone told her at work a couple of days ago.

"*Smooth*," I mouth and roll my eyes at her once my mother opens the fridge to pull out the butter, and my brother takes another bite of his sandwich.

"Great, thanks, man. I know I said I was okay with spending it alone, but I was kind of bummed about it. I'm really looking forward to spending the holidays with you and your family." He says it to Vinny, but I know it's directed at me. He's admitting that he wasn't looking forward to it, that he would be lonely, and telling me that he can't wait to spend the week with *me* and my family.

"Yeah, sure." Vinny clears his throat now, uncomfortable with Matt's change in the tone of his voice. "Any time, man."

So, I guess I'm spending Thanksgiving week with my secret boyfriend and my family.

Chapter Nineteen

MATT

MATT

> Whoops, I guess I didn't see this in time.

BUT IT'S A LIE. I READ HER TEXT WHILE I WAS ON THE CALL with Vinny—before he asked me to spend Thanksgiving with him—and I still agreed to go.

I know it was wrong to say yes when she specifically asked for me to deny the invitation, but honestly, I don't care. I'll pretend like I didn't read it in time—it's what I'm good at, anyway. All I've been doing for the past month or so is pretend. Pretend I'm not dating Liza. Pretend I'm not in love with her. Pretend I'm not the worst friend in the world for constantly lying to Vinny about the fact that I've spent almost every night since Halloween at his sister's apartment. Pretend like it's not killing me to hide all of this. Pretend like I totally get where she's coming from.

Frankly, what's one more lie?

I just don't think that she's thinking clearly, because this Thanksgiving thing can actually end up being a really good thing for us. Besides the fact that we'll actually get to spend time together, I don't get why she can't see that this can earn me some serious points. I can bond with her mother, get her on my side—Danielle already confessed to saying that Catterina wasn't opposed to the idea of us being together.

Vinny might even see us together and think we would make a good couple. He could see how I make her smile and how incredibly happy she makes me feel and think what a great idea it would be to set us up. Maybe things will turn out so well for us that we actually decide to come clean that same trip, and everyone will be happy for us.

Yeah, yeah. I know what I sound like, okay? I know I sound a bit delusional. But I have to keep the dream alive because I am *so* over this childish sneaking around. Sure, I'm positive that secretly hooking up that week will be hot as hell, slipping into her childhood bed in the middle of the night and fucking quietly, watching her bite her lip as she tries not to make a sound when she comes. But still. Can't we be grown-ups here? Is it so fucking wrong to want to spend the holidays with my girlfriend, whom I love very much?

LIZA

It's not a big deal. We just need to be really careful when you're there.

MATT

Of course. We'll be super discreet. Don't worry about it.

AND I REALLY WILL TRY TO BE DISCREET. I'LL TRY NOT TO kiss her neck and wrap my arms around her waist while she cooks or stare at her ass when she bends over. I'll do my best not to kiss her first thing in the morning when she's at her most adorable, all groggy and sexy with bedhead. But I also won't be super disappointed if we get caught, you know what I mean? I won't feel like it's the end of the world—the way that she seems to think it is. Especially since we'll be so close to December 1st, the date she picked for her stupid "checkpoint" and reevaluation of our relationship—the day *she* chose for us to determine whether we would go public or not, which pretty much seems like a given, right? *Right?* What's a couple of days ahead of time anyway?

Regardless of whether or not her family realizes I'm fucking head over heels in love with her, I think it's important for her to see me in her familial environment, for her to see that I can fucking handle myself.

I love her, and I'm not going to go down without a fight.

Chapter Twenty

LIZA

MATT WILSON IS CURRENTLY HUMMING. *HUMMING.* Humming to the tunes of *The Beatles* as we drive down the Long Island Expressway on our way to my mother's house.

Normally, this wouldn't surprise me, as Matt tends to be a very happy guy, and he does love music, but after the DEFCON-1-level freak-out he had last night while packing, I expected some nervousness before leaving the city this afternoon—some lip biting, brow furrowing, or mumbling—but I got nothing.

Last night was the first night we spent at his apartment, and it was only so that he could show me what he was thinking of packing for the trip. He started pulling out outfit options to show me, trying things on while I made fun of him —something he didn't really appreciate—telling me how important this trip was for him and for us. When we finally finished outfit planning for him (adding an extra one just in case a baby vomited on him or something), I tried to calm him down by kissing him senseless, but that didn't even work, which really concerned me. He went to bed tired, grumpy, and nervous. I went to bed annoyed and sexually frustrated.

Which is why I expected a nightmare scenario when I met up with him this afternoon at the car rental. But there he was, standing in all his glory, broad shoulders, freshly cut hair and trimmed beard, pressed pants and clean shirt, smelling *amazing*, waiting for me with a massive smile. He kissed me until my brain fogged and I lost my balance and told me to get in the car in the same voice he uses sometimes in bed—all of this right in front of the parking attendant, making me blush deep crimson.

I have no idea why he's so excited, and it's freaking me out. Now *I'm* the one who's nervous. Does he know something I don't? Because I'm trying not to focus too much on the fact that my secret boyfriend and I are about to spend four days and four nights in my childhood home with my mother, brother, sister-in-law, and their toddlers while he's looking like an absolute *snack,* and I'm not going to be able to touch him.

"Why are you so damn happy?" I ask, narrowing my eyes at him, unable to keep the question in any longer.

Matt stops singing about Lucy, and how she's in the sky with diamonds, and smirks. "I love driving. I don't get to do much of it in the city."

"*No one* likes driving this much. Not even Lewis Hamilton, and he's an F1 driver." Something's definitely up.

"A Formula-1 reference?" He brings a hand to his chest. "Be still my heart!" He laughs and glances at me. When he's met with no reply, he says, "I'm just excited, is all. Aren't you?"

"Uh, no? Not really. Concerned? Nervous? Anxious? Check, check, check. Excited? Nope. Hard pass."

He chuckles at me and shakes his head with a broad smile on his face, eyes glowing.

What is going on here?

"We're almost there. I need to stop and get your mother

167

some flowers. Do you know any place nearby that might still be open?"

I check the clock on my phone and see that it's only 6:30 pm. We've made impressive time given that it's the night before Thanksgiving and the expressway is usually packed. I direct him to the nearest flower shop, and we park across the street. He reaches for my hand as we cross, but I pull it away.

"What are you doing?" I hiss. "Someone could see. What if we run into someone in town?"

He rolls his eyes at me and opens the door to the shop, letting me walk in first.

I help him pick out the flowers, mainly because he's a guy with no idea what to choose but also to give me something to do, to distract myself from thinking about how incredible he looks and stop myself from wondering why he's being so weird, giddy, and flirty. He waits for the shop attendant to turn her back on us and then pinches my ass, stealing kisses as we watch her pull the flowers from tin buckets. Then, he wraps his arm around my waist as we check out.

"What's up with you?" I ask.

He looks at me like he's never looked at me before. His eyes are soft but gleaming, his smile buoyant, his eyebrows raised. "I'm just happy," he says simply with a shrug. He bends to kiss me on the lips, but I separate after a moment.

"You know, you can't really do this once we get to my mom's house. You need to stop." I smile against his lips.

"Then I better make it count, don't you think?"

His lips come crushing down on me with much more force than before, giving as much as he takes. He parts my lips with his tongue and sweeps it across mine, tasting me, claiming me. I hear myself whimper a little as he turns me and presses my back to the cash register. Somewhere in the back of my mind, it registers that this kiss might not be appropriate for the general public, seeing as I can feel him half-hard against my stomach, and our breathing has grown ragged, but I couldn't care less at the moment. I feel the heat pool in between my thighs, and it takes everything in me not to wrap a leg around his hip, my body aching for some friction. Matt pulls me tighter into him, and I dig my fingers into his hair with one hand, cupping his face with the other, feeling his soft beard. I tell myself to screw it, because he's right—we probably won't get a chance like this again for the entire weekend—and I just follow his lead.

Eventually, someone behind me clears their throat, and Matt releases his hold on me, coughing up an, "Excuse me," to the sales clerk. He pulls out his wallet from his front pocket, surreptitiously adjusting himself, and pays for the flowers.

My head is spinning so much that I have to use the counter at the register to prop myself up. I'm so worked up now I feel like my skin is tingling all over. I chance a look at Matt, and he looks as affected as I am. His entire face, neck, and ears are bright red, and he exhales a deep, stabilizing breath. All I have to say is *thank God* for Matt's coat because, based on what I felt pressed against me down there, we would not be able to walk out of this flower shop until he settled down.

Damn. That kiss, though.

WE SPEND THE REST OF THE CAR RIDE TO MY HOUSE IN silence. I look out the window and play absentmindedly with my necklace while he keeps his hands firmly on ten and two. I spend it thinking about how incredible that kiss was, and Matt just keeps quiet, expression solemn. He doesn't sing anymore; he doesn't joke anymore—I think the nerves have finally hit him.

"You okay?" I ask at a red light a few blocks away from the house.

"Just...kind of nervous. I don't know how I'm supposed to keep my hands off you after that," he says quietly. I laugh, but his expression doesn't change.

"Hey," I say, reaching out and placing a hand on his arm. He jumps slightly at my contact.

"Please," he groans, accelerating once the light turns green. "Don't touch me. I feel like I'm going to spontaneously combust. I might actually need to use the extra pants and underwear I packed."

I laugh again, but he seems to be completely serious.

Matt pulls over just before turning onto my street. He turns off the engine, and we don't say anything for a few minutes. "I need to say something before we go in there."

My stomach churns, and ice-cold water shoots through my veins. *Now* I'm really nervous.

"You don't have to say anything," I say. I think I know what he wants to tell me, but I don't want to hear it now. Not like this. Not when he's upset, and I can't do much about it.

"No, you don't understand," he says. "I want you to know before we go in there that—"

"Stop." I hold up a hand, my heart racing. "It can't be like this. It can't be in reaction to you being scared about what might happen this weekend."

My suspicions are confirmed as I see his pupils dilate, his eyes widen, and a soft smile appears on his face.

"I told you I was committed to this. I'm not freaking out or leaving you. I'm in this," I say firmly.

"Really?" His smile is almost blinding. "Well, then why can't we tell him now? It'll be fine." He reaches for my hands and kisses them. "It'll be so much easier to just tell him tonight."

He's losing his mind, but I don't think he would appreciate

me telling him. Instead, I try to reason with him, to explain why right now is the absolute worst possible time to announce that we're together—that we have been for quite some time.

"Not now." I shake my head. "Not over the holiday." Matt lets go of my hands and sits back in his seat, sighing in exasperation, running both his hands through his hair.

His eyes are closed when he says, "I'm so fucking tired of lying, Liza." His voice is cold, angry—a tone I've never heard him use before. Chills run up and down my spine, and for a hot second, I think he might give me an ultimatum again. But he wouldn't really do that to me, would he? Not on Thanksgiving, right? The holidays are already dramatic enough. There's no reason to add more drama to it. "I have to do it every fucking time I'm with him. In his home. Under his roof. When we're playing with his kids. I have to tell him that I'm not interested in seeing anyone when he suggests setting me up with someone. I have to lie to him when I'm at your place and he asks where I am." He sighs.

"He's my *friend*. My best friend. And I feel like an asshole. I feel like a really bad fucking guy. And I keep telling myself that that's not who I am—at least not anymore—but actions speak louder than words, don't they?" He shakes his head and squeezes his eyes shut. "I care about you a lot, Liza—you know that—but I can't do this for much longer. You need to promise me that it'll be soon."

"Matt..." I reach for his hand, but he leaves it on his thigh where it was resting. "Hey, look at me." He turns his head, but his expression is impassive. It makes me anxious to see him like this, especially when I know that it is completely my fault. "Next week. I promise. It'll give him enough time to cool down and for the dust to settle for everything to be absolutely fine by Christmas, okay? I just want us to be careful and not ruin the holiday season."

171

He pulls his hand from mine and rests them both back on the steering wheel. He takes a deep breath and then another. I examine his profile and take in his worried brow and frown, stare at the newly formed wrinkles on his forehead and his now-messy hair. His back is tense, and his muscles are flexed, veins popping on his neck. He looked so put together before we left the city. Now he looks like he's about to have a nervous break-down, or scream, or I don't even know... I can't stand to look at him like this, so I unbuckle my seatbelt and crawl onto my knees so I can reach out and kiss his cheek, lightly cupping his face.

"Hey, stop overthinking this. You're important to me, and nothing is going to change that," I whisper against his skin before releasing his face.

"And you're everything to me," Matt says with a sigh. He smiles half-heartedly at me, eyes sad. My heart aches, and I'm trying to think of ways to make him feel better, to assure him that I'm here, that I'm not going anywhere, that all the lying is temporary, but I can't think of anything else to say or do at the moment that I feel would be right. And now we have to spend the entire long weekend with my family, feeling the way we feel, not being able to do anything to fix it.

He starts the engine up again, and I sit back down, buckling myself back into my seat.

Neither one of us says anything as Matt parks the car in the driveway behind Vinny's car. Luckily, my brother and the twins decide to run out and greet us, filling the void our previous conversation left.

The twins' excitement at our arrival cheers me up, bringing

a smile to my face. However, when we both exit the car, it's not me they run to.

"Uncle Matt!" they say in unison as they barrel toward his legs.

What? When did this happen?

Matt smiles and ruffles both of their hair. He picks up Clara in his arms, propping her on his hip, and she wraps her little arms around his neck, monkey style. Leo huffs as he sees his sister getting more attention than him. I guess he really has been spending quite a lot of time with Vinny—the kids are absolutely smitten.

"What's up, little man? Where are your toys?" he asks.

My chest tightens at how incredibly adorable he looks, my ovaries screaming to lock this guy down. I tell them to calm the fuck down, that I'm working on it.

Leo pulls Matt's jeans toward the door, begging him to come in and play with him.

"Hold on, kid. I gotta take your aunt's bags into the house first." He shoots me a smile, and I'm about to say something flirty until I realize that, oops, I can't anymore. I check to make sure no one noticed Matt smiling at me like that before smirking back at him.

"What am I, chopped liver? You don't care about your aunt anymore?" I mean, I am the one who is *actually* related to them here.

Clara reaches out for me from Matt's arms, and he passes her to me. *This is how it could be,* I think and then promptly squash that thought before more start popping up and tearing me apart.

We're not there yet.

Danielle and Vinny manage to wrangle the kids up, leaving us free to take everything out of the car and into the house. Matt gives my mother the flowers we just bought, along with a basket of Italian holiday foods he purchased from *Eataly* earlier this week. To say he knocked the gift out of the park is an understatement—Matt definitely came to win. It seems he figured out that the way to my mother's heart is through a ton of imported Italian fine pastas, risottos, and cookies, along with one phenomenal bottle of wine. It looks like everyone in the Castelli family is in love with Matt Wilson.

For now, at least.

Chapter Twenty-One

LIZA

I'm trying to sleep, but I'm just too uncomfortable. My childhood bedroom is too hot, the bedsheets too itchy, and the springs on my mattress too squeaky. Every time I flip from one side to the next, it sounds as if someone has crashed into a truck full of doggy chew toys.

To be honest, it's not the sheets or the mattress keeping me up. It's the fact that my boyfriend kept sneaking kisses and getting handsy tonight behind everyone's back, causing me to almost have a heart attack by the end of the night. Every time I'd slap his hand away, he'd smirk like it was a joke, like it would be funny to get caught.

It was incredibly annoying.

After dinner, I volunteered to do the dishes so my mother could rest before tomorrow, and Danielle and Vinny could put their kids to bed. Matt came into the kitchen behind me and just wrapped his arms around my waist as if we were alone in my apartment. I shoved him off as gently as possible—for which I should receive an award because, *my God*, that man is a fine work of art, and I have been craving him ever since that ridiculously hot kiss in the flower shop—and he just laughed as if it wasn't a big deal. I wanted to ask him what had happened to the man who'd had a near breakdown two blocks away from my house? I wished he'd channel the cautiousness of Nervous Matt for the rest of the week, because Horny Matt was becoming a problem.

Danielle thankfully put an end to it. She came in looking for me because Clara was asking for her Auntie Liza to read them tonight's bedtime story, thus interrupting Matt's lapse in judgment. So I went upstairs and *Goodbye'd Moon* with Clara and Leo, showered, and changed into my pajamas. I texted Matt that I was going to bed and put my phone on *do not disturb*, switching off all of my alarms, planning to sleep in until noon before having to spend the entire day cooking for our family with my mom.

I'm finally drifting off, in that weird state of half-awareness, when I feel—and *hear*—the mattress dip next to me. I feel Matt's familiar arms wrap around me, pulling my back to his chest, kissing me on the shoulder, his beard tickling me.

"What are you doing?" I whisper as I start to clear from my kiss- and sleep-induced haze.

"Kissing you," he says against my suddenly very heated skin.

I turn to look at him over my shoulder, and his lips catch mine, arms tightening around me. He groans, and the mattress squeaks loudly as his hips thrust just a little against me.

Matt is *very* excited to see me.

"Matt," I plead, pulling away from him. "We can't do this here, now. These walls are *paper thin,* and the mattress is comically loud. This isn't happening tonight or any night that we're here," I whisper as low as I possibly can, aware of my mother's superhuman hearing capabilities.

Matt groans in frustration. He loosens his grip around me, and I turn in his arms, burrowing my face in his neck. I breathe in his signature scent and hold it in for a few seconds before exhaling.

"Were you just taking a hit of me? Like a joint?" he whispers in disbelief.

I stifle my laugh against his shoulder, and his body shakes against mine as he attempts to restrain his. I shrug and say, "You smell nice. What can I say?"

He kisses my neck and sighs. "I missed you. I couldn't sleep. I was lying in bed alone, and it just felt really weird." Is that what was missing? Why I couldn't sleep? I missed Matt's body curled behind mine? "We haven't spent many nights apart, you know."

"Sure we have." I look up at him, trying to think back to the last night we didn't sleep in the same bed, but I come up short.

"Nope." Matt shakes his head with a smile on his face. "Not since Halloween, we haven't. Maybe one night apart here and there, but we've spent almost every night after that together."

"Oh my God, you're right," I say in wonder. Matt kisses my shoulder again, distracting me momentarily from the fact that we've barely spent one night apart in the past month. "How stupid do I have to be to not realize that you have basically been living with me?"

I see his smile flash in the darkness. "Not stupid, just... focused on other things. Which has worked to my benefit."

I kiss him lightly and smile before pushing him off me.

"What's wrong?" he asks, brow furrowed.

"Nothing's wrong, but you should probably go back downstairs. I don't want us to get caught." I pull back a little—as far as I can in my twin bed.

Matt looks down at me for a beat and then rolls onto his back to groan in frustration, the mattress spring squeaking loudly. "Why are you doing this? Is it so fucking bad for me to want to spend the night with my girlfriend whom I haven't been able to touch or kiss or anything since getting here?"

"What are you even talking about? You've been completely inappropriate and handsy all damn day. I had to keep pushing you away because your hands were always touching me behind people's backs, and you kept trying to kiss me while other people were in the room." I hear the edge in my voice, my exasperation bleeding into it.

"I'm so fucking tired of this, Liza," he says in a low voice for the second time in the day. "I don't think I can do this much longer."

My heart starts racing, beating fiercely against my chest. Surely he can see it against the thin fabric of my tank top. The anxiety creeps in, crawling up my back, so I climb on my knees to look down at him. Matt avoids my gaze, his expression scaring me. He's cold, distant, lips thin, and I can feel him emotionally start to pull away from me. The tears well in my eyes, and a sob forms in my chest.

I'm going to lose him.

Patient Matt has left the building.

I try to swallow the knot in my chest and press a small kiss to his lips. He doesn't move an inch, doesn't respond in any way.

"Matt..." my voice cracks, and a tear runs down my cheek. He turns to look at me now, and his expression turns into one of concern, of guilt, because no matter how mad he is at me, Matt will always be a gentleman first. He will always put my care first. The thought of losing him grips me harder still, and the tears start coming freely.

I know he's struggling, and I know it's my fault, but I need him to be patient with me—at least for the next couple of days. He's not wrong in that we need to come clean soon, but now's not the time.

"Hey." He sits up, cupping my face, swiping away the tears

with his thumbs. "I'm sorry. I didn't mean to be so cold. I'm just upset." He shrugs. "I'm so sorry."

I squeeze my eyes shut and shake my head. "No, I'm sorry. This is all me. You're right—I already told you so. And I know you're mad and frustrated, but I just need you to go along with this for a couple of more days. I don't want to mess things up between us, but I also don't want to ruin the holiday with our drama."

"It's not *drama*," he says bitterly. "It's our fucking relationship, Liza."

I sigh, exhausted with this conversation. He's hurt right now, and anything I say has a high chance of making the situation worse, so I stick with simple. "Let's not talk about it anymore. Not tonight. Stay with me," I capitulate, "and then you can sneak out of bed before the twins wake the entire house up at six. Let's spend the night together."

I catch a glimpse of Matt's smile. "That's a *Stones* song, you know?"

I snort, rub my eyes, and sniffle before saying, "Do you have your phone on you? Set your alarm so you don't forget."

"Don't worry—I won't oversleep." He pulls out his phone, scrolling and tapping before sliding it carefully onto my nightstand. I lie back on my side with my back to him, and he pulls me close, breathing me in. "Thank you, Liza."

I smile with my eyes closed in the darkness and drift off into a comfortable sleep in Matt's arms, his heat enveloping me, warming every corner of my heart.

"Liza!" I hear Danielle from the other side of my door. *"I'm starting breakfast. Do you want French toast or waffles?"*

I try to push through the morning fog, but the pillow I'm using is too comfortable, and the comforter is too heavy, holding me down. I take a deep breath as I hear Danielle pound on my door one more time, and the familiar cedar smell hits me like a freight train—a super-sexy freight train.

"Shit!" I whisper-yell, sitting up straight. Matt's arm falls from around my waist, and he wakes, his eyes groggy and sexy as hell.

"LI-ZA! Are you dead in there?" She jiggles the door, trying to open it, and I thank God that Matt locked it before slipping into my bed.

What do I do? I need to get him out of my room without anyone noticing, but I have no idea how to do that! Did we sleep through the alarm? Did he not set it properly? Or is the rest of my family waking up unusually early these days? Danielle's going to kill me, but there's no way I can get through this without her help.

Matt stares at me with wide eyes, scratching the back of his head, sitting up. He mouths, *"Fuck,"* to me, and I roll my eyes. I want to kill him because setting the alarm was his responsibility, getting up before everyone else was his responsibility. Did he just turn the alarm off and keep sleeping?

I walk over to the door and take a deep breath before unlocking and opening it just a little bit, enough for Danielle to see my eyes and desperate plea. "Dani...I may have...fucked up?"

"Gawd, what did you do?" Her hands fly to her hips, eyes narrowed.

"So...Matt may have come up last night and fallen asleep, and now he's kind of stuck in my bedroom."

A pause. "You are both such idiots. It's like you want to get caught. Are you serious?" She's not laughing or teasing me, which honestly has me kind of concerned. Is it the stress from Thanksgiving, or is she genuinely upset?

"Please, Dani, we need your help," I plead.

"Fine, I'll distract your brother, and you distract your mother. I don't know how you're going to get her out of the kitchen on *Thanksgiving morning*, but whatever." She rolls her eyes at me. I frown. Shit. The door to the basement is in the kitchen. She's right. "I'll just tell Vinny one of the toilets is clogged. Gimme a minute." She walks away, screaming for my brother to come and help her in the bedroom bathroom.

While I wait to hear Vinny come up the stairs and go into his bedroom, I turn to Matt. He's checking his phone, completely carefree, and something about his body language makes me suspicious of him.

"So what's the deal? How am I getting out of here?" He sounds bored, completely uninterested.

"It's like you want to get caught."

"Oh my God." I stare at him in horror. "You did this on purpose." My hand flies to my mouth.

He looks up to meet my gaze, and for a split second, I see it in his eyes before he controls his expression. "Did what on purpose?"

I groan. "You are such an idiot." He leans back slightly on the bed as if I'd pushed him.

"Excuse me?" His brows furrow, his anger from the previous night returning easily. But what did he expect? That I would just be okay with this exhibit of childish behavior? "I didn't do anything on purpose. Plus, would it really be so bad? If we were publicly dating, this wouldn't even be an issue. So we come clean. So what?"

"Even if they knew we were dating, this would not be cool

by my mother's standards, Matt! I dated Jeremy for *three years,* and he was never allowed to stay in my room whenever we were over here. He always slept in the basement or the study. And he certainly did not try to sneak into my bedroom at night." My mother is incredibly conservative, and though she knows I am not a virgin, she definitely does not want any of that in her own home.

"You're gonna fucking compare me to that loser? Seriously? I'm at that level in your eyes?" He's angry, raising his voice.

"Shh, Jesus! Vinny's on his way up."

"No, seriously, I want to know. Is that what I am to you, then? Another Jeremy? Less than that?" I know he's hurt, but right now, I couldn't care less. What I do care about is the fact that he's pretending he doesn't know what I'm talking about by deflecting. But still, I have to defend myself. I don't ever want him to believe that what I feel for him is similar to what I felt with Jeremy, because it is absolutely not true—not even close.

"You *know* that's not true, Matt. You *know* that. You *know* that I—"

I'm cut off by the sound of Vinny coming up the stairs, complaining to Danielle about her inability to unclog a toilet and how simple it is.

I sigh, exhausted all of a sudden and feeling much older than my years. "We need to go," I say when I hear the door to their bedroom close. "I'm going to lure my mother away from the kitchen so that you can go back into the basement through there."

Matt gets up, scoffing, shaking his head. He rolls his eyes at me and says, "Whatever," and I hate this right now.

We proceed to sneak down the stairs, tiptoeing like cartoons, until we reach the door just outside the kitchen. I tell him to hide in the guest bathroom while I speak to my mother and make something up to pull her out of her Thanksgiving meal-prep station. I tell her I need her help in picking an outfit, and she gives me a look like I've lost my goddamn mind, because I have never asked my mother for help with a look since being able to dress myself, and we both know it. My mother and I get along swimmingly, but something we do not agree on is fashion. I aim for trendy-casual, and my mother is more classic—she hates trends.

She looks up at me with wide and hopeful eyes and says, "*Ma certo.*" But of course.

I catch Matt sneaking into the kitchen from the corner of my eye as my mother and I make our way up the stairs. I'm so angry at him I don't even want to speak to him. I'm having to control the fire building in my chest, the absolute indignation, but it's tricky. Yesterday, I had to put all my focus on stifling how much I loved him. Today, I'm going to have to pretend like I don't want to kill him.

Who would have known that it would be easier to hide love than to hide a lovers' quarrel?

Chapter Twenty-Two

MATT

I'm such an asshole, I know. But it's like I couldn't control it. Like it was word vomit.

I don't know what the fuck I was thinking. I know I'm not like Jeremy. I know that she's never felt this way before. That what she felt for him doesn't even come close—because she's told me so, and I've felt it.

But we haven't even been here for twenty-four hours, and already it's been absolute torture. I don't know if she feels the same, but it's been driving me crazy. I'm on edge, having to think carefully every time I address her in front of people, wondering whether what I want to say is too flirty or intimate for a brother's best friend who doesn't happen to be secretly dating her. I've had to pretend like I didn't know certain things about her life and restrain myself from answering things like, "Yeah, she told me" or "I know." Like I don't know her or spend almost all of my free time with her, talk to her every day, have had my hands all over her body, memorized every inch of her skin.

It's frustrating and hurtful, and frankly, I'm tired of it. I want to be able to say that she's mine and I'm hers completely out in the open.

She was upset that I was being too flirty behind everyone's back, but honestly, I wasn't doing it maliciously or *because I wanted to get caught*. I just wanted to cheer her up since she looked about ready to have a panic attack all night (and now I know that I was making it worse). I was just trying to relieve some tension but also feel close to her. All night, I felt like she was slipping through my fingers. So, yeah, I guess I overdid it. I guess I was a little too handsy or forward. I guess sneaking into bed with her might not have been the best fucking idea ever.

But I *missed* her. I missed her, and we'd only been at her house for a few hours, and the thought of going to bed in a damp, cold basement without her was just too much to bear. I want her with me always. I guess, last night, I didn't care enough about getting caught so long as I got to spend the night with the woman I'm in love with.

But we almost did get caught. Danielle had to bail us out—again. I see now how stupid and irresponsible it was to turn off my alarm instead of hit snooze, telling myself I wouldn't fall back asleep and that I'd be able to sneak off in time. She was just so beautiful, asleep in my arms, warm and soft, and I couldn't bring myself to leave her. And...if I'm 100% honest...I really couldn't have cared less in that moment if they'd caught us in the throes of something more. I was just lying there, looking down at her, thinking about how I'd have to endure another fucking day of pretending, and for one split second before falling back asleep, I thought, *Fuck them and fuck this*.

In that moment, it felt like the right thing to do. And now, after our stupid morning fight, I just want to take it all back. I don't want to spend the rest of the day feeling this way, like I

000000

messed everything up. I didn't mean the things I said. I was just frustrated and scared.

And I want to tell her that. I want to apologize and talk to her, tell her the truth, but by the time I finish showering and get dressed this morning for breakfast, everyone is already seated at the table, eating. When I arrive to the dining room, everyone turns to look at me and says good morning except for her. Liza's eyes are stuck on her French toast, concentrating deeply, cutting it into precise pieces.

She looks so sad and won't even look at me. I have to sit next to her all through breakfast, feeling her warmth on my side, smelling her coconut scent, and not being able to say anything. I try to reach out at one point, to hold her hand under the table in silent apology, but she pulls it away from me, excusing herself to start cleaning up.

I'm miserable and uneasy, trying to hide the fear and sense that things will soon come to an end, that I should be preparing myself for a life without her. I don't see this going much further, to be honest. I don't see her fighting as hard as I am. I know she loves me, but does she love me enough to overcome her fears?

I don't want to fucking be here anymore. I'm hurt and upset and just want to get back to the city, to my apartment, and sulk. I feel like I'm two seconds away from snapping, losing absolute control over everything. I'm exhausted from doing my best to hide my frustration, and I'm clearly failing by the looks of Danielle's face every time she shoots a glance in my direction.

After breakfast, the women retreat into the kitchen to start prepping everything while Vinny, the twins, and I play in Catterina's backyard. I'm trying to be cheerful Uncle Matt, but I'm having trouble concentrating here. We've been playing *Mickey Mouse Clubhouse* for almost two hours, but I can't get into the whole hot-dog-diggity-dog of it all.

I decide to make up a medical emergency so I can leave and go back to New York, because I think that my presence here is just making things worse. I'm just about to stand and go to the bathroom, where I intend to come back saying that unfortunately there's been an emergency with one of my patients and that I need to leave, when Catterina comes out into the backyard.

"Matt, *amore*," she says. "Would you mind going to the supermarket and getting a few things for us with Vinny and the twins? I know you're going through a hard time now, but we need you to go with my son." She looks at me intently, and my eyes widen. She couldn't possibly know, could she?

I need to get outta here.

"Actually, Catterina, I was just coming to find you because—"

"I don't know what happened between the two of you since you arrived," she leans closer and whispers, interrupting me, "but don't leave just yet. Whatever it is, you can fix it. I'm sure of it."

My jaw drops. I knew Catterina was supportive about the *idea* of us being together, but I wasn't aware that she knew it was actually happening.

"Did Danielle—"

She shakes her head with a soft smile on her lips. She looks so much like Liza it's insane. They both have the same perfect smile, full lips, and dark-brown eyes—though Liza's have more gold in them, more to get lost in. "Danielle didn't say anything. We just talked about how good you looked together when you were here last. I realized you must be seeing each other, because it was incredibly obvious the second you arrived last night—I don't know how my son hasn't noticed." She snorts.

"I don't know what to say except that this hasn't been about sneaking around for me. I know Vinny has...*opinions* about the type of guy that I am..." I feel my cheeks heat. "But it's not like that with your daughter, I swear. I care about her."

I'm frustratingly in love with her.

She smiles and pats my hand, holding it between both of hers. "One glance at the way you look at her, and no one could doubt that. I can see you love her." I inhale a sharp breath. "It's been a while since I've seen her this happy—with the exception of today, of course." I wince.

"I don't know what you two are fighting about, but it will be okay. And when it comes to my son, don't worry about him. Once you sit him down and explain, he'll come around. But you two have my support. Ever since his father passed, he's had this impression that he's the head of the household now." She scoffs. "He doesn't seem to realize that this is an Italian family, and in Italian families, it's the women who are in charge."

The relief I feel is immediate. The weight on my chest has lightened, and if it weren't wildly inappropriate, I'd wrap my arms around this small woman with the accent and kiss her on the forehead. Instead, I tell her, "I don't know how to thank you. For...everything. Having me here and for your support. It hasn't been easy," I admit.

She shrugs and smiles. "Love is *never* easy." I remember that was exactly what I told myself back in October, before Halloween. She hands me the shopping list and walks away saying, "Don't forget to get the *right* kind of cranberry sauce," over her shoulder.

"Dude, that's the wrong one." I take the can of cranberry jelly from Vinny and put it back on the shelf.

"What's the difference?" He picks it up again and dumps it into the cart. I pull it out and put it back on the shelf for the second time.

"Your mother was very specific. I don't want to upset her," I say. I have somehow won her over, and I am not going to do anything to risk losing her approval. It might not matter to Vinny, but Catterina takes her food seriously, and there is no chance I'm going to bring back the wrong kind of anything when she specifically asked me not to.

I ignore him, scanning the shelves for the right one. I pull the right brand from the Thanksgiving-themed shelf at the supermarket, and Vinny snorts.

"What's up with you? You've been acting weird all day. You look...I don't know. Depressed?"

I sigh, pulling two containers of fresh cranberry sauce from the shelf and placing them gently in the cart next to the extra marshmallows. "It's nothing," I mutter. "Just a little anxious, is all."

"Hey, I, uh... I know it must be tough to spend the holidays without family. But I hope you're not having a horrible time." He looks so uncomfortable, scratching the back of his neck, and my jaw almost drops. This is as deep a conversation of my feelings that we've ever had. It's not that our relationship is superficial, because it's not. But we are careful to steer clear on the topic of absent parents, both dead or alive. It's a lot to handle for the both of us.

I realize he must think that my overall depressed demeanor might be interpreted as me missing my father or being disappointed in my mother for abandoning me over the holidays to go on a trip, but I haven't really even thought about that. I absolutely miss my dad, but we were never too big on Thanksgiving.

And my mother... I've kind of given up on my mother being a mother to me, if you know what I mean. What she did for me with Liza's necklace was an amazing favor, but it was probably done mostly out of guilt. Do I wish my mother were more like Catterina? Of course. But I've learned to live with the fact that my father's death and her behavior after it changed us forever. We both know what type of relationship we have now, and I've come to terms with it.

I think.

Regardless, it's not my mother's neglect nor my father's death that has me looking miserable. It's the fact that I got into a fight this morning with his sister, and I feel like I'm dying because we haven't been able to clear the air since. I just can't tell him about it.

"No, I'm having a great time," I lie. I do my best to sound happy, but even to my own ears, I sound flat, lifeless. "Thank you again for inviting me. I just didn't get a lot of sleep last night, but it's okay." I take the cart from him and keep pushing it down the other aisles, glancing down at the paper in search of the next item on the list.

Whipped cream.

He grimaces. "Yeah, I'm sorry about that. The basement can be kind of uncomfortable to sleep in. It's freezing in the winter and boiling in the summer. But the pull-out wasn't too bad, was it?"

"No complaints here," I say. At least that's not a lie, considering I didn't spend the night there.

How refreshing.

He calls Leo and Clara to follow us, as they've fallen behind, and he turns to me. "It's not just you." He sighs. "I don't know. Maybe I'm going crazy or getting just being paranoid, but I'm just getting a weird vibe today, you know? I get that it's Thanksgiving, and like, by law, everyone is supposed to be stressed out, cooking, fighting. And I know my mom misses Dad, and so does Liza, but I thought things were better. For the past month, I finally got to see her be the Liza she used to be, and now she's almost back to where she was last year."

"What do you mean?" I ask, sounding maybe a little too interested. I stop pushing the cart and park myself in front of the dairy department. The cold from the open fridge is freezing my butt off, but I don't care—I'm much more interested in this conversation.

He shrugs. "I don't know, man. I'm just saying it's like a switch flipped inside of her lately and turned her light back on. Except now she's just...*out* again."

Guilt punches me hard in the stomach, knocking me breathless, making me want to throw up. I love knowing that she's been noticeably happy this past month and that there's a chance that it's because of me. But it kills me to know that this fight with me has affected her so much that Vinny is claiming she's back to being the same depressed person she was last year when she was still dealing with her dad's death.

"Uh...I don't know what to say, man." Not a lie, either. Should I say I have no idea or tell him that she's sad because I was an asshole to her? Yeah, right.

"Yeah, it's just a bummer because I thought she was making progress, you know? I felt like, for so long, she was just stuck in life with that fucking loser, Jeremy, because Dad 'liked him'"— he air-quotes—"and then she wasn't really living or doing anything."

My heart races. "Wait, hold up. What do you mean 'liked him'?"

"Well, he didn't. He hated the guy. Thought the same as all of us. But he was dying, and Liza *said* she was happy, and he wasn't about to ruin her relationship by being the father who tells her he thinks her boyfriend is a complete douche on his deathbed." Vinny rolls his eyes at me, but I'm horrified.

What?

I can't believe this. Deep down, I know this is the main source of her hesitation with us, whether she knows it or not. She had her father's approval to date this other man, then her dad passed away. She wasn't into the guy, but she didn't want to go against what her father's fucking dying wishes were. I don't understand why no one thought to tell her that after her father had died. She could've saved herself a couple of years of a relationship with that asshole. Vinny himself said he didn't even think she was happy with him! If he had just *told* her, just clarified that her father thought he was a dick, everything would be fine. She could come to terms with the fact that the last guy she dated was not who her father hoped for her to be with, because I think she feels like she's disappointing him by dating me, and she doesn't want to disappoint her brother, too. I think that's what I'm up against here.

"But she stayed with Jeremy for that long because of it. She said that was the main reason she didn't break up with him earlier," I say as calmly as possible (but I'm definitely about to lose my mind).

"How did you know that?" Vinny asks, his eyes narrowed in my direction.

I almost panic, but then I remember what Liza told me: *stick as close to the truth as possible.*

"She told me when she took me out to dinner as a thank you, remember? It was the night I helped her move her stuff into her apartment. We ran into her ex, and he was a total tool to her. She kind of told me the break-up story." I shrug, trying as hard as I can to play it cool. I start putting random items into the cart, keeping my head down, pretending like I did not obviously just reveal myself.

"Hmm." He looks like he wants to press me for more information but is momentarily distracted by two toddlers attacking his legs, running up to him, begging for cookies.

I silently thank God for saving me from another close call—I cannot put into words how much I love those kids now—and decide that, as soon as we get back to the house, I'm going to pull Liza aside and apologize for being a massive asshole to her.

Chapter Twenty-Three

MATT

When we drop off the groceries in the kitchen, I notice a couple of things. First, everything smells *incredible*. Second, except for the store-bought pecan pie and a marshmallow-topped sweet potato casserole, the Thanksgiving dishes they're preparing do not look conventional in any way. It's not your regular scalloped-potatoes-and-string-beans dinner—even the turkey looks different. I ask Vinny what this is, and he says it's how his mother marries everyday Italian flavors with Thanksgiving food. Third, Danielle is only allowed to assist and perform small tasks (i.e., passing of bowls, stirring of sauce, cleaning of vegetables). Fourth, the three women of the family, led by their fearless leader, Catterina, are cooking with the same concentration, dedication, and energy of someone competing for the Iron Chef title.

There is absolutely no way I'm going to be able to pull Liza aside now. I see her chopping zucchinis into coins like she's on fast forward, and I marvel at her. How did I not know she was so skilled? Sure, we order take-out most nights because we both have busy schedules, but on nights we do cook, she's never been this precise or seemingly skillful in the kitchen. We've cooked basic stuff together—rice, chicken breast, steamed broccoli, or salmon—nothing like whatever it is they're doing with that turkey breast and prosciutto.

"Thank you, boys. You can go back out now and leave us to it. The hors d'oeuvres will be ready soon," Catterina informs us, practically shooing us away.

"Catterina, would you like some help? I'm not a skillful cook, but I know the basics, and I can help," I offer. Everyone in the kitchen bursts out in a chuckle, even the kiddos, and I raise an eyebrow in question.

"*Amore*, don't worry about it." She pats my cheek with her soft hands. "In this house, I do the cooking, Liza helps, and Danielle...*tries* to help." Catterina chuckles, and Danielle blushes.

"Are you sure? Isn't it a little sexist to just—"

Vinny pulls me by the arm and says, "Dude, it's just tradition. It's not a sexist thing. My mom is very particular about her cooking, and she's just trying to teach her daughter and daughter-in-law—the women in our family—so that they can learn the recipes and pass them on." He rolls his eyes. "Italians are very into tradition." With one final look in Liza's direction, Vinny pulls me and the twins out of the kitchen and into the living room, where we proceed to finish watching the last quarter of the second game that day. During that time, Danielle brings a full charcuterie and cheese board, along with some roasted tomato and ricotta bites and bruschetta with roasted squash and ricotta cheese.

If Liza and I ever get over this fucking fight and settle down into a serious relationship, I think I'm gonna end up gaining *at least* a good thirty pounds just by visiting her family twice a month.

Jesus, this shit looks incredible.

I'm scarfing down my third bruschetta when we're called to the table. As I've been doing since I first came to this house in October, I make my way to what I have now assumed to be my seat. Vinny, however, has different plans for me this time around.

"No, man, why don't you let Danielle sit there. That way, the girls can talk during dinner," he says tightly. All three women and I look at Vinny, confused. What's with the sudden change?

"I just spent the last three hours cooking with Liza—I think we're caught up," Danielle says, narrowing her eyes at him. What is he playing at?

"Fine, then I'll go sit next to Liza. I haven't been able to spend much time with her anyway." He starts to make a move around the table when Catterina interrupts.

"Vinny, this is my house, my table. You do not get to tell people where to sit," she says firmly in a very scary tone I never want to be on the other end of. "Go back to your seat. I will sit at the head of the table, Liza will sit on my right, as she always does, and Matt will sit next to her. You and Danielle need to sit together to feed the kids."

Vinny doesn't look happy about this, and I know that it's because I officially blew my cover at the grocery store. If he didn't suspect that I had feelings for his sister before, he does now—especially since Liza and I have literally not spoken to each other in front of them since last night, and it is getting awkward. Everyone takes their seats—the twins included—and I'm finally able to take in the decadent feast in front of us.

"Whoa," I say, my mouth literally watering. I've never seen a more unique array of Thanksgiving dishes. "What is this?"

Catterina smiles proudly at the fruits of their labor. "Well, when Pietro and I first moved to the U.S., we wanted to embrace American culture but never forget our roots. We never hesitated in celebrating an American holiday because our children are American, and this country has been very good to us, but we always added a little Italian spin to it."

"We even make sure to have at least some pasta during Fourth of July," Liza says with a smile, and it's the first time she's talked to me or even looked in my direction all day. I smile broadly back at her, thanking her enormously for this white flag she seems to be waving. Because that's what this is, right? She's not pulling away or going back to ignoring me. She's smiling.

"That's so awesome," I reply to her, never removing my eyes from her beautiful face. It feels like I haven't looked at it all day, like she's hidden herself away from me, even when we were in the same room.

I'm snapped back to reality when she kicks me under the table—I guess I was staring? I turn back to Catterina and tell her, "This is incredible. You really do manage to marry the two. I don't know where to begin!"

"Here," Catterina says, pushing a dish to me. "Start with the prosciutto and spinach-stuffed turkey breast, and then make your way through to the zucchinis, rosemary and goat cheese potatoes, and the meatballs in cranberry sauce."

Holy shit.

"I also made the risotto you liked from when you were here last time. The butternut squash one," she adds. "I don't usually make it for Thanksgiving, but I know you liked it."

Liked it? I fucking loved it.

"Don't forget about my dish!" Danielle points to the sweet potato casserole with the crispy marshmallow topping. It looks so good.

"My mom let's Danielle pick *one* American side dish to do each year, since she *isn't* Italian, and this is an American holiday, after all," Liza whispers in my ear, trying to control her laughter at Danielle's eagerness.

"What are you guys whispering about?" Vinny asks, his eyes narrowed in our direction, bouncing between both of our faces.

Easy, officer.

I feel like I should be raising my hands in front of me, showing that I'm holding no weapons, but Liza shrugs and casually reaches for the risotto. "Just telling Matt about Danielle's gastronomical contribution to our table."

So simple and absolutely true, but Vinny doesn't buy it. I can see his trust in me fracturing by the second, putting together every tiny detail and coincidence of the last month and a half, none of which would be easy to connect were it not for the fact that I expressed interest in his sister six weeks ago in this very house.

Vinny stares at his sister through narrowed eyes as she steadily holds his gaze and serves herself a generous helping of risotto. She passes the dish to me, and mercifully, Catterina distracts her son by asking how the game was.

"I'll go get another bottle of the red," Liza says, getting up from her seat. She makes her way into the kitchen, and I wonder whether this could be my shot to talk to her alone, even if it's only for a few seconds. I just want to ask her if her comment and smile at the beginning of the dinner was really a white flag or not? Are we done with our fight? Can we go back to talking?

"Oh, no," I say, patting my pants pockets. "I left my cell phone downstairs in the basement," I lie (it's in my pocket). "I'm so sorry, Catterina, but would you excuse me? I just need to have it on hand, but it's only for emergencies, of course."

I don't know whether Catterina knows that I intend to sneak off and see her daughter or whether she really buys that crap, but she smiles and tells me, "Of course you're excused."

I get up and walk around the table, doing my best not to run to the door.

"Hey," I say, *finally* alone and addressing her directly, "do you need some help with that?" I see her struggling with the bottle opener and the red wine and walk over to her.

"Nope, I got it." She smiles weakly at me, it fading as fast as it came.

"Liza," I start, sighing. "I know now probably isn't the best time, but I've been going crazy here. I hate that we're fighting. Today has been the longest fucking day of my life."

She inhales sharply, her eyes meeting mine, filled with sadness. "I missed you so much," her voice cracks. "I missed you so much, Matt. I'm so sorry."

"Hey, no." I reach out and pull her into my arms. "Shh, it's okay. I was an ass. I think that, deep down, you were right—I did want us to get caught. We had agreed not to say anything, but here I was, just blatantly going against what we talked about."

Liza shakes her head against my chest. "But I'm the one making you lie every day to your best friend. You wanted to come clean, and I've made you a liar, and that's just *horrible*, Matt. I don't know how you can forgive that."

"Don't—please stop crying," I whisper against her forehead before kissing it, inhaling her coconut scent until my lungs are filled.

God, I missed her.

"I was just freaked out, and I'm so sorry." Tears flow easily out of her now, and I hold her, rocking her gently from side to side. After a minute, she calms down enough for me to remind her that we should probably get back soon before we raise any further suspicion. "I want to tell them tonight," she says with full confidence.

"You what?" I breathe.

"I want it to be tonight, together. I want to do it over dessert and tell them how much you mean to me and just have it be out in the open." She smiles, wiping at her eyes.

"Liza..." I kiss her, smiling against her lips. "Yes, that would be incredible."

She sniffles and laughs once. "Okay, I just need to get this stupid bottle open." She places the tip of the corkscrew on the cork of the bottle and presses down, but her hand slips, and the sharp end slices across her palm instead. Liza yelps in pain, and a shot of adrenaline shoots through me.

"Are you okay?" I ask, freaking out as the blood starts dripping down her hand. I pull her hand to me to inspect the wound while my heart races. I'm a fucking doctor, for fuck's sake, why do I feel like I'm about to have a panic attack? "It doesn't look too bad, but I want to run it through water to get a clearer view —see if you need any stitches." She's crying again, and I feel a pang in my stomach at the look in her eye. Pain. I want to take it away.

I turn on the water at the kitchen sink and hold her hand tightly in mine because I know she's going to want to remove it, and I need to get a clearer view before I wrap it up. "This is gonna hurt a little," I say, preparing her. She looks down at our hands, both covered in her blood, and she buries her face in my neck as I push her hand under the stream of water.

Liza yelps louder this time, screaming, "It hurts!"

"I know, baby, I'm—"

Suddenly, something pulls me back by the shoulders with incredible force, pushing me against the counter, the edge of it painfully hitting my spine.

"What the—"

I don't understand what's happening until I see a fist headed for my jaw a split second before feeling the white-hot searing pain all throughout my face, completely disorienting me, leaving me in a haze.

Oh, fuck.

Chapter Twenty-Four

LIZA

I feel Matt quickly pull away from me, the sudden disappearance of his body—which I was using as my support—causing me to trip and almost fall flat on my face. It's only after I hear a loud crash and look up that I see him being pushed up against the kitchen counter. Vinny has him by his shirt, pulling and pushing his back against the counter over and over again. Matt is clearly in a lot of pain.

I scream and tell him to stop over and over again, but Vinny won't listen. He completely ignores my pleas.

Finally, he stops pushing Matt enough to ask, "What the fuck were you doing to her? Why is she crying? Did you hurt her?" I see rage and betrayal in Vinny's eyes, and my heart starts racing.

"He didn't hurt me!" I yell, trying to stand up for him. But Vinny ignores me, pretending like I'm not six inches away from him.

"I saw you! You were forcing yourself on her, hurting her, and she was crying!"

"Are you kidding me?" Matt looks like he's about to lose it, and I imagine weeks of frustration and tension are catching up with him. "I would never hurt Liza!" Matt says, shocked at the suggestion. Anyone who knows my relationship with Matt would never say that. He's always been incredibly attentive and loving to me, putting my care above anything else.

"Oh yeah? Then why the fuck is she crying, asshole?" He grabs Matt by the shirt and pushes him again. I wince, running to Vinny, pulling on his shoulder with my good hand.

"She cut her palm open, you idiot," Matt tells him. I wave my hand in front of Vinny's face to show him the pooled blood dripping down my wrist, and Vinny loosens his grip on Matt's shirt. "Jesus, you okay?" Matt asks. My brother just punched him in the face and pushed his spine against the sharp edge of a kitchen counter over and over again, and he's asking me if *I'm* okay?

I'm crying now, the shock of seeing my brother hurting Matt hitting me hard. I ignore Vinny and run to my boyfriend's side to see how he's doing. His back must be in a lot of pain. "Am I okay? What about you? Are you okay?" I ask between sobs. "Oh my God, Matt." He wraps his arms around me, panting, whispering that he's okay, he's okay.

"What the fuck is going on?" Vinny asks, his breathing coming fast.

My mother and Danielle walk into the kitchen at this point, looking back and forth between the three of us until realization dawns on them on what must be going on.

Matt ignores him, picking up a clean kitchen towel, wrapping it around my hand. "I need you to put pressure on this, okay? I don't think you need stitches, though."

Mom gasps at the sight of blood on my hand and runs toward me, asking what happened, but I don't reply—I'm too focused on what's about to go down.

"Matt." Vinny's voice is no longer angry. It's cold, calm.

"This is the last time I'm going to ask you. What the fuck is going on here?"

Matt sighs and runs his fingers through his hair. "This isn't how we wanted you to find out, obviously. We were going to tell you over dinner tonight."

Oh no.

Something turns in my stomach, the pain in my hand long forgotten, overpowered by this huge sense of danger headed our way, like a semi about to T-bone us.

"Tell me *what* over dinner?" He narrows his eyes at us, but he knows. I don't know why he's stalling, though. He's giving us an out, a chance to not tell him, to end things.

Matt shakes his head and shrugs. "I love her, man," he says as if he can't help it. "I tried not to, but I really fucking love her."

It's the first time he's said it out loud, and I'm torn between wanting to kiss him, to say it back, and to stand right in front of Matt to protect him before my brother punches him in the face again.

There is a collective charged pause where no one in the kitchen says anything. My mother continues to help put pressure on my wound while she stares at both the men, and Danielle looks like she wants to stay and make sure this doesn't turn into a fight but needs to go back and make sure her children are safe. My mom whispers to Danielle that it might be best if she goes to take care of her kids, and I agree. The last thing we want is for the twins to run in and see their father in the middle of a physical altercation—which I assume at this point is a big possibility.

Finally, Vinny breaks the silence. "You fuck my sister?" he asks, and Matt winces, then straightens and looks him in the eye.

"It's not like that, man. I told you. I love her. It's not about just sex with us."

Fuck, Matt. You shouldn't have said "just." Now you've definitely admitted to us having sex—something Vinny could have happily lived in denial of.

"Yeah, right. I'm supposed to believe that. I'm supposed to believe you didn't just fuck my sister and put her in the same category as your other conquests." Gone is Vinny's calm voice. Now it's raised in warning.

"What other conquests?!" Matt raises his hands in frustration. "That was fucking med school, Vinny. I was a fucking kid going through a really fucked-up time. I don't get why you think I'm this horrible person who just wants to screw women over. I love and respect your sister very much. This isn't a fling or something casual to us." He takes a deep breath. "This is real." He says it with such strength and determination that I melt.

I love him so much.

"I'm not this awful villain you seem to think that I am."

"Oh, yeah, asshole?" Vinny challenges.

I pull my hand from my mother's so I can walk over to Matt, but I stop in my tracks as I see Vinny's fist fly across and hit Matt's jaw with surprising force. A wave of coldness washes over my body, and I'm shaking in fear.

"Oh my God!" I hear myself scream. My mother is yelling expletives in Italian at her son, but again, he ignores us.

Matt's body is propelled against the kitchen counter once more, and I throw myself at Vinny's back, doing my best to pull him off my boyfriend. He comes away easily, seemingly done with hurting his (now former?) best friend.

"If you're such a stand-up fucking guy..." he says as Matt looks off into space, confused from the blow he received in the face. My mom tries to pull Vinny farther away from Matt, but he shakes her off. "Then why did you go against my wishes when I specifically asked you to stay away from her? Or why did you lie to me for this long? No, you're absolutely right, Matt. You're actually a great guy."

That one hits me close to home in the chest because it's *my* fault we didn't speak up sooner, and it's *my fault* we didn't come clean. Matt wanted to tell him. He was tired of lying. It was tearing him up inside. *I'm* the one that made everyone lie to my brother, and it definitely did not end up well.

I help Matt straighten as much as he can considering the back pain he must be feeling right now. He brings his hand to his mouth and pulls it away with blood. I start crying again.

"I want you to get the fuck out of my house," Vinny says with a hard edge to his voice. "I want to you to leave, and I don't ever want to see you again."

"You don't get to—" I start to say but am cut off by my mother.

"*Elisabetta,*" she says in a calm and collected voice. "I think it would be best for everyone if Matt leaves right now."

"What?" I turn to look at her, confused. Wasn't she the one who thought it would be a good idea for us to get together? Why is she kicking him out?

Matt looks down at the floor and nods a couple of times before looking at me. I start to protest, but he shakes his head and tells me that my mother is right, that he should go. He pulls my injured hand to him and carefully unwraps the kitchen towel. "This looks better. It looks like the bleeding has stopped almost completely—you don't need stitches." He takes a deep breath. "Just make sure you take a look at it," he says to Vinny, looking like he wants to say more but holds back. *I don't know what to say or how to feel. Do I offer to go with him back to the city?* I feel like I should stay here and do damage control, speak to Vinny, give him a piece of my mind. I also need to be here as back-up for Danielle, because if my brother finds out that his wife knew all along, it'll be a shit storm.

"Thank you for hosting me, Catterina. I really enjoyed my time here, right up until a few moments ago." He leans down to kiss her on the cheek but seems to remember last minute that he has blood on his lips and pulls back.

Vinny rolls his eyes and walks out of the kitchen in exasperation. I think he's trying to convince himself that Matt is a bad guy, but then he sees stuff like this, and it makes him angrier. Who thanks and kisses the hostess after being beaten by her son after dinner?

We hear the engine to a car start up and pull out of the driveway—I guess Vinny needed his space.

Matt walks out the door with his head hanging low, and I watch him leave. My mother and I stand still as we hear his car start and pull out just like we did with my brother.

We don't say anything as we look at each other, trying to process the events that have happened in the last ten minutes, until I realize, "He left without his stuff."

Chapter Twenty-Five

MATT

I PULL INTO THE PHARMACY PARKING LOT AND PARK RIGHT by its front door. I don't get out of the car yet, though. I can't move—and it's not just because my lower back is currently screaming in pain from being repeatedly thrown into the sharp edge of the kitchen counter. I'm just in shock of how absolutely horrible that went and how bad I left things with Liza, her brother, and her mother. This is definitely one of the worst possible ways things could have worked out.

I hit the steering wheel in frustration a couple of times, scaring a mother and her daughter walking in front of me. I press back into my seat and feel the acute pain in my spine. Yeah, there's no fucking way I'm gonna make it through a minimum two-hour drive like this—especially now that the adrenaline is leaving my body. I check my face in the rearview mirror and see how it's already starting to swell by my jaw under my beard, the blood on my lip dried in the corner of my mouth. I look like a vampire who just had dinner and missed a spot during clean up. My eyes are still a little wild, wide and alert, like I'm preparing myself for the next hit. I lick the blood clean from my lip, grimacing at the taste, and try to fix myself up a bit before walking out in public. I don't want to scare anyone else today. I squeeze my eyes shut and take one deep, calming breath.

I can feel my heartbeat in my jaw, the throbbing intensifying.

I struggle a little to get up from my seat, my car too low and unforgiving on my injured spine, and make my way toward the first-aid aisle. I need some painkillers, a bottle of water, a large wrap, and instant icepacks for my back. I should also start icing my face if I want to make it into work on Monday morning with little to no swelling or bruising. Vinny *really* put his weight into the punch, though. I doubt I'll come out without a reminder of it for at least a couple of days.

I find what I'm looking for and decide to buy some arnica cream to help with the bruising on my back as well. I walk over to self-checkout (I don't want to talk to anyone now; I have a feeling it will hurt too much), pay quickly, and make my way back to my car to wrap myself up.

I must look like a nutcase, removing my coat and sweater in the middle of the parking lot, but whatever. I raise my shirt up on my chest, holding it between my teeth as I activate two separate instant icepacks. I plan to secure them around my lower back with the wrap, hoping it will help alleviate the pain by numbing my back until the pain killers kick in. Once they're secured, I pull my shirt back down and get in the car. I turn the engine on but make no move to back up and get on the Long Island Expressway back to Manhattan. I press my forehead to the steering wheel and take another deep breath. And then another. And then another.

The feeling that I've fucked everything up doesn't seem to fade, only increasing with each passing second. Would things have turned out better if I hadn't listened to Liza's wishes and just sat down with Vinny myself? If we had had a conversation man to man? Or would he have reacted as poorly as he did? Surely not. I'm almost positive his violent reaction was a result of seeing his sister crying and the suspicions he must have already had that something was going on.

I was so happy when Liza decided we should announce at dinner that we were in a relationship together, so happy to end the lies and the sneaking around. I thought it would be a great moment. We would have all been in a food coma after having spent a great day together. It would've happened in front of Danielle and Catterina, both supporters of this relationship, and I think they would have helped as buffers. I'm sure Vinny might have felt like he was betrayed a little, regardless of the scenario, but it would have been better than this. Anything would have been better than this.

I think about what he said, and he might be right. I might not be as good a guy as I think I am. I was really selfish by pursuing this with Liza. I ignored my friend's request and, in doing so, created a break in the relationship between him and his sister—all because I wanted her.

But I see now that there was no way I could've resisted falling for her—even from the first second I saw her, that split second before she was covered in Clara's vomit. This was always going to be a lose-lose situation: Vinny's friendship or a relationship with Liza.

I pop two painkillers into my mouth and wash it down with water, my jaw hurting with every facial movement. I pull out another instant icepack, rub it fiercely until it activates and cools, and press it to my jaw, wincing, head resting against the seat.

Fuck!

In my haste, I completely forgot to take my stuff with me, leaving my weekend bag full of clothes on top of the pull-out in the basement. I want to call Liza and let her know, but I know she's probably dealing with much more important things right now than my fucking clothes.

I didn't want to leave without her, but it's for the best. They need space to settle this as a family, and having me there would have made things infinitely worse. I don't blame Catterina for agreeing with Vinny that maybe it was best if I left.

I don't know what's going to happen now, but I know it can't be good. Like I said, it was always going to be a lose-lose situation—I just picked the one I couldn't live without.

Chapter Twenty-Six

LIZA

"Ow, ow, ow, ow!" I scream. "Mom, you're being too rough! Gentle pats, *gentle!*" I beg as she presses more hydrogen peroxide onto the gash on my palm.

"Are you sure this doesn't need stitches?" she asks, concerned. She loosens her grip on my hand, and her pats grow gentler.

I shrug. "I think it's fine. Matt said it was fine." I sigh sadly.

"Matt was a little fucked up at that point," Danielle says beside me, cursing for possibly the first time ever in front of my mom. My mother and I give her a look like she's lost her mind, but she doesn't see us. Danielle is too busy staring out the window, back ramrod straight, waiting for her husband to come back.

"Fucked!" Leo yells from the floor where he and Clara have been playing with their toys. Danielle is so far gone she doesn't reprimand her son or curse herself for breaking her own rules.

My mom and I both look at each other and shrug, deciding not to say anything about it.

"Still," I say, "I really don't want to go to the ER or Urgent

Care on Thanksgiving. I'll be there for eight hours, and I have to get back to the city."

"What?" my mother asks. "You're leaving?" She stops patting the cotton ball on my hand, tossing it into a plastic grocery bag she's been using as garbage.

"Mom, I *have* to. He's not answering my calls, and he was really beat up. I'm concerned about his back. I think Vinny really did some damage." I pick up my phone and check it, but still no missed calls or texts. Is he mad at me? He has every right to be. This is my fault, too—much more than it is his. "Plus, I don't think it would be such a good idea if I stay here. Vinny's going to want to go back to New York if I do, and you don't get to see him this Christmas, so I should go."

As if we've summoned him, we hear his car come up the driveway and freeze, waiting for him to come in. He walks through the front door and makes eye contact with me first then with my hand. He sighs and walks over to us. Vinny takes a seat on the coffee table, pulling my hand from my mother's.

"Let me see," he says quietly, not unkind but definitely not my brother's normal fun tone of voice.

He examines my hand and asks my mom what she used. She answers, but he shakes his head, telling her he needs bacitracin before he can wrap it up. She hands him the first-aid kit, and he rummages through its contents until he finds whatever it is he's looking for.

"Danielle and I are going to give the twins baths. Right, Danielle?" my mother says.

Danielle looks at her husband with furrowed brows. She looks like the last thing she wants to do is leave him in his current state, and I marvel at how much we all underestimate the love they share for each other. Just because Vinny and Danielle bicker does not mean that they don't support and care for each other, that they're not partners. She's looking at his right hand, and I notice for the first time that Vinny's knuckles are red and swollen.

Jesus.

"*Danielle,*" my mother says with a slight edge in her voice. My *mamma* wants her kids to solve their issues, and right now that takes priority for her.

Dani reluctantly takes her children upstairs, throwing Vinny one last longing look in his direction, but he doesn't notice. He's too busy putting on gloves to place the ointment on my hand. He spreads it carefully on the cut with the concentration of someone performing heart surgery. We both know we need to talk, but neither of us knows where to begin.

Screw it.

"He's a good guy, you know. Good for me," I say softly, trying really hard not to get defensive or raise my voice. The key here is to keep calm, show Vinny that this isn't a whim and that we've taken this seriously.

Vinny scoffs and shakes his head, keeping his eyes on my wound. He opens his mouth and starts to say something but stops himself, removing the gloves with a snap.

"What? What were you going to say?"

"You really don't get it, do you? It's not just about the fact that he was a total player in college, and I don't want him to treat you that way." I start to interrupt him, but he holds a hand up to me and keeps going. "It's also about the fact that I specifically asked him not to do something, and he did it anyway. He lied to me—you both did—and he betrayed my trust. I basically lost my only friend today, and I'm...I'm hurt and pissed that you took him from me, and he preferred you over me."

My jaw drops, and I stare at him, wide-eyed, as he opens up a gauze package. I see Vinny flush in embarrassment at his admission.

"What are you talking about? Your only friend? You have *tons* of friends."

Vinny sighs and sits back a little, hesitating to meet my eye. "Liza, they're...colleagues. I don't know. The only people I know in the city nowadays are people I went to school with and never left the city. We graduated, and it's like everyone flipped a switch. Or maybe we were all pretending to be friends in school, and now we just use our past relationships for networking, you know?

"I guess because Matt left, he never transitioned from friend to colleague or peer. It kind of froze that relationship, and at the same time, it became something different because we're older. I don't fucking know." He sighs. "Whatever, he's a dick who went against what I asked him to, and now I have to find a new friend." He places the gauze directly on the gash and then wraps it snugly around my hand.

"Thanks," I mutter. I didn't realize that my brother had the emotional ability to express—let alone feel—everything he just told me. It's... kind of cute that this is mostly about friendship and not all about his delusional sense of being the "head of the family."

"But why are you being so dramatic about this? Matt loves you. He hated lying to you. This is all my fault," I say. I don't know if this will make things worse between my brother and me, but I know I owe them both the chance to be able to fix their friendship.

Men are much more sensitive than I thought they could be.

"I can't be friends with a guy who's fucking you." He grimaces. "And I *definitely* can't be friends with him after he dumps you."

I sit back on the couch like someone's pushed me. He said it so matter-of-factly, like it's the most given thing that has ever existed in the world. "Excuse me? Why are you so sure he's going to dump me?"

"Come on, Liza." He rolls his eyes at me. "Don't make me say it."

"What do you mean, Vinny?" I ask again, my voice sounding like venom now. I'm not letting him off easy here.

"You know," he says nervously now.

"Obviously not, since I'm still asking." I'm not going to back down until he clarifies what he meant. I know it won't be good, but I need to know exactly why he thinks our relationship is going to fail. It's somewhat perverse, but I have to know.

"Because of how the both of you are in relationships." He shrugs like he didn't just sound like an absolute ass. "I just mean that he's going to get bored after two weeks, like he always has, and you don't really ever get attached to anyone. You basically didn't give a shit about Jeremy breaking up with you, and you were *engaged* to him. The only reason you were pissed is because he cheated on you."

I scoff and get up from the couch. "Are you kidding me? Thanks for thinking so highly of your sister that you think Matt would only be able to stay with me for two weeks—"

"Come on, that's not what I meant, and you know—"

"For your information, we've been together for about six weeks, and I am deeply in love with Matt."

He stops and gets up from the table as well. "Six *weeks*, Liza? Are you fucking kidding me? You've been lying to me for *six fucking weeks*?"

I recoil and take a step away from him. I think he just grew a foot taller. "I—I thought you just *assumed*. I mean, it kind of started when he came here in—"

"So literally the *day* I told him to stay away from you?" His voice is raised, his face angry now. "I thought maybe this was a recent thing."

"I told you I loved him," I say in a small voice. "He—he said he loved me. Did you think it'd only been a couple of weeks or what? What did you expect?" My voice is shaking, and I hate it. I should be able to own up to this. I'm a grown woman!

He laughs dryly once. "What did I expect? I expected for my best friend to stay away from my little sister and for none of this to happen." His voice must have carried upstairs, because Mom and Danielle run to the commotion and stop at the top of the stairs. He looks sad and shocked, and I regret that this hurt him, but I can't regret Matt. It's what Vinny's waiting for, though. He's waiting for me to say sorry and to promise I won't see him ever again. But that's never going to happen.

I exhale. "Listen, I understand that we hurt you. But the fact remains that Matt and I are a real thing. I am really, truly sorry about how this has affected you, and I'm really sorry about how poorly we handled things—which was basically all my fault —but you also need to consider my feelings here, Vinny. I have never been this happy before—at least not since before Dad passed away." I take a deep breath and say what I know will hurt most, what will seal his anger, but it needs to be said. "You're just going to have to deal with it."

"*Deal with it?*" He stares down at me in anger, chewing on the inside of his mouth, and I'm suddenly terrified that he's going to start yelling at me, but what happens is worse. Vinny says nothing as he turns around and walks out the door for the second time today.

Chapter Twenty-Seven

LIZA

IT'S LATE, BUT I HAD TO COME BY AND DO A WELLNESS check. He hasn't answered the phone or any of my texts, and I've been extremely concerned. All I got was an, *"I'm okay,"* an hour ago, but I was already on my way here. I slip the key he gave me just a couple of days ago into the lock and open the door to his apartment.

Matt's place is minimalistic. It has no paintings or photos hanging anywhere, completely devoid of decoration except for the one succulent sitting in the middle of his coffee table. It's clean and cold and shows no evidence of any inhabitants whatsoever. I don't know if it's because that's his personal style, or if he just never put the time or effort into it.

I don't like it very much. It's cold and generic and a stark contrast to who Matt is. My boyfriend is none of those things. He is loving and inviting and caring and is constantly showing me those feelings through little actions every day.

Vinny was right. I didn't know what love was until I met Matt. And there is no fucking way I'm letting him go now over some drama my brother will eventually get over.

I walk into the living room and see him sitting on his black leather couch. He looks groggy and exhausted. "Hey, sorry," I whisper. "Did I wake you?" The TV is on, the Macy's Thanksgiving Day parade from earlier today playing on low volume in the background.

He nods and smiles—a small smile, but a smile nonetheless. I guess that's a good sign?

"What are you doing here?" His voice is low, quiet, gravelly with sleep.

"Oh, sorry. Did you want me to leave?" The pain in my chest is visceral. I wouldn't blame him for not wanting to see me. It's my worst fear realized, but after tonight, I totally get it.

"No!" He sits up and winces, one hand flying to the left side of his face and the other to his lower back. "No," he says again softly, gently settling himself back into his seat. "Was just wondering because it must be really late. Thought you were going to spend the night at your mom's."

His voice sounds different, like he can't open his mouth wide enough to enunciate the words properly. I drop both our bags by the entrance and walk over to the couch, taking a seat next to him. "No way," I say. "I wanted to see how you were doing—especially after you stopped responding to my messages."

He grimaces and reaches for my injured hand and cradles it between his, softly running his fingers over the gauze. "Sorry. It's..." He sighs. "It's obviously been a day." It's the understatement of the century, but he smiles softly. Up close, I can see the difference in size between both sides of his face. I place my other hand gently on his left side, wondering idly how bruised the skin underneath his beard is.

"Should've made arrangements for you to get back home," he says. "So sorry."

Home.

I shrug and kiss his cheek as softly as possible, barely touching him, his beard tickling my lips. I marvel at the fact that this man is so obviously in pain and distraught over his fight with Vinny, and he *still* manages to be concerned with my well-being. He looks anxious and guilty over the fact that he couldn't arrange alternative options for my return, and it's just crazy.

I love him.

And I haven't even told him yet.

"Don't worry about it," I say with a shrug. "I took the last train into the city, and it was fine."

He nods softly but shrugs. "Still."

He looks so tired, so...*beat up*. I'm afraid of touching him, hurting him more. He doesn't look mobile, and I wonder how long he's been sitting on the couch for.

"How *are* you?" I ask. He looks stiff with pain.

"Not great." He shrugs, and I frown. Is that all I'm getting? He's probably so disappointed in me, so angry. I would be pissed at me too, if I were him. I *am* pissed at myself. We could have definitely avoided this—at least the fight with Vinny—if I had just agreed to tell my brother when Matt wanted to.

"I'm sorry, Matt. I'm so sorry." Tears well in my eyes, but I know I don't deserve his forgiveness right now. Vinny could have really hurt his spine. What if he needs to see a doctor? Plus, if Vinny never forgives him, will he ever forgive me? Will he hold it against me? Technically, he's the one who broke the rules, though. I didn't force him. Still, the phrase *bros before hoes* comes flying into my brain—the golden rule of the bro code.

The freaking bro code.

I don't think I've hated anything more.

He wraps an arm around my shoulders and brings me carefully into him. I do my best not to put too much of my weight on him, not to shake him too much, even though I feel like burying my face in his neck, surrounding myself with his scent, seeking comfort. "Don't worry," he whispers.

"You're not very verbose tonight," I say softly, my heart beating wildly in my chest. He's not acting like himself. Maybe he *has* come to his senses. Maybe this whole fight was too much. "Are...are we okay?" I hold my breath.

He smiles a little and points to his jaw. "Hurts to talk," he says simply, and I want to slap myself. *Of course* it does. Of course it hurts to talk. My brother just delivered, not one, but two stunning right hooks not four hours ago.

"Sorry," I say sadly. "I'll only ask you *yes* or *no* questions from now on. That way you can nod or shake your head and don't need to speak." His smile flashes, broad and warm, eyes shining with humor.

"Did you eat?" I ask. Matt chuckles and immediately winces. I slap his hand slightly in reprimand, but I know why he's laughing. "I know we ate dinner already, but we finished at seven, and it's"—I check the time on the cable box—"just after eleven pm."

He shakes his head and pulls both my hands in his hand now, carefully readjusting the bandage wrapped around the injured one.

"I'll make you some soup." I stand, but he pulls me back by my good hand.

"Don't have to," he says, shaking his head. "Come back." He frowns, tugging again. "Missed you," he sighs. My heart squeezes in my chest, a knot catching in my throat. It's ridiculous since we were only apart for a few hours, but I missed him, too.

"Shh, don't talk." I lean down and kiss his forehead, his skin soft and warm beneath my lips. "Let me take care of you the way you always take care of me." I pause. "Let me love you."

He inhales sharply, his eyes wide. "Liza…" My name on his lips sounds reverent.

"Shh," I say again, kissing him lightly on the lips. "I know." He kisses my hand once before releasing me so that I can make him some food that won't hurt for him to chew.

I heat up a can of tomato soup and put it into a coffee mug, hoping to make it easier and quicker for him to drink. It's gone in under five minutes, and I make fun of him for inhaling his food. He kisses my cheek and pulls me close into his side again, but I pull away. He looks at me in alarm, but I reach out and grab his hand to calm him down, reassuring him that I'm not going anywhere, not tonight, and not any night after that—at least for the foreseeable future.

"I just want to apologize. Tonight was my fault. If I had listened to you—if we had told him earlier—it would never have gotten violent. I think that us acting suspiciously plus the fact that he found me crying in your arms as you held my hand under the water was just not an overall good first impression." He shakes his head, seeming to agree with my statement.

"Not all your fault," he says, but I lift a hand to stop him. What part of *don't talk* does he not understand?

"I can at least take seventy-five percent of the blame here," I say. He frowns at me but doesn't argue. Maybe because he finally realizes that it hurts too much to talk, or maybe it's because he knows he won't win this argument, or maybe it's even because he agrees. Regardless, I'm sticking to how big a role I played in what happened tonight.

"I'm sorry about everything." I look down at our intertwined hands before looking up into his eyes again. "This never would've happened if I had just listened to you, if I hadn't been so freaking scared. Honestly, I think I made it an even bigger deal than it was. I'm starting to agree with Jeremy on some things about me, and I think me being a tad bit too dramatic is one of them." My last statement seems to spark something in him, his dark-green eyes almost black.

"Not true." He shakes his head. "Even if you are a bit dramatic, it's one of the things I love about you. Plus, Jeremy was an asshole." He winces, his hand flying to his jaw again.

"Stop talking!" I sigh, exasperated. "I'm getting you more ice."

I walk over to the kitchen and pull an icepack from the freezer. I find a kitchen towel and wrap it around the pack to keep it from burning his skin. When I get back to the couch, his head is leaned back against the headrest, eyes staring up at the ceiling.

"Don't want you to blame yourself," he says without looking at me. "Takes two to tango."

"I *told* you to stop talking!" I say, sighing deeply. "I'm trying to take care of you here, and you're being an awful patient." I *tsk*. "I know doctors make the worst patients, but *damn*."

He looks into my eyes and grins, taking the icepack from my hands, placing it on the side of his face. "Can I say one more thing?" he asks, and I roll my eyes at him. He takes this as a yes. "I love you." He smiles.

I try to control the goofy grin on my face, but really, what's the point? Despite everything that's happened today and every other crazy moment in our relationship, he loves me, and I love him. "I love you, too." I kiss him on the lips. It starts off soft, slow, but it's like wildfire between us. And I know he's hurting, and I know he really shouldn't be kissing me like this, but he does anyway. He parts his lips, slipping his tongue into my mouth with a groan, and I separate immediately, unsure whether that was a good sound or a bad one.

Matt's eyes are hungry, pupils dilated, and he definitely wants more. He looks me slowly up and down, raising goose-bumps on my skin, smirking.

"Nuh-uh. Nope." I shake my head. "You're hurt, mister, and I'm not gonna do anything to jeopardize your well-being." I shake my finger at him. "I love you too much to hurt you just because you're smoking hot, and I want you, too."

He rolls his eyes at me and groans again, wincing in pain immediately after.

"See?" I point at him, completely exasperated. "You need a shower, anyway," I tell him. "The hot water on your back will be really good for you, and then we can place an icepack on it after. Do a little thermal therapy." I help pull him up off the couch with my good hand.

"You a doctor now?" he asks, amused, his eyes shining.

"No, but I know enough of them." I smirk.

WE'RE IN MATT'S BATHROOM, WHERE I HELP HIM UNDRESS himself while the water heats, pulling his sweater carefully over his head, unbuttoning his shirt while he does his pants. I gently push his shirt over his shoulders without meeting his gaze because I know what I'll find there: the look in his eyes he gets right before he kisses me like I'm the only thing he needs to survive, like he needs me more than oxygen. I can hear it in his ragged breathing, in the way his chest is rising and falling faster and faster. I can practically *feel* his heart race, and I'm not even touching him.

"Stop," I whisper, keeping my eyes on his bare chest—not really the best idea, considering how lean and defined Matt's chest is with his sprinkle of dark hair. I'm so close I can see every single freckle on his skin, even in the dim light. Just like that first night, I want to lick him.

"What?" he asks in his gravelly voice.

"You know what," I admonish him. "I can practically *hear* your smile." We both chuckle. I push down his pants and underwear, and he stands naked in front of me. It's taking everything in my power to remind myself that Matt is hurt, because, right now, I *really* want to tackle him. Especially when I look down and can see just how happy he is to have me here in his bathroom.

"Shower with me?" he asks, his eyes pleading, a different kind of hunger in them now. I get where he's coming from, because I feel it too. It's not about sex. It's about needing to feel me close after the awful day we've had. It started with us getting into an argument and not talking all day and then ended in a physical altercation with my brother. I need his arms around me just as much as he needs mine.

"You gonna behave?" I ask, because this will only work if he controls himself.

He smiles sheepishly and nods, tugging on my sweater, silently instructing me to take it off. I undress completely, slowly, in front of him. I know it's cruel of me, but I can't help teasing him a little. I place our clothes on top of the white marble countertop and turn back to face him.

"I'll change your bandage before bed anyway, but try not to get it too wet," he says, grimacing from the pain.

I shake my head at his inability to follow orders and nod. "Fine, come on. Let's go."

He smirks and grabs my good hand, opening the glass door to his massive shower. I gasp at the sight of his lower back, and he turns to face me with a questioning look.

"Your back! The bruises! Oh my God," I say. He walks over to the mirror and twists in front of it to get a better look, the movement causing him pain. I walk over to him and wrap my arms around his waist, leaning my head on his chest, breathing

225

him in, doing my best to keep the tears from falling. "I'm so sorry," I say again, kissing his chest. He wraps one arm around my waist while his other hand goes into my hair, holding me to him. After a while, when the hot water from the shower completely fogs up the mirror, he leads me into it, and we proceed to spend a good half hour in there. We don't talk. We don't kiss. We only hold each other under the stream of water in complete silence. I only break the comfortable silence when I remind him just how late it is and that we should probably go to bed so that he can get his sleep.

Once we're out of the shower, have dried ourselves off, and he's redressed the gash on my palm, I have him lie facedown on his bed in his boxers, shirtless. I softly rub some arnica cream on the bruises that are slowly forming on his lower back and place a large icepack on it after I've let the cream dry for a bit.

I lie down on my side next to him, wearing only one of his t-shirts, and I stare into his dark-green eyes. He looks exhausted. I settle my head on my bent arm, and he reaches out for my hand. I don't think I've ever loved him more.

We've just spent the entire night taking care of each other—me helping him with his back and jaw, and him redressing my wound. We've settled easily into our roles as partners and lovers and best friends, and even though today was a mess—a complete and total shit-show—I wouldn't change it for the world.

"I love you," he says seriously, his eyes smoldering. "I don't regret anything about us—not if everything we've been through has led us to this exact moment in time." My heart soars at his reassurance, at the knowledge that he feels exactly the same way.

I know saying that must have hurt him in more ways than one—physically, obviously, but emotionally as well. Having to admit out loud that he doesn't care how awful today was because this was all worth it must not have been easy. He might have potentially lost his best friend over me, but he's saying he doesn't regret it.

Once again, I remind myself how lucky I am to have found someone as incredible as Matt, and I resolve to try and reconcile him and his best friend. I owe him at least that.

I kiss his hand, and we close our eyes, facing each other, fingers intertwined, as Matt's sweet cedar signature scent and the sounds of his deep breathing lull me to sleep.

Chapter Twenty-Eight

LIZA

MATT AND I SPENT THE ENTIRE WEEKEND LOCKED UP IN his apartment while I took care of him. He woke up Friday morning with back spasms, unable to move. So, guided by his medical knowledge, I did my best to help him through it. At one point, the pain was so bad that he had to call his boss and ask for a prescription for muscle relaxers. I picked them up for him, and we spent the entire next couple of days switching up ice and heat therapy on his lower back, eating take-out from containers, and binging really bad reality TV on the couch while he dozed next to me.

It was hell for Matt but heavenly for me. I got to spend the entire weekend with him, and I loved every second of it. I loved taking care of him and showing him how much I love him. I loved going to bed next to him in his king-sized bed and showering together in his massive bathroom.

I asked him why he had always insisted on spending the night at my apartment when his bed is so much more comfortable than my full-sized one and his shower is more spacious than mine. He simply shrugged and said it never felt like home to him, that my apartment smelled like me, and it made him happier than being alone in his own space. I rolled my eyes and told him he was ridiculous, but my heart was beating wildly in my chest. That definitely earned him a big smooch.

By Monday, Matt was feeling well enough to go back to work as planned, which was good since I was about to begin three weeks of complete and total hell at school and wouldn't have been able to help him as much. Finals were fast-approaching, and I had to study for tests, write papers, and finish my touch-base with my thesis advisor. I was about to be buried in work, so I wanted to resolve this problem with my brother before essentially being forced into disappearing under a mountain of work.

The truth was, I missed my brother a lot. It had only been a few days since the last time I spoke to him, but I was used to regular communication with him, especially since our father's death. It was weird to not have heard from him all weekend—and I didn't like it.

By Monday afternoon, I decide to show up to his apartment to see if we can clear the air, if we can make up. Maybe, if I'm lucky, I can convince him that Matt isn't a bad guy, and they can go back to being friends—or at least be civil. But when I knock on the door, it isn't Vinny who answers the door—it's Danielle, and she looks like shit.

"Hey," I say, a little taken aback. "Oh my God, what's wrong?" Dani looks exhausted, bags under her eyes, hair a mess. I don't think I've ever seen her this disheveled—not even after giving birth to the twins. As soon as the babies were out of her, she made sure to brush her hair and do her makeup before letting anyone besides Vinny see her.

Danielle sighs and waves me into the apartment. "It's been a bit hard around here," she explains as I follow her into the living room. We both take a seat on the cream couch, and she sighs deeply. "I don't think any of us actually considered the fact that this wasn't all about the stupid bro code or the fact that Vinny seemed to think he was the head of the family and was being protective."

I raise an eyebrow at Danielle. "I don't think I understand what you mean?"

"I didn't realize just how lonely he was in terms of needing a friend," she tells me. I think back to what Vinny told me, before he stormed out for the second time, about me stealing his only friend, having not really understood why he was so hung up on that idea. "I guess when your dad died, he was caught up in the twins—he had to be, you know? Your dad died when I was about a month away from giving birth, and then we had to focus on *two* newborns, and I think that, now that they're older, the grief has caught up with him, and it has made him really lonely." She exhales. "I don't think he ever really had time to process it. He was just trying to keep us all together. You, your mom, me, and the babies."

I feel like an idiot now. Of course.

"He never took care of himself," I say, and Danielle nods.

Vinny has always been an incredibly charismatic person, one of those people who everyone naturally gravitates toward. He's never been someone to struggle with making friends or fitting in, like me. But his true, one and only best friend was always my dad. They would talk about everything and nothing, and he respected his advice above everything else. I guess I never truly realized how superficial his other relationships were or how deep a friendship he had developed with Matt. I never completely understood why Matt was so wracked with guilt over our relationship and how it would affect my brother, but I finally get it.

"Anyway," she says. "He's not exactly happy with me right now—or your mom, for that matter. He feels like everyone kind of betrayed him," she says sadly. "I hate that," she whispers.

"Dani, you didn't have to tell him you knew. I never mentioned the fact that you were aware that Matt and I were dating. I didn't want you to be dragged into it." I reach out for her hand to hold it.

She shrugs. "I was the one who told him, don't worry. Your mother and I both thought we should stand up for you and tell him how ridiculous he was being, and it came out that we both knew this was happening. Obviously, this was before we knew what was actually going on with him."

I shake my head. "I'm so sorry." I frown at her joined hands, unable to look her in the eye. "So where is he now?" I ask, hoping to God he hasn't done something crazy.

She sees the expression on my face, and her eyes widen. "No, no. Don't worry, he hasn't *left* me or anything. He just had an emergency with a patient." She sighs, looking terrified. "He's not *that* angry—I don't think." She mutters that last part under her breath. "We've just been talking *a lot*, staying up late, and I've been a teensy bit sleep deprived and overwhelmed. I'm feeling guilty that I didn't notice that my own husband, who I see and talk to every day, has spent most of our marriage grieving." She sniffles and shakes her head. "We'll get through it, though."

My heart aches for her and the absolute catastrophic damage this whole thing has left in my wake. "I'm so, *so* sorry, Dani," my voice breaks.

"Don't be. In a way, what happened was a good thing. It helped us talk things through, have him finally express himself. I don't think *he* even knew what he was going through, you know? It's like he's been in fight mode all this time and hasn't given himself time to break down. It just sucks that it had to be this way." I nod and tighten my grip on her hand. "You want to stay for dinner? The twins are with my mom and should be back in a little bit," she asks after a few beats of silence.

I smile and thank her but tell her that I'm going to have to pass.

"I never planned to stay here. I didn't think my brother would want me to. So, I made plans with Matt and Barbara for dinner so that they can get to know each other better."

She smiles and sniffles, wiping her nose with the back of her hand. "The best friend and the boyfriend." She snorts. "You nervous?" We laugh.

"Nah, they've met each other already. Although, I think the last interaction they had was when Babs drunkenly and repeatedly called him a dick at her Halloween party." Danielle laughs, and I reach for her hand again.

"I hope they get along. Matt's already been through enough because of dating me," I say.

"Preach," she agrees and nods.

"I love you. Thank you for being so supportive." I kiss her on the cheek.

"Love you, too. Just know that your brother needs a little space. I'm sure it will all be okay in time." She smiles.

"Will you tell him I stopped by? That I miss him?" I ask as we both stand. I want to make sure he knows that I don't care that he's upset with me, with us. I want him to know that I care and that I'm sorry that I hurt him. That I'm making an effort to see him.

"Of course," she says as she walks me to the door. I give her a hug before leaving and thank her for being such a great sister-in-law.

Chapter Twenty-Nine

MATT

IT'S BEEN ALMOST THREE WEEKS SINCE OUR ARGUMENT with Vinny on Thanksgiving, and neither Liza nor I have managed to speak one word to him since. It's been really difficult for the both of us to cope, but we understand that he's hurt and needs time, and we're sad he's taken it so personally. I tried to reach out to him several times, even showing up at his office one day, but it was fruitless. He won't pick up the phone or see me, and I don't know if he ever even read the letter I left with the receptionist at his practice.

It hasn't been easy, and the guilt over the part I played in the chasm in the relationship between Liza and her brother never fades—it has increased over time. Not to mention the fact that I miss my best friend, too. I love my girlfriend very much, but I also miss hanging out with Vinny, having a beer, and talking about absolutely nothing. Sometimes a guy just needs guy time, you know?

I hate that he hates me.

But what was I supposed to do? I couldn't help falling for

her, and I meant what I said to Liza the other day: things might suck right now, but I don't regret anything because it led me to being with her, to loving her.

Still, it's hard.

I sigh and run my fingers over the strip of photos Liza and I took in the photo booth at the cardiology department's holiday party last weekend and smile. I've taped it to a frame on my desk right next to my computer screen. We're making funny faces in the first two photos, but the third in the bunch is of me holding her close, grinning into the camera while she looks up and smiles at me, beaming. She's *glowing* in the picture, and I marvel at the fact that I can make anyone—especially someone as incredible as her—look at me like that, like I'm everything to her, just like she is to me.

We did two more sessions in the photo booth that night, but I wanted to keep this particular strip because of the look in her eye in that third photo, that smile that can bring me to my fucking knees. I wanted it in my office to look at every damn day and remind myself that, no matter what, I have her with me. Yes, her brother is still mad at us. Yes, it's caused a lot of familial drama. But we are finally openly together and really happy. The rest is just noise, in my opinion.

I know it will work itself out sooner rather than later—I know that—but I hope that Liza and Vinny reconcile soon—before Christmas. I don't want her to go into the holidays without being on speaking terms with her brother. Christmas is already hard enough as it is for Vinny and Liza, because of their dad's passing, without adding their fight to it. I want us to be able to enjoy the holiday together at her mother's without the underlying drama of it all. I want us to be able to enjoy my gift to her (a three-day getaway starting the day after Christmas at a cabin in Vermont), and I want things to be okay enough for me to ask her to move in with me.

I think it's time.

I already spend every night at her place when she isn't at mine, so what's the difference? Some of her stuff is already at my place—this would just be adding to it, right? Plus, she's still a student, and it would be better if she saved the rent money by moving in with me and putting it toward her loans. I already own my place, and she wouldn't have to spend a dime. I know she thinks my apartment is cold, but it's bigger than hers, has more closet space, and I'd let her redecorate it however she wanted to—I don't care if I have to pay for it.

I want her stuff in my closet, her makeup on my bathroom counter, her almond milk in my fridge, and her awful paint-by-numbers art on my walls (preferably in the bathroom, but whatever). I'm tired of overnight bags and pretending like we don't *already* live together. Sure, some people will say it's too soon to make it official, but I don't care anymore about what other people think regarding my relationship with my girlfriend. All I care about is that she's happy and safe and healthy—something she's been struggling with lately, which is why I can't ask her to move in yet.

We've been happy, sure, but I think the stress of this fight with her brother plus the stress of school is really getting to her, and I'm concerned. I don't know if it's just the stomach flu or whether it's the anxiety from everything going on her life, but she hasn't been able to keep anything down this entire week. I've asked her to slow down multiple times, to study at the apartment instead of in the school library, to come home a little earlier, sleep in more, but it's like talking to a wall. She's determined and driven, and it's definitely sexy—until it makes her throw up like a woman possessed by a demon.

I want her to be happy, but she is not doing okay, and I'm incredibly concerned for her. She keeps telling me this is normal, that this is her body's reaction to stress, but I'm a doctor, and vomiting all day, every day as a reaction to stress is not fucking normal. I'm so fucking happy today was her last day of school. I'm hoping now she can relax and feel better.

"Dr. Wilson?" I hear Jenny, my receptionist, through the phone's intercom.

I press the button and speak. "Yes?" I ask.

"Dr. Parker is on line one. He says he needs to speak to you urgently," she says.

"*Shit,*" I mutter under my breath. I press the button again and thank her.

I think I'm in trouble with him because I didn't actually ask if it was okay for me to switch shifts with the other doctors in order to have the whole week of Christmas off. The general rule in the hospital is if you aren't on-call for Thanksgiving, you cannot have Christmas off, and vice-versa. It's a way to keep things fair for every doctor and make sure that we have some sort of work/life balance. Generally, he doesn't police shift schedules since we're adults and should be able to manage them on our own, but someone could have complained. I'm still new to the hospital. Maybe another doctor is having to work extra and is not happy about it?

I pick up the phone and hold it to my ear, clearing my throat. I just need to remember to stay strong and remind him that the doctors who switched with me *made the choice* to do so, and I didn't force their hand. Did I bribe them by promising to take at least one of their weekend shifts this January? Absolutely. But he doesn't need to know that.

"Dr. Parker," I say, trying to keep my cool. "How are you?"

"Ah, Dr. Wilson. How...how are things?" he asks, unsure. Something in his tone irks me—he sounds off.

"Um, great. Everything's going great," I say in my most confident voice. It's not a lie, either. Work *is* going great. My practice has been growing, and I'm really enjoying working in this new hospital.

"So, you're at the office now, right?" he asks, and now I know something is wrong, because fucking *duh*, that's where he called me.

"Yes?" I answer like I'm not sure, but of course I am. I'm seated at my mahogany desk, surrounded by stacks of paperwork that I've been neglecting for the last couple of weeks. I've been too focused on my relationship with Liza to want to stay late and finish, choosing instead to run home to her as soon as possible every single night.

"Right, right..." he says, followed by an awkward period of silence. I hear him cluck his tongue on the other line, a nervous tick he uses when debating a course of treatment with a patient that might end up going either way.

"Can I... Can I help you with something, sir?" I ask finally.

I hear him exhale deeply and then clear his throat. "Are you still, by any chance, dating that lovely girl I met at the hospital function? The one who also came to our department holiday party?" he asks quietly.

I furrow my brow in confusion. Why is he asking me this? Does he want to ask her out or something? I know he was super flirty with her both times he met her, but dude has a wife! This is really weird.

"Uh, yes." I clear my throat. "I am, and it's very serious," I clarify, just in case he has any weird ideas.

She's mine, buddy.

"Right, right. *Good.*" Silence again. This is the weirdest conversation I have ever had with my boss. Why the hell is he asking me about Liza?

"Is there a reason for your question, Dr. Parker?" I realize there's an edge to my voice, but I can't help it. He can't really be interested in her, can he? This is ridiculous. Also, something about this conversation in general is giving me the creeps.

He sighs. "Dr. Wilson...do you happen to have the number for her, er, next of kin, perhaps?"

I sit up straight in alarm, cold water running through my veins. I know what he means by asking me that question.

Chapter Thirty

MATT

"Excuse me?" I choke out.

No, no, no, no.

He can't tell me what's happened to her because of HIPAA and because it's a conflict of interest, but he's just told me that *something*'s happened to her, because why else would he ask me that?

"Dr. Wilson, I am currently at the hospital ER where I was doing a consult for one of my patients, and I happen to need your girlfriend's next of kin contact information," he says as calmly and professionally as possible, as if he were asking to borrow a pen. "Do you have it?"

"I—I don't," my voice is shaking. I'm torn between wanting to run out of this office and sprint the two blocks to the ER and staying on the phone so I can see what I can get him to tell me without necessarily breaking the law.

Fucking landlines.

"Actually, I do. I don't have her mother's number, but I have her brother's. I can call him!" But then I remember that he's not picking up my calls and almost lose it.

Parker clears his throat again. "Well, would you mind texting me the contact information? There is a nurse here *by bed eleven* in section B of the ER who needs it."

I fucking love Dr. Parker.

"Yes," I say, getting up and pulling my cell and wallet from my desk drawer, making sure I also have my hospital badge with me—I'm gonna need it. "I'll do it immediately, sir." I hang up and rush out of the office, leaving my winter coat behind— there's no time for that now. While I wait for the elevator, I text Vinny's contact info to Dr. Parker.

I start running once I'm out the building, the cold December air cutting into my lungs sharply like small shards of glass—but I don't give a shit. Liza's in the emergency room, and I don't know what's wrong with her, so I push through.

They can't tell me over the phone because I'm not related to her, but I can probably find out from the hospital, get one of my colleagues to pull the chart up, let me "accidentally" read it while they leave it open on the screen.

I don't know what's wrong with her, and it's killing me.

Dr. Parker was the one who called, though. Does that mean that she was his consult? Did they need a cardiologist? My heart starts beating out of my chest, and I'm suddenly breathless, but it's not from the two-block sprint. I start thinking how familiar this situation is, how I lived through it with my dad and *his* heart. I remember perfectly how my mother called the house, told me to find my way to the hospital somehow—even though I was just a kid—because my dad was sick. By the time I got to the ER, my father was already gone. My mother had lied. He had already passed away when she called. She had just tried to get me to use the trip over as a way to mentally prepare myself for the possibility.

Was that what Parker was doing?

Oh, God.

A wave of nausea hits me at the thought of losing Liza. I cannot stomach the thought.

Right before entering, I place my KN95 mask over my face as hospital policy dictates everyone wear one nowadays. I finally make it to the ER entrance and flash my badge at the security guard as I make my way inside. He's unfazed by my rush—this is the emergency room, after all.

I make my way through the wing, and it's a maze of beds and machines, but I know my way around by now.

Bed eleven, bed eleven. I need to make it to bed eleven.

I power-walk through the different designated areas, trying not to draw too much attention to myself, until I finally reach the curtain outside her bed. I slide it open a little too aggressively, scaring the patient in the bed across from her awake.

"Liza!" I run to her and take in her condition. She's asleep— or passed out? Her skin is pale, and her lips are chapped, and they've already changed her into a gown and covered her with a blanket in her hospital bed. How long has she been here? Is she alone? I take her wrist in my hands and check her pulse. She's in a resting position, but her heart is racing. I place both hands on the sides of her face and say her name, but she doesn't wake. There's an IV hooked up to her arm, and I wince. I'm a fucking doctor, but the sight of her like this is driving me crazy and making me nauseated all over again.

I try calling Vinny before looking for a nurse who can help me, but he doesn't pick up. I walk up to the nurses' station, still wearing my white lab coat from work and, as casually as possible, ask for some more information on the patient in bed eleven. I need to be careful here and not reveal who she is to me. The second they find out my personal relationship to the patient, they'll shut me out of receiving any type of medical information without her next of kin present.

But there's no need for any of that, thankfully.

"Dr. Wilson." I hear a voice behind me and turn to see my boss standing in his lab coat with a stethoscope around his neck. His pants are pressed, his shirt neat, and hair styled—probably a stark contrast against what I must look like right now. I practically run to him, feeling the strange urge to wrap my arms around him.

"I can't thank you enough for calling me, Dr. Parker. I'm—I don't know what to say. I just want to know what's wrong with her." I'm a desperate man, dude. Just fucking tell me.

I know he technically can't because of my relationship to her, but there must be a gray area for boyfriends who are doctors in the hospital where their girlfriends are being treated. A loophole he's willing to take? I'm too new here to ask any of the other doctors, having not become as friendly with them yet, but isn't there some sort of unofficial code?

"I haven't looked at her chart yet. She wasn't my consult," he explains.

I exhale a deep sigh at this brand-new piece of information. It's as if I've been holding my breath since running out of the office.

It's not her heart.

It could be something way worse, of course, but the thought that it was related to her heart had me so concerned. The similarities of what's happening right now to the day my father passed are so intense that the relief almost brings me to my knees, almost makes me cry.

I choke down a sob, and I do my best to swallow it down. I don't think I've ever been this scared. The cheerful holiday decorations that cover the nurses' station and the twinkling lights above us do nothing to lighten my mood or ease the tension caused by the fact that my girlfriend is currently lying in a hospital bed, and I have no idea what's wrong with her.

"I was down here to check on a patient of mine that was

brought in and saw her lying there while they inserted an IV and drew some blood. After about an hour, when I didn't see you or anyone else with her, I thought it would be acceptable to give you a call and talk to the nurses about her case."

"*Thank you,*" I say again, my voice cracking. I feel a bit light-headed, the adrenaline slowly waning after having made sure that she wasn't in some sort of horrible accident and that it might not be as awful as all the scenarios that went through my head—all of which included having to face a world without Liza in it.

I don't think I've ever experienced this completely crippling anxiety over the possibility of losing someone and the ability the mind has to race and imagine the worst.

It's fucking horrible. I feel like I'm having an anxiety attack.

"Sit down," he says in a surprisingly gentle voice. "Let me go find a tablet so I can look at her chart."

This is the trouble with going digital—the files are no longer hanging on the patients' beds for everyone to see. Sure, it's amazing because files are easily accessible now for all of the patients' doctors to see in one place, but it leaves an electronic trail of who's seen your chart and when—which means that if I were to try and access her chart and someone found out, I could get into a lot of trouble.

I sit on the chair by her bed and reach out for her hand, running my index finger over the red scar forming on her palm from Thanksgiving night. I call Vinny again, but he sends me to voicemail after one ring.

I make a mental note to kill him the next time I see him and hope to God he at least picked up the hospital ER call, because I don't even have her mother's phone number.

When Parker comes back, he takes a seat next to me, scrolling and tapping away at the tablet screen.

"Right, here it is. Bed eleven," he says, and I sit up straight, steeling myself for whatever may come. "'Patient was found passed out in supermarket aisle,'" he reads. "'Brought in because patient had trouble coming to. Possible concussion and dehydration.' It says here that the doctor on call wanted to take a CT scan but didn't because..." He stops and looks at me, wide-eyed, but doesn't finish the sentence. "I—I think it's best if we wait for her next of kin."

"What?!" Is he insane? "Give that to me!" I practically scream and rip the tablet from his hand. I don't fucking care if he fires me. I need to know whether she's okay or not.

"*Dr. Wilson*, I hardly think that's appropriate—"

But I don't hear him anymore because I'm shocked. I can't talk. I can't think. I can't fucking breathe anymore.

"*Suspected concussion, but CT not possible. Patient is est. 6 - 7 weeks pregnant. HCG levels found to be at 7,500 mIU/mL. Suspect morning sickness as cause of dehydration.*"

I sit back in my chair and look up at the ceiling, completely awestruck.

Pregnant.

Morning sickness.

It wasn't the stomach flu.

My face hangs in my hands as I attempt to steady my breathing and try to understand how I feel about this whole situation. Parker left me a couple of minutes ago with her chart to give me some space to think, for which I thanked him.

A baby.

It's so soon. *Too* soon? I mean, I obviously would have

wanted some time for us to just enjoy each other before having kids, but I can't deny that I haven't thought about it. It's kind of hard not to. When you decide you want to move in with someone, you think about what that means for your relationship long-term—and that includes marriage and maybe kids.

I love Liza, and I know this is all fast, but I feel like we've always been kind of fast, living by our own timeline of what we think is appropriate for our relationship.

So, do I want this kid? I drop my hands from my face and sit back in my chair, staring at my girl asleep in her hospital bed.

Fuck yeah, I want this kid.

I want everything with her. I always have. Since the moment I held her as we danced in her apartment, since the pumpkin patch, since the fucking vomit—okay, maybe not then, but I was definitely a goner by the pumpkin patch after lunch.

How will *she* react, though? Does she even know? Did they tell her already? Was she in the supermarket buying a pregnancy test or something?

It's so soon—I didn't even notice the signs—but it seems so stupid now, so obvious. I mean, we've been having uninterrupted sex for seven weeks now—no periods or anything. And she just started feeling a little sick this past week. But finals and the stress of the fight with Vinny coincided, so I didn't think much of it.

I should've noticed or suspected something. It's my job to take care of people, and I can't even take care of my girlfriend, make sure she's eating or drinking water when she's been so sick lately. How am I going to take care of a baby?

Shit, what kind of dad will I be? What kind of mom will Liza be?

She's going to be amazing. She's already so caring and loving, and family means everything to her. She will never neglect our children in any way—she'll never be like my mother. I'm not worried about what kind of mom she'll be. She'll be the best mom in the world. She won't be like my mother—cold, distant, unattached. Nope. She'll be like Catterina, sometimes too involved in her children's lives but incredibly supportive and understanding, loving and dedicated. And she'll make them incredible Italian food every day. I'm not worried about what kind of mom she'll be. She'll be the best mom in the world.

Will we get married?

I would *love* to marry her. To be honest, if I weren't so scared she'd say no, that it's too soon, I would've already asked her. It's why I was planning on begging her to move in with me —so she'd at least be with me always.

I see a doctor I've never seen around the hospital making rounds and curse under my breath. I'm never gonna get away with getting information on her with some doctor I don't know.

I pull out my phone and call Vinny one more time. Voicemail.

"Your sister is in the hospital, asshole! Get your ass over here!" I hang up in anger before realizing I didn't even tell him *which* fucking hospital she's at. I groan and lean back against the chair again. I'll call him back in a minute. I need to breathe for a bit. I text my scheduling assistant and ask her to cancel all of my appointments for the next two days due to a family emergency.

After that, I lean forward in my chair and reach for Liza's hand again, just staring at her while I imagine the next steps in our life.

"Hey." I hear Vinny's voice beside me and jump. It's the first time I've seen him since he pushed me repeatedly against his mother's kitchen counter and punched me in the face. *Twice.* "I got a call from the hospital saying Liza was here. How is she?" He frowns and walks over to her side, putting his fingers to her wrist, checking her pulse just like I did.

Would a normal person just walk up to their loved one in a hospital bed and do that? Probably not. We're doctors; we can't help it.

I take a deep breath and run my fingers through my hair. "She's...I don't really know. I haven't seen a doctor yet. I just read her chart." I lock the tablet screen before Vinny has a chance to see it open on the chair bedside me and ask to read it. I don't want him to find out she's pregnant this way—before *she* even knows.

"*And?*" he asks with a raised eyebrow. "What did it say?"

"Dehydration and possible concussion. She's...been sick these past couple of days," I say, ashamed of myself. I should've taken better care of her, made sure she was staying hydrated and resting properly, and I know he's thinking the same thing.

"The least you could do is make sure that my sister is staying healthy, Matt." He rolls his eyes at me and checks the IV bag.

There it is.

"I was," I growled. "She's just been very stressed with school and this whole fight with you." I don't mean to put the blame on him, but I also don't *not* mean to blame it on him, because he really has played a big part in her general well-being.

Vinny sighs. Half his face is covered by his mask, but I can tell that he's frowning, his brows furrowed. "I know." He takes the tablet and hands it to me so he can sit next to me. "Everything got so messed up in the most ridiculous way possible. I mean, you guys were assholes for hiding it from me and you for going against my wishes, but I don't fucking know what got into me over Thanksgiving, man. I don't think I've ever gotten into a physical fight before." Vinny shakes his head.

"Well, it definitely didn't seem that way. Your right hook is insanely good," I deadpan. Vinny chuckles and leans back in his seat.

"I guess I *kind of* wanted to apologize? But the more time

went on, the stupider I felt, you know? Like, I don't even know why I reacted that way. I mean, I *know* why, obviously, because the both of you are liars, but still." I nod and stare at the floor. I don't even try to deny it.

"It's really gross that you're dating my sister, Matt," he says after a few moments of silence with a smile in his voice.

"*I* don't think so, but it's okay if you do."

"And I don't really know if I would feel comfortable enough going back to being your friend in the same way that we were before I found out." I frown, disappointed, but completely understand. "But it's mostly because I need to put her first in the event that you ever hurt her, you know what I mean? I don't ever want her to think that I'm picking you over her. Because she's my sister, after all. I will always choose her."

"That's fair," I say, trying really hard to control the hope in my voice. "I clearly picked her over you," I say with a shrug, trying to make a joke out of the truth.

"Right," he sighs.

"So, what are you saying?" I ask carefully.

"I'm saying..." He sighs and turns to look me in the eye. "I'm saying this is really fucking weird for me, but I think I'm okay with the two of you being together." I can feel a smile spread quickly across my face, my chest about to burst. Liza will be so happy. "I realized that you guys weren't the only ones who were being selfish. Yeah, in the beginning of your relationship you definitely put yourselves ahead of what I wanted, but I guess after you...fell in love"—he grimaces and playfully gags—"it was kind of a dick move for me to be mad about it. I care about the both of you, and I should have understood where you were coming from as well." He runs both hands through his hair. "I just kind of felt abandoned all over again, you know?"

My jaw drops inside my mask, unable to grasp the amount

of emotional maturing that Vinny has undergone these past three weeks in order to be able to admit that he wasn't completely right about me and Liza.

"Don't look at me like that," he says gruffly. "I had a lot of help from Danielle, so you should thank her for this."

I laugh—mostly in relief—and clasp him on the back for a brief and very awkward moment. I know I owe Danielle for so much more than this huge emotional growth of Vinny's, and I plan to find some way to make it up to her.

"For the record, I never planned on 'abandoning' you, Vinny. I never stopped wanting to hang out with you or be your friend. Dating Liza and being your friend aren't mutually exclusive concepts—both can happen at the same time. I hope that they do." This conversation is making me just a teensy bit uncomfortable. It's not often Vinny and I discuss feelings on a nitty-gritty level, but I guess it was absolutely necessary for this situation.

We both clear our throats and sit up a little straighter in our seats. "Well, then. But I don't want to see any touchy-feely things in my presence, alright?"

"Agreed. We'll keep the PDA to a minimum in front of you."

"Thank you," he says.

I decide to take advantage of this moment and go for broke. "You should know I plan on asking her to move in with me, Vinny. And eventually, for her to marry me."

We're quiet, neither of us saying anything, not moving an inch—I don't think I'm even breathing. He turns to look me in the eye, and I stare on back because I'm not backing down. I don't know what he's looking for in there, but he finds something. "Okay. But you're gonna have to do a better job at taking care of my sister."

I smile and open my mouth to thank him but am interrupted by someone clearing their throat.

"I don't understand why you insist I need taking care of," Liza says from her bed.

Chapter Thirty-One

LIZA

"LIZA!" MATT AND VINNY GET UP FROM WHERE THEY'RE sitting at the sound of my voice. Matt *gently* wraps his arms around my waist, burying his face in my neck, and I melt in my hospital bed. Every time I see him after a long period of time, it's like instant relief—even more so now that I'm lying in the ER with the worst headache imaginable. I breathe him in, closing my eyes, trying to hold his sweet cedar scent in my lungs as long as possible.

"Dude! You promised there wouldn't be any PDA!" I hear Vinny protest beside us.

I sigh, still a little disoriented, and Matt softly pulls away from me. I prepare for Vinny's anger, but I can see the smirk in their eyes.

What?

Did they make up? Oh my God.

I'm so happy I could cry, except I really shouldn't because I remember the doctors saying something about dehydration when they brought me in. I take stock of myself and see an IV line attached to my arm.

Ew, needles.

"I'm gonna go get your doctor—see if he can update us on your status, although you seem to be doing okay," Matt says, leaving Vinny and me alone to talk.

"So," he says awkwardly, shuffling uncomfortably between his feet. "How ya feeling?"

"Really?" I laugh once. "I mean, not great, but okay. Feeling a little nauseated. Have a headache. No biggie."

He expels a puff of air as he crosses his arms in front of him, eyes on the floor. "So...I'm sorry?"

"Is that a question or a statement?"

Vinny groans. "Fine. Definitely a statement. I. Am. Sorry. Like I told Matt, we were all selfish and lacked a bit of understanding and consideration for each other, did we not?"

I agree and apologize in turn, for the second time, for lying to him. We agree that we should apologize to our mother, since she was also hurt by this fight, and it wasn't fair to her. Vinny and I also agree to put it completely behind us, but he doesn't let it go without warning me that if Matt were to ever hurt me, he will not hesitate to kick his ass again, not stopping at one punch.

A nurse comes by during our conversation to change my IV bag, and I grimace throughout the entire process even though she's as gentle as can be. Vinny rolls his eyes at me, calling me a baby, making fun of me the entire time. When Matt comes back, my brother leaves us to call my mom and tell her I'm at the hospital but that I'm okay. I think he wants to give us some time alone as well.

"Hey," Matt says, kissing my cheek through his mask, taking a seat, scooting the chair closer to the bed. "How are you feeling?"

"Tired, but better. They just changed my IV bag." I look over my shoulder, and he follows my gaze to the full bag.

"That's good," he says, nodding, his brow furrowed. I can see the anxiety in his eyes.

"What is it? What's wrong?" I ask, and he raises an eyebrow. "Besides the obvious, I mean."

"Nothing, nothing. Just waiting to hear from this doctor. I know I work here, but I have no idea who he is." He looks over at the nurses' station, as if expecting him to magically appear in front of us.

I suddenly grow very nervous, my stomach turning again for the millionth time today. There's something I need to tell him, something I only realized today when I walked past a bagel cart this morning and had to throw up in a trashcan on the corner of the street. It's something I'm afraid the doctors might already know and will tell us in a couple of minutes. I don't want him to be blindsided, even if it means giving him just a couple of minutes to process it before someone else comes up and tells us.

"Matt?" I start, my voice soft. "I—I think I know why I've been so sick, and I don't think it's the stomach flu or stress."

Matt stares back at me, eyes red-rimmed, a smile in his gaze. "Yeah, I know," he chokes out behind his mask.

"You—you know? What do you mean *you know*?" I can't breathe. Does he suspect it too? He *is* a doctor. He could just be making this assessment based on symptoms, same as me. I have been throwing up all damn week, and I honestly can't remember the last time I got my period, but it was definitely before Halloween.

"I read your chart." He takes off his mask and kisses me on the lips, slow, deep, and...salty?

Oh. I'm crying.

"Oh my God," I breathe when we separate. "So, just to clarify...?"

He laughs. "Yes, you are, in fact, pregnant. But it's super early days—obviously," he says, and I know he's referring to the fact that we haven't been sleeping together for long—just under two months. Suddenly, I'm extremely anxious because I remember that Matt and I really haven't been together for that long. I don't even know if he wants kids! And now I'm pregnant? This is insane.

"Well, this certainly accelerates things for us," I state in my role as Captain Obvious.

"I don't care, actually," he chuckles. "I mean, I *do*, but I was gonna ask you to officially move in with me over the holidays, anyway, so I'm not mad about this *acceleration*." He smiles wickedly. "I'm actually really fucking excited." He's beaming, hopeful, and it knocks me breathless.

"*Really?*" My heart is racing, and my face hurts from smiling so wide.

"Are you kidding me? Of course." He laughs, and I feel like it's a weight off my shoulders. I don't know what I would've done if he wouldn't have been on board with this baby, but I'm so glad that he isn't just okay with it—Matt looks *elated.*

"We should probably just keep it between us for now, though," he says, interrupting my train of thought. "You're only at around six or seven weeks—most people don't say anything until week twelve."

The hand that isn't attached to the IV flies to my stomach, even though I know there's no way I'll feel anything, not even a bump. But still, just putting my hand there makes it real, like I can feel a baby growing inside me.

Matt tells me how he found out I was in the hospital, and I rub in how much of an impression I left on his boss, teasing him, asking him if it made him jealous. Obviously, we both owe a huge thank you to Dr. Parker and his willingness to bend the rules—something that will never be publicly spoken about again.

"Oh my God, Matt," I say randomly at one point. "I'm

gonna look *huge* at graduation!" He laughs at where my priorities are at the moment, but I tell him I'm gonna look like a circus tent in my graduation gown. He starts to argue with me, but we're interrupted by the arrival of my doctor.

"Ms. Castelli? I'm Dr. Chang. I see you're finally awake." A short, middle-aged man in scrubs stands at the foot of my bed with a tablet in his hands. He has kind but tired-looking eyes that smile when he addresses me. "Are you feeling better?"

"Yes, thank you," I say, sitting up higher in my bed. Matt helps adjust the pillows behind my back as we prepare to hear the doctor's assessment and suggested course of treatment.

Dr. Chang walks me through what happened since I arrived at the hospital and the tests that were performed. I remember some of what he's talking about but not everything. My lapse in memory can just be from me having passed out or from the concussion they suspect I have. They weren't able to confirm whether I have one or how bad it is—because I'm pregnant (!)—so they're keeping me here for observation for one night, which isn't horrible news.

Matt makes plans to stay overnight as well and works on getting me a private room. It pays to date a doctor who works in the hospital, especially one who just found out he's gonna be a dad and has suddenly become crazy overprotective and relentless.

Just as we're packing things up for them to move me upstairs, Vinny comes back to meet us. "They releasing you now?" he asks, shoving his phone back into his pocket. "Mom's coming into the city to see you."

Shit.

"Actually, they're asking her to stay the night for observation," Matt says, stuffing my clothes into the plastic bag the hospital provided. He's not happy that we have to lie to Vinny again, but it's different this time around. It's a *baby* we're talking about, not a relationship. I think this is justified.

"Stay the night? For a little dehydration and a concussion?" He furrows his brows in confusion. "All she needs is an IV, which they gave her, and to be monitored from home. What did the CT show? Is the concussion really that bad?" Matt continues to pack up my stuff for me, ignoring my brother and biting the inside of his cheek. Vinny takes in Matt's sudden nervousness, and his eyes widen. "Shit, how bad is it? But you look fine—just a little beat up."

"They didn't make me get a CT," I say to Vinny, trying to remove the heat from my boyfriend.

"No CT, but they think she has a concussion? What kind of hospital do you work for, Matt?" Vinny jokes, albeit nervously, and again, Matt doesn't respond.

"I don't know, they didn't want to do one," I say, shrugging. Matt looks at me, eyes wide with panic, and I realize immediately I've said something wrong, but I don't understand why.

"What do you *mean* they didn't want to do one?" Vinny narrows his eyes at me, upset. He looks like a hysterical woman at a restaurant right before threatening to call the manager, craning his head left and right, looking for a doctor to speak to. "What doctor in their right mind..." His voice trails off. "Unless..." He gasps. "Are you *pregnant*?!"

Chapter Thirty-Two

LIZA

"You know, I can walk just fine, Matt," I whine as he helps me out of the elevator with an arm wrapped around my waist the following afternoon.

"I know that," he huffs. "But the doctor said you need bedrest for *two weeks* until your first check-up with the OBGYN. I'm not taking any chances with you or my kid." I roll my eyes at him, but I'm truthfully thrilled. Matt's taken the news of my pregnancy extremely well. He's happy—*buoyant*, even—which makes me even more excited to be having this baby with him.

Matt came completely out of left field to me. I don't know how I got so lucky to find a guy who cares for me in the right way, loves me in the right way.

As a teenager, I often daydreamed about being with Matt, but never in my wildest dreams would I have ever imagined *this*. If you had told me then that I would be in a committed relationship with Majestic Matt, I would've laughed in your face—probably hysterically. Add the fact that we're about to start a family together? I don't think I would have been able to take the news without losing my mind.

I think both Matt and I believed that Vinny was going to crack at the news, but he definitely did not take it as we had expected. Once my brother put two and two together and realized what was really going on—that I was actually pregnant—he started crying. Matt and I stared at him in shock, not understanding what was happening. After everything that happened between the three of us, we were just afraid of more familial drama, and we didn't want to poison what we thought was happy news with more negativity.

But we were wrong. Vinny turned out to be extremely happy. He told us that the reason he was coming around to us being together was because he had just been reminded how important family was. Only a few days ago, he and Danielle had found out that she was pregnant. He was ecstatic that our kids would be growing up together, that they were going to be around the same age.

So, now we won't just have one more baby in the family, but *two*.

It's been a surreal last twenty-four hours, I tell you.

Matt throws a nervous look in my direction, and I gaze quizzically at him. He slides the key into the lock of the apartment with shaking hands and pushes the door open. I am immediately hit with a wave of his signature scent—except, this time, it's mixed with the almost overpowering one of pine. His arm is still around my waist when I walk into his apartment and gasp.

"Matt! When did you do all of this?" The entire living room looks like Christmas has thrown up on it, with twinkle lights strung around the TV and windows, holiday-themed throw pillows on the couch, poinsettias on every surface in quirky and festive pots of every size, and a massive Christmas tree in the corner of the living room (which makes me wonder how in the world he ever got it into the apartment—do they even sell trees this big in Manhattan??) with a pile of gifts underneath.

"I may have had a little help from some people you know." He smirks, wiggling his eyebrows. "Plus, since you're on bedrest, we can't go out to Long Island to your mom's for the holiday, so I suggested we do it here. She's gonna stay at your place, if that's okay. And..." He exhales. "If you're still up for it, I want you to move in here."

"*Of course* I want to." I beam, placing a kiss on his cheek. I feel his breathing increase; it's coming in jaggedly.

"I also asked for their help because I want this place to feel like your home, too. I don't want it to feel like you are moving into *my* apartment. I want you to feel comfortable and to bring some of your unique Liza-ness into it. Make it *ours*. A place where we can start a family together."

A family!

My heart soars. It's trying to jump out of my chest, my ribs struggling to keep it inside.

"I love you, and I know things have been crazy with us, but I think it's just the universe's way of saying *screw it*. I can't wait to have this baby with you. I can't wait to move in with you. And..." He walks to the table by the front door, opens the drawer, and pulls out a black velvet box.

"Oh my god." My hands fly to my mouth.

"And if you'll have me..." He swallows hard as he kneels in front of me. "I can't wait to marry you and spend the rest of our lives together." He pulls the lid of the box open and reveals a simple oval-cut solitaire on a platinum band. It's beautiful and elegant and just right. Although, he could have given me a rock and some duct tape, and I still would have loved it—even if it had been heart-shaped.

"When did you have time to buy a ring?" I ask.

He furrows his brows. "I've had this for some time. I, uh...

bought it at the same time I got the necklace," he admits, face heating all the way to his ears.

Excuse me?

"*What?*" I ask. "That was, like, over a month ago! And you bought it from your mom? Did she know how long we had been together for? Oh my God, I can't believe it. She must think we're crazy—unless she thought it was romantic. Oh, wow, I can't wait to meet her and—"

"Hey, Liza." He stops me before I go on a bigger tangent, brows furrowed. "Do you think you could maybe answer my question real quick?" he asks, anxiety oozing from every inch of his body, still down on one knee. "You can go back to freaking out after." He grins, but I can tell he's nervous, like he doesn't actually think I'm gonna say yes.

I roll my eyes at him and laugh, throwing myself into his arms. "Of course I'll marry you, you loon! How could I not?"

He wraps his arms around me, kissing me on the neck, both of us kneeling on the floor. "I'm so happy right now," he laughs in my ear. "I can't believe this."

"But wait." I push off him gently. "We don't need to do this just because we're pregnant, Matt." A little thrill courses through my body again at the thought. *We're pregnant.* "I don't *need* to be married. I don't want you to feel like I'm forcing you into this whole thing."

He stares at me in confusion. "Did you not just hear me tell you that I've had this in my drawer for about a month? You're not forcing my hand at all. If anything, this baby means I get to have you sooner than what is socially acceptable." He grins. "I want this. I want you. I've wanted you since the second I saw you splattered in vomit." I snort through tears. "I love you, Liza."

Epilogue

MATT

"COVID HAS REALLY PUT A DAMPER ON EVENTS LIKE THIS, hasn't it?" Catterina says next to me. "I hate that we can't actually be there with her when it happens, that we have to wait for her to come home." I smile sympathetically at her.

Liza's whole family, Barbara, and I are sitting in our living room while we watch Columbia's post-grad ceremony from our apartment. The twins look bored out of their minds, fighting over who gets to play with the iPad first. It's definitely a little cramped in here, but I don't mind. I love seeing how loved and supported Liza is, how supported *we* are as a family. It's something I haven't had since before my dad died and never thought I would ever get back.

It's strange to think that a year ago today I was almost done with my fellowship, looking at new job opportunities and thinking about moving to New York. Now, I have a beautiful and smart fiancée, a baby on the way, and have been brought into a loving and gregarious Italian family that I'll soon get to officially be a part of. My life has definitely changed for the better.

Even my mother, who I had barely had a relationship with for well over a decade, has been making more of an effort to be a part of my life. Since finding out about the baby and the engage-ment, she's come to visit at least once a month, wanting to get to know me better, wanting to be part of my kid's life.

It's unbelievable what grandkids do to a family, how they bring them together.

"I know," I say, exhaling deeply, impatiently waiting for Liza's name to pop up on the live-stream of her graduation. They wouldn't allow non-students at the actual ceremony because of health regulations, so this is the only way we could see her graduate.

She's eight months pregnant, and it's incredibly hot outside under the early-June sun, and you could say that I'm a bit worried about her—I always am these days. I don't want her to pass out from the heat or get tired from having to stand too long on her feet. Plus, I'm terrified of Liza getting sick from being in such a large crowd of grads. She's been vaccinated, but what if she gets the virus anyway? What if the vaccine doesn't protect her?

This whole parenting-and-being-in-love-with-someone-unconditionally thing is exhausting sometimes. It's like my brain is now filled with these worst-case scenarios, where my worst fear is losing one of them—or worse, both.

Is this normal? Or is this new-parent jitters? Am I going to live with this anxiety for the rest of my life, or will I eventually get used to it?

Liza and I had a huge argument last week about her attending this ceremony, but ultimately, she won and was right to stick up for herself. She's worked so hard, managed to complete her schoolwork, thesis, *and* required internship all while battling morning sickness that has lasted throughout her entire pregnancy. She deserves to be able to celebrate this moment with her friends, to bask in the achievement—even if it turns me into a nervous wreck, even if it's a little hard for me to let go. Plus, it's probably one of the last things she'll do just for herself before the baby comes and we get married, which we plan to do in October.

People often ask us why we want to marry *after* the birth of our child, but the truth is, once we knew we were pregnant and decided to get married, we thought it would be so great to have our baby boy or girl present with us. The reality is that Liza and I were always going to get married, start a family, and share a life together—it just probably wouldn't have happened as quickly as it's happening now without the baby. We want to honor him or her by having them there with us, thanking them for bringing us together even quicker than anticipated—we really don't mind.

Plus, she really wants to get married in the place where we first actually fell for each other, and Tom's Pumpkin Patch looks better in the fall (my future wife's favorite season). There are plans for there to be *a lot* of pumpkins in our wedding pictures, obviously. Maybe even a picture with the famous giant turkey, but I know she's not fond of *that* idea.

"Elisabetta Angela Castelli, Graduate School of Psychology," the school provost announces. Vinny, Danielle, Catterina, Barbara, and I all cheer for her as if she can hear us all the way from campus. We watch her waddle all the way to the center of the stage to get her diploma and smile broadly as she takes it from the dean and then, just as quickly, disappears from the screen.

I'm so fucking proud of her.

"I gotta pee again," my future sister-in-law says with a frustrated groan. "This kid is more of an annoyance on my bladder than the twins were. It sure loves doing jumping jacks."

Danielle being pregnant at the same time as Liza has been an incredible experience. The two girls were already close, but this has definitely brought them much closer together. I know Barbara has been getting some serious FOMO about the whole situation, but she's been really supportive, and I know she's going to be the best godmother to our little monster.

With Babs, I'm confident that my kids will all grow up with a fun, loving, kooky aunt. I know that they'll be surrounded by love and affection and want for nothing in terms of emotional support. I know that they will never, ever feel abandoned by the members of their family. Will we be overbearing? Meddling? Absolutely. But better that than nothing at all.

"Did you get everything for dinner tonight? We should probably start prepping so that it's ready by the time Liza gets back," Vinny says nervously.

Tonight, he and I plan to cook dinner for the girls for a change—show them how much we appreciate everything they do. We're gonna try to make a summer caprese pasta salad, which Catterina says is so simple to do that even Danielle can make it (her words, not mine), and I'm looking forward to doing it here, in our home.

Catterina snorts and says, "Vinny, this dish only takes about fifteen minutes to make. Do not exaggerate." She rolls her eyes at him, and he blushes. I laugh and refill her wine glass. Catterina pats my hand in appreciation, thanking me with a smile. I owe a lot to this woman for everything that she's done for me, and I'm not just referring to the amazing cooking lessons she's given both me and Liza, but the maternal affection she's shown me and how she brought me into the fold.

I'm so happy to have her and everyone else join me in celebrating my future wife in our apartment. I've owned it for almost a year now, but it wasn't until Liza moved in that it started to feel like my place. She's turned my generic and sterile apartment—and life, to be honest—into a warm and inviting home. She's filled it with quirky touches and decorations, including her paint-by-numbers paintings, her bright and vibrant throw pillows, her laughter, the scent of Italian herbs coming from the kitchen at dinnertime, and the continued love and support she shows me every day.

I send her a selfie of me and her family in the background and a text:

MATT

> I love you so much, Liza. I'm so proud of you.

THE END

Keep on reading for the Castelli Family Thanksgiving Dinner Cookbook!

Thanks so much for reading Liza and Matt's story! I hope you enjoyed reading their story as much as I enjoyed writing it. If you did, please drop me a review and follow me on Instagram to stay up to date on all future releases and cat pictures.

Want to hear Barbara's story? Make sure to read Book 2 in the Seasons of Love Series by clicking here.

The
CASTELLI FAMILY
Thanksgiving
Cookbook

Spinach and Prosciutto-Stuffed Turkey Breast

Ingredients:

- Salt & Pepper
- 4 Pound Turkey Breast, Boned
- 1 package of Frozen Spinach, Thawed and Squeezed Dry
- 1/2 small onion, finely diced
- 12 pieces of thinly sliced prosciutto di Parma
- 1/2 Cup of grated parmesan cheese
- 6 Tablespoons Olive Oil
- 1 Teaspoon Italian Seasoning Mix

- 1/2 Cup Dry Wine
- 1 1/2 Cups Chicken or Turkey Broth
- 1 Teaspoon Fresh Thyme
- 2 Tablespoons

Directions:

1. Heat 2 Tablespoons of oil and sauté the onions until they are tender, then remove the onions and place in a small bowl.

2. Add 2 more tablespoons of oil to the pan, sauté the spinach until heated through.

3. Season with salt and pepper, then add the spinach to the onions, and mix well.

4. Add the grated cheese, and mix.

5. Butterfly the breast and lay flat open, pounding with a meat tenderizer to create even thickness throughout.

6. Spread the spinach mixture across the breast, leaving 1 1/2 inch border all around.

7. Lay the prosciutto slices over the spinach layer.

8. Beginning at one end, firmly roll up the turkey breast, and secure with twine.

9. Place into a small roasting pan and rub the surface with the remaining oil, and season with Italian seasonings, salt, and pepper.

10. Roast in preheated oven for about 1 hour and 20 minutes, or until turkey breast reaches and internal temperature of 150 F.

11. Remove the breast roll from the pan and cover with a tent of foil.

12. Remove the pan from oven, and drain off all excess oil.

13. Place pan on stovetop, add white wine, and scrape up all the browned bits from the bottom. Cook until reduced by half.

14. Remove a few spoonfuls of the broth to a separate cup,

and pour the rest into your roasting pan with fresh thyme, and mix well.

15. Mix together flour and remaining broth, and whisk this mixture into your gravy.

16. Season with salt and pepper, and strain through a sieve.

17. Cut off twine around turkey and slice into 1/2 inches. Arrange on a platter.

18. Serve, offering a little sauce or gravy on the side.

source: italianfoodforever.com

Roasted Tomato and Ricotta Bites

Ingredients:

- 10 - 15 cherry tomatoes
- 2 Garlic cloves, finely minced
- 1 teaspoon of sugar
- Salt & Pepper
- 2 tablespoons of chopped basil
- 1/4 cup of olive oil
- Puff Pastry
- 1 cup of fresh ricotta
- Pesto Sauce
- Muffin tin

Directions:

1. For the tomatoes, preheat oven to 275 F.

2. Halve tomatoes and place skin-down on baking sheet.

3. Sprinkle over them the garlic, thyme, salt, pepper, and sugar, and drizzle with the olive oil and place in the oven.

4. Bake for about one to one and a half hours or until they have shriveled yet still remain moist.

5. For the bites, preheat the oven to 375 degrees F.

6. Lightly grease the muffin cups.

7. Cut the puff pastry into squares slightly larger than muffin cups and center one into each cup.

8. In a small bowl, mix together the ricotta cheese and fresh herbs.

9. Season with salt and pepper.

10. Spoon a couple of spoonfuls of the ricotta mixture into each muffin cup and then bake for about 15 minutes or until the ricotta has puffed and set and the pastry has turned golden brown.

11. Cool to room temperature.

12. Carefully remove from the muffin pan and place on a platter and add a bit of pesto before serving.

source: italianfoodforever.com

Roasted Squash and Cheese Bruschetta

Ingredients:
- 2 Cups seeded, peeled, and diced butternut squash
- 2 Tablespoons of Olive Oil
- Salt and Pepper
- 1 1/2 cups of freshly chopped sage
- Sliced crusty baguette
- 4 Oz of Goat Cheese, room temperature
- 2 Oz Cream Cheese
- 1/4 cup of pancetta bits
- 1/4 dried cranberries

Directions:
1. Preheat oven to 375 F.

2. Toss diced squash with oil, then season with salt and pepper.

3. Line baking sheet with foil, and scatter the squash onto the sheet.

4. Bake for about 20 minutes, or until fork tender, tossing twice during cooking time.

5. Cool to room temperature, after tossing it with the chopped sage.

6. Preheat the broiler, and lay the baguette slices onto a second baking sheet.

7. Lightly brown the bread slices on both sides.

8. In a small bowl, mix together the goat cheese and cream cheese.

9. Spread one side of each slice of bread with the cheese mixture and arrange on a platter.

10. Spoon the roasted squash onto each slice, then top with pancetta bits and cranberries.

source: italianfoodforever.com

Meatballs in Cranberry Sauce

Ingredients:

- 1 Lb ground beef
- 1 cup crushed cornflakes
- 1 tablespoon minced onion
- 1 tablespoon of soy sauce
- 3 tablespoons of ketchup
- 1 egg
- 1 minced garlic clove
- 1/4 minced parsley
- Salt and Pepper
- 1 cup of cranberry chutney
- 1 cup chilli sauce
- 1 tablespoon brown sugar
- 1 tablespoon lemon juice

277

• Yield: 6 - 8 servings

Directions:

1. Preheat oven to 350 F.

2. Mix beef with cornflakes, onions, soy, ketchup, egg, garlic, salt and pepper to taste, and parsley.

3. Shape into small balls if using as appetizer, larger if for an entree, and bake until brown and cooked through.

4. In large skillet, combine cranberry chutney, chili sauce, sugar, and lemon juice.

5. Add browned meatballs to sauce and simmer gently for 20 - 30 minutes.

Source: family recipe

Butternut Squash Risotto

Ingredients:

- Butternut Squash Risotto:
- 3 tablespoons Olive Oil, divided
- 1 small yellow onion, chopped
- 2 cloves of garlic, minced
- 4 cups (32 oz) vegetable broth, divided
- 1 cup of water
- 1 1/2 cups of brown arborio rice
- 1 small butternut squash (about 2 lbs), peeled and sliced into 1/2 " cubes
- 1/2 cup dry white wine
- 3 tablespoons unsalted butter, diced
- Salt and pepper
- 1 Teaspoon of red pepper flakes (optional)
- Fried Sage:
- 1 tablespoon extra-virgin olive oil

- 16 - 20 fresh sage leaves, chopped

Directions:

1. To prepare: place oven racks in lower third and upper third positions (we're going to bake the risotto on the middle rack and roast the squash on the upper rack at the same time), then preheat oven to 375 F. Line a large, rimmed baking sheet with parchment paper for the butternut squash. Reserve 1 cup of broth from your container and set it aside for when the risotto is out of the oven.

2. Heat 1 tablespoon olive oil in a medium-to-large Dutch oven (if you don't own Dutch One use a large saucepan instead, then carefully pour the boiling broth and rice mixture into a casserole dish. If the casserole dish has an oven-safe lid, use that; if not, cover it tightly with foil. Bake as directed) over medium heat until shimmering. Add onion and a pinch of salt. Cook, stirring occasionally, until softened and turning translucent, about 5 minutes. Add the minced garlic and cook until the garlic is fragrant, 1 to 2 minutes.

3. Add 3 cups broth and 1 cup water, cover, and bring to a boil over medium-high heat. Remove from heat and stir in the rice. Cover the pot and bake on the lower rack until rice is tender and cooked through, about 65 to 70 minutes. It will seem pretty dry when you take off the lid, but don't worry!

4. Immediately after placing the pot of risotto in the oven, toss the cubed butternut with 2 tablespoons olive oil on your lined baking sheet. Sprinkle with salt and some freshly ground black pepper and arrange the butternut in a single layer on the pan. Roast on the upper rack until the butternut is fork tender and the edges are deeply caramelized, tossing halfway. This took 55 to 60 minutes for me, but start checking for doneness around 40 minutes.

5. While the risotto and butternut are in the oven, fry the

sage: Heat 1 tablespoon olive oil in a medium skillet over medium heat. Once the oil is shimmering, add the sage and toss to coat. Let the sage get darker green and crispy (but not brown) before transferring it to a plate covered with a paper towel. Sprinkle the fried sage lightly with salt and set it aside.

6. Carefully remove the Dutch oven from the oven. Remove the lid and pour in the remaining cup of broth, the Parmesan, wine and butter. Stir vigorously for 2 to 3 minutes, until the rice is thick and creamy. Stir in the salt, a generous amount of pepper and a pinch of red pepper flakes.

7. Stir in the roasted butternut. Taste and add more salt and/or pepper, as needed. Divide the risotto into bowls and top each with a sprinkle of fried sage.

source: cookieandkate.com

Rosemary-Goat Cheese Potatoes

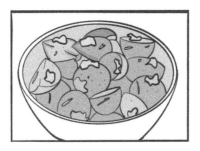

Ingredients:
- 2 lbs of potatoes, cut into big squares
- 1/4 Stick of butter
- 4 Tablespoons of fresh rosemary, chopped
- Olive oil
- Salt and Pepper
- 4 Oz of Goat Cheese, room temperature
- 3 cloves of minced garlic.

Directions:
1. Preheat oven to 400 F.

2. In ovenproof casserole dish, mix together potatoes, olive oil, salt and pepper, and freshly chopped rosemary.

3. Cook for about 45 minutes, or until potatoes are fork-tender, and are beginning to brown.

4. In a mixing bowl, mix together garlic and goat cheese.

5. Once potatoes are ready, toss in goat cheese mixture until lightly covered, and transfer back into casserole dish.

6. Serve hot.

Source: family recipe

Sweet Potato Casserole with Marshmallows

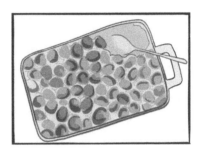

Ingredients:
- 5 sweet potatoes, diced
- 3/4 stick of butter, unsalted
- Pinch of salt
- 1/2 cup packed brown sugar
- 4 Tablespoons of orange juice
- 1 pinch of ground cinnamon
- 1 pinch of ground nutmeg
- 1 pack of marshmallows (any size, depending on preference)

Directions:
1. Preheat 350 F.
2. Place sweet potatoes in pot with enough water to cover (about 1.5"). Bring to boil and cook until tender.
3. Drain sweet potatoes and mash.
4. While potatoes are still hot, combine all remaining ingre-

dients except for the marshmallows and blend with an electric mixer.

5. Spread mixture onto baking dish and top with marshmallows

6. Bake for 25 - 30 minutes until heated through and marshmallows are golden brown.

source: family recipe

Zucchini and Tomato Toss

Ingredients:
- 10 - 15 cherry tomatoes
- 5 to 6 medium zucchinis
- 1 garlic clove, minced
- 1 - 2 Red Pepper Flakes
- Salt and Pepper
- Dried Rosemary
- Olive oil

Directions:
1. Slice zucchini into thin coins and half cherry tomatoes.

2. Place zucchinis and tomatoes into a bowl with olive oil, salt and pepper, rosemary, minced garlic, and red pepper flakes.

3. Pour vegetable mixture onto heated pan and sauté until fork tender.

source: family recipe

Ultimate Charcuterie Board

Personal note:

I live for a cheese/charcuterie board! There is no wrong way to make one so long as you have at least one cheese, one meat, and some dried fruit and/or nuts.

Below is what I like to include whenever my big family and I get together, but honestly do whatever you like!

Ingredients:

- Prosciutto di Parma
- Honey
- Seedless grapes
- Dried Fruit
- Nut mix
- Genoa Salami
- Triple Cream Brie
- Mozzarella
- Water crackers
- Cranberry-Fig crackers, if you're feeling fancy!

• Anything your heart desires!

Directions:

1. Assemble to your liking, although I try to put each category on opposing sides, creating separation between each cheese or meat with crackers or grapes.

source: personal preference

Also by

CAROLINE FRANK

Seasons of Love Series (Open-Door Romantic Comedy):

Fall Into You (Book 1)

Shall We Dance? (Book 2)

Happily Ever Disaster (Novella - Book 2.5)

Second Chance Snowmance (Book 3) **Coming Soon!**

Standalone Women's Contemporary (Open-Door):

In For a Penny

Acknowledgments

This book would not have been possible without the love and support of my husband. K, you've always been my biggest supporter, and for that I thank you. There's not a day that goes by that I don't thank the universe for leading me to you.

I want to also give a shoutout to the Booksta community. Never in my wildest dreams could I have imagined that I would have made such great friends and received such love and support from a group of strangers. So many of you offered such kind words of support and wisdom, telling me it's okay to throw your WIP out the window and start from scratch, even if you are 12 chapters deep.

Special shout-out goes to Barbara (aka. @fancyshman-cyreads) for the advice and amazing friendship. This book would not have been possible without you.

Jenn Lockwood, my editor, thanks again for all the hard work and detail you put into revisions and feedback. I am so lucky to be able to work with you.

To M for teaching me how to use PhotoShop (lol) and for inspiring the character of Danielle (even though I didn't realize until 3/4 of the book that she reminded me so much of you).

Lastly, I want to thank my two best friends, A and E, for their constant love and support. I'm so proud to know the two of you.

About
CAROLINE FRANK

Caroline Frank is an indie author and self-proclaimed shoe addict. She currently resides in Massachusetts with her husband and two crazy cats, Señor Kitty and Salem.

She spends her days reading, crocheting, crafting, writing, and biking. Her favorite things include the first sip of a Coke on a hot day, crocheting, and using self-deprecating humor to get through the day.

Though she always planned to eventually take over the world, she thinks writing fun stories every day is pretty freaking awesome and plans to continue to do so for the foreseeable future.

Milton Keynes UK
Ingram Content Group UK Ltd.
UKHW031003020924
447770UK00006B/378